MW01135500

BEFORE *the* MEMORIES FAIL

THANK YOU

This is Ed Eby. Thanks so much for purchasing *Before the Memories Fail*. As a thank you gift, I would like to give you a free PDF copy of the sequel, *Marna*. As of this writing, the rough draft has been completed and the novella is in the editing phase. Send me an email at AuthorEdEby@gmail.com to sign up.

I've also completed the rough draft of the third book of the series, *The Dementia Encryption Enigma*. I don't yet have a release date, but I'll keep you informed if you join the mailing list. I promise I won't spam your inbox.

BEFORE *the* MEMORIES FAIL

ED EBY

POWER HOUSE PUBLISHING

ALEXANDRIA
VIRGINIA

Before The Memories Fail

by Ed Eby

Published by:
Powerhouse Publishing
625 N. Washington Street, Suite 425
Alexandria, Virginia 22314

info@powerhousepublishing.net
703-982-0984

ISBN First Paperback Edition: 9781790424450

First paperback printing December 2018
Printed in the United States of America

Eby, Ed
Before the memories fail

1st paperback ed.

ISBN-13: 9781790424450

DEDICATION

I dedicate this novel to my mother who is in the final stages of dementia.
Love you Mom. You are my hero.

ACKNOWLEDGEMENTS

I'd also like to thank my wife Sue for her patience with me as I bounce from hobby to hobby. I'm not always easy to live with, but I'm trying really hard to be better. I couldn't have published without her support.

I would like to thank Chris Mixon for his awesome work as an editor. He had terrific suggestions on changes and fixes for the novel. My wife Sue and our friend Kathleen Law also helped with the editing process.

I've collaborated with several author's clubs. I specifically want to thank Judy Rose and Erin Szalapski. The input and perspective of other authors is invaluable.

DISCLAIMER

All people in this book are entirely fiction. In some cases, you will find similarities of people in real life. For these characters, names have been changed.

AUTHOR'S NOTES

My protagonist, Jaqueline Saeed Scott was born in 1952. She, Richard, Turner, and Williams would have been eighteen in 1970. Our contemporary kids may not understand, but young marriage was common for Jackie's generation.

After her birth, Jackie's parents moved to Basra, Iraq which was a bustling city in the '50s. The port city loaded oil onto tankers which fed the nations of the world. I tried to keep the events of Jackie's childhood as accurate as possible for her historical context. Although I only hinted at it in my story, the history of the Middle East as it was formed by the industrialization of oil is a fascinating read. In the '50s, the area was still feeling the impact from World War II.

I have Jackie's father transferred from Iraq to Fairfax County, Virginia when she was thirteen years old. During the twenty years that I worked at the USPS Engineering Center in Merrifield, Virginia, the Exxon/Mobile Headquarters was just around the corner on Gallows Road. The oil company headquarters has since moved to Houston.

Although Abigail has already passed, she plays a large role in the story because of Jackie's name confusion. Abby was born in 1979 and died in 1998, at the age of 19, in a car crash as Richard was taking her to college. Her brother Charles is a few years older than her.

The events of the first Gulf War are historical fact that can be read anywhere. I fictionalized Jackie's actions and her role in the events.

Aaeesha dies on the first day of that war as they flee from the palace guard who had come to arrest her husband.

Jackie's house in Vienna is just a few blocks from where I attended church for many years, so I know the neighborhood quite well. Like Jackie, I've eaten at Ledo Pizza.

The central theme of this book is Jackie's dementia. There are several different forms of dementia. Many people are familiar with the term Alzheimer's, but that's just one of the specific types of the disease.

Every person's dementia experience is different. My grandmother would be much like Jackie. She would loop off into her childhood and happily tell everybody that it was time to go out and milk the cows. Then when she came to herself, and realized how far she'd been gone, she would sit and cry.

My wife's relative has had dementia for ten years. She can't remember anything that happened today unless she looks at her notes. Then she can tell you, "Oh, I sang in choir today." Once her memory is jogged, she can often tell you details of what happened. She's brilliantly managed the effects of her disease by learning to take notes. Her decline has been slow. In her dementia years, she has remained a sweet and loving person that everybody adores.

My mother's decline has been precipitous. As I write these Author's Notes, I can tell you that a year ago she was walking a mile every day, feeding the cats and dogs, and helping on the farm. Then she had a fall. We don't know if she fell because of the dementia or if her rapid decline was because of the fall. Probably a little of both. Now she sits in the nursing home with her eyes closed and her mouth open in an almost perpetual sleep.

Some dementia patients become violent and lash out at people who are trying to help. Some are happy and others are angry. Some can tell you details of events years ago, but can't remember your name.

Inappropriate comments are common. The normal filters that govern the tongue disintegrate.

The government has a real problem with people who knew state secrets. Dementia can cause people's lips to be loosened. The problem from the patient's perspective is that nobody ever believes anything she says. We can see that borne out in Jackie's story. She knew the treasure existed and held important secrets, but everybody thought she was batty.

As I was telling the plot outline to a friend he said, "You're describing my neighbor!" Apparently, she was the secretary for a high-ranking government official in the Intelligence world. She told my friend some very interesting stories. Who knows how many of them are true?

Dementia patients frequently feel ignored and rejected. What they have to say is important to them, but others don't take them seriously. I gave Jackie a loving family environment. We can see how Katrice went beyond the call of duty by helping Jackie with her bathroom needs. In this case, it was because of the injuries to Jackie's hands. In real life, many people revert to diapers for their senior years.

The opening scene is a heavily modified version of a story from a coworker many years ago. My own mother had a similar experience. She went out to get her hair done. She got lost and tried to turn around in a farmer's lane. She drove off the road and got stuck. The farmer came and helped her get out and figure out where she needed to go. When she got home, she gave up her license willingly and never drove again.

The family members of dementia patients go through hell with their loved ones. Some people can't bear to watch the progression of this terrible disease, so they stick them in nursing homes and abandon them. Other family members walk the painful journey with their mom or dad.

In my opinion, it's okay to put your parents in a nursing home. There comes a point where a child or spouse just can't handle the pressures of the care that's required. Put them in the home if you need to. Get your life back, then you can be fresh and rested when you go to visit them. But whatever you do, don't abandon your loved one—they still need you and you still need them.

I have to confess that as I did my final reading before sending this manuscript to the editor, I wept the entire way through the book. As I climbed into Jackie's head, I saw the world through Mom's eyes. I felt her frustration as she tried to do simple things and couldn't remember how.

Many of the examples of Jackie's experience came from my own mom. She would put her clothes on inside out or tell us that her clothes just wouldn't act right. A sock would go on the hand, or two legs would try to go into the same hole in her pants.

Mom's sundowning wasn't as pronounced as many dementia patients', but she had it. For some people, the daily experience is traumatic.

You'll see other little things in the book that are commonplace for dementia patients. At one point, Jackie puts her earrings in the refrigerator. If you live in a household with a dementia patient, you'll find weird things in the most interesting places.

Writing this book was challenging. No dementia sufferer is writing novels, so we really can't know what goes on in their heads, but we can observe from the outside. I have anecdotal experience with loved ones. I have read and researched extensively to hear what the experts had to say. Also, every patient's experience is different. So, I tried to create a plausible journey for Jackie. I wanted to put my reader into Jackie's head. Obviously, Jackie is just in the beginning stages of an early onset of dementia—she's young for the disease, but that sometimes happens. She is able to interact with those in her life. She has lucid moments, and she has bad days too.

Jackie struggles with names. This is common. Sometimes Jackie knows who the person is, but can't remember the name. Other times, she has no clue who her son is.

One day I told my own Mom that I loved her. She got very angry, began stuttering, and told me that she was a married woman! She thought I was making a romantic advance on her. She didn't know who I was and was very offended by my presence. I had no choice but to walk away and let the nursing home staff intervene. I'm not mad at Mom for the misunderstanding. I know it was the disease talking, not Mom. The next morning, she lit up when I walked into the nursing home. She was so glad to see me and knew who I was. She had no recollection of the events the previous evening.

I have a cousin who said that dementia is a blessing that helps to hide the painful memories of the past. I'm not sure that I totally agree, but I appreciate the perspective that there may be a small blessing hiding in the pain of the journey.

One criticism of the book will be that Jackie is aware of the disease's progress. Often the patient doesn't know what's happening to them. However, for the sake of the reader, I let Jackie see her own condition. She would say things like, "My brain is turning to Fruit Loops." In reality, the process is often baffling to the patient. They may not even be aware of what's happening to them.

To underline this point, I remember a story of my wife's relative watching a documentary on Alzheimer's. Afterwards, her comment was, "Oh those poor people." She didn't realize that the documentary was about her own disease!

I took some literary/artistic license to let Jackie be aware of her dementia. This knowledge created an urgency that propels the reader through the novel. She has to find the treasure before her brain is gone. She knows this and so does everybody else in her life.

I hope this book has been helpful to you. Your dad's experience is going to be different than Jackie's, and also different than my mother's. But my goal was to help the reader see the world through Jackie's eyes.

I know that I didn't get everything right. Probably the best person to write this novel would be Marna Hunt or another home helper. I'm sure that after I'm published, many of my readers will have corrections for my story and will share their experiences and knowledge with me. I would love to hear your stories and weep with you about your own parent, grandparent, or spouse.

Now, go give your dad or mom a kiss and tell 'em you love 'em.

PROLOGUE

February 17, 2003

It was Abigail's birthday. "She would have been 23 today," Jackie thought to herself as she followed the diminutive servant. Jackie wondered if her own death would mark her dead daughter's birthday. She hoped whatever happened today wouldn't come back to haunt her best friend Aaeesha.

The gaudy opulence was sickening. She was walking through the Presidential Palace of the Butcher of Baghdad. The day after she'd dropped the note to the colonel, he'd told her that she had an audience with Saddam for the following morning.

Jackie had dressed in her chador. Woven into the sleeve, there was a plastic knitting needle that had been sharpened into a thin dagger. As she had gone through security, the weapon hung like a 50-pound lead weight in her hand. The metal detector and the pat-down hadn't revealed it. Which was fortunate, because it would have meant a bullet to the head before she'd even had a chance to meet with the man.

Now she was walking through the marble hallway. Money dripped from the walls in the form of art and decorations. Ribbons of gold were wound through the ornate sandalwood trim. Jackie recognized original paintings by Salvador Dalí, Botticelli, and Jacques-Louis David. The sound of a fountain babbled in the courtyard below. From this vantage point, there was no poverty outside the palace walls, nor was there the threat of war in the air.

Jackie followed the functionary, whose heels clumped loudly even through the deep carpet. The man leading the way had asked her if she preferred to speak Arabic or English—obviously, they had done their research on her. In deference, she had chosen Arabic.

She had not come with the expressed intent to kill Saddam, but she wanted the option. If negotiations failed, she wanted to be ready. She knew that thousands were about to be slain in the coming war. She knew that if she tried to kill the man, she would die, but she was willing to exchange her life for the thousands if she had the opportunity.

The man turned left into a room that was bedecked in red. It was an anteroom complete with pastries and the sharp scent of Arabic coffee. He motioned her to a plush, ornate chair and offered her a refreshment. Jackie accepted a dainty cup of coffee.

The bone china cup was as decadent as the room in which she found herself. She was sure that the entire set could be traded for a new Rolls Royce.

Inside the big double doors, she could hear the voice of the tyrant berating an underling. Although she couldn't make out the words, Saddam's voice was angry. She thought she heard the slap of a riding crop on a desk. Then the gilded doors burst open, and a man strode furiously out of the inner sanctum. He didn't look her direction, but Jackie recognized Lieutenant General al-Hamdani as he passed. She had met him once at a function—she couldn't remember where. But she didn't have time to reminisce; the Lilliputian palace-guide was speaking.

"His Excellency will see you now," the servant said. Jackie bowed her thanks to the man and followed.

"Your Excellency," the man proclaimed as he stepped into the room, "I present Jacqueline Saeed Scott, unofficial emissary from President George W. Armstrong** of the United States." The man bowed deeply and backed out of the room, closing the doors behind him.

Jackie sucked in her breath and fought to control her emotions. She had never been in Saddam's presence before, and his powerful mien was overwhelming. She averted her eyes deferentially.

**Some names have been changed to allow the author literary freedom.

The mustachioed ruler was sitting behind a desk that looked like it came straight out of Buckingham Palace. If the bone china outside was worth a Rolls, this desk could have bought an entire dealership. There were a few papers and reports strewn about. The riding crop sat ominously across the clutter. A surprisingly feminine lamp sat on the left corner.

The dictator was dressed in a military uniform that added to his perceived potency. On either side of him, stood a soldier the size of a small, foreign car. Each was festooned with military decorations and bristled with weapons.

Jackie thought of the futility of the thin, plastic knitting needle in her sleeve—she had risked her life for nothing. She bit her lip to quell the trembling in her knees.

"So, the Great Satan disrespects me by sending me a woman," Saddam said, leaning back in his chair. He laced his fingers behind his head. It was obvious that he could see her trembling and was truly enjoying the moment.

She nodded, not yet trusting her voice. Her appropriately submissive eyes were on the desk.

"What unofficial, backdoor message would the pig, George W. Armstrong, like to relay to me through this insulting messenger?" the big man asked. He picked up a cigar from the ashtray and pulled a drag. He breathed out smoke. For a moment, he looked like a dragon who was preparing to devour the young maiden before him.

"Your Excellency," she managed to find her voice. In impeccable Arabic she said, "Unless things change, a great war will begin on Iraqi soil in a few weeks or months. Many will die. President Armstrong would like to avoid this conflagration if at all possible."

He shook his head. "I will paint Iraqi sands red with the blood of the American swine. In the first war with Armstrong's father, I underestimated his strength. But this time, I know his weaknesses. Mark my words, this time, I will not fail."

"Is there any way that we can avoid this conflict?" Jackie asked, ignoring the man's bravado. "Whatever it is, I will relay your message to President Armstrong."

Saddam leaned across the desk at her and jabbed an index finger into its ornate surface. "I know my people, Saeed! Even if the Great Satan were to kill me, my followers will rise up to drive fear into the heart of the American beast! If he doesn't back off, I promise a war of terror that will never end!" He apparently preferred to call her by her Iraqi name—her father's surname.

"But sir..." Jackie's words were cut off by the slap of the riding crop on the desk.

The man sat back studied her for a moment. "Today would have been your daughter's birthday."

The words rocked her foundation. She forgot her decorum and looked Saddam in the eye. Shock filled her face. Not only had the man read her file, but he knew details of her family and her life.

"And you're staying at the house of Aakav Aswad, one of my officials. His wife is Aaeesha, your childhood friend."

She swallowed hard at the bile that rose in her throat. No! Not Aaeesha! Please don't make her pay for my visit with you today! But the words would not escape her lips.

The tyrant shuffled a paper on his desk to find a note. He held it up and read, a grin spreading across his face. "My sources say that you took out a hit on the man that killed your daughter and husband." He looked at her over top of the paper. "You are a formidable woman, Ms. Saeed."

Jackie felt the blood run from her face. How could he know? Her knees grew weak and she grabbed the desk to stay vertical. Only one man in the world knew that secret—the guy who had carried out the hit. Had he talked? Couldn't be. Had to be! Who else knew?

Her mind shot to every relationship in her life. Charles? Did her son know? What about the President? His wife, and Jackie's dear friend, Laura, did she know?

Saddam was obviously enjoying her discomfort. "I don't allow people into my office unless I know who they really are," he said in way of explanation. "How many weapons did you bring today?" he asked, the mirth bright on his face.

Jackie ran the options through her head. If she leapt fast enough, she might have a chance to drive the plastic spike into the man's throat before the guards' bullets riddled her body. She glanced at the soldier on her right and saw his readiness. She knew she'd die before she made it half-way across the desk.

She didn't answer his question. She could only blink dumbly under the dictator's gaze.

"Not only did you pass through a metal detector, but you also passed through an x-ray machine," the dictator said, studying his cigar. "I know about the plastic dagger in your sleeve."

She stood in silence. The man had allowed her in, knowing she was armed. She fought to control her bladder.

"Many people coming to see me have a fantasy of killing me. I have to know everything." He shrugged and took a drag on the cigar, expelling a perfect ring of smoke toward the ceiling. "It is a difficult position."

He swiveled in his chair and stood. "I think I shall use you to send a message to the President of the Great White Satan," Saddam said as he leaned across the desk, baiting her to strike. "I shall have you skewered with your own weapon, and hang your naked body on the Palace wall," he laughed. "That will be an excellent message indeed."

She wanted to leap and stab, but the strength had left her knees. Instead she stared with her mouth agape.

He sat back down and stubbed his cigar in the ashtray. The soldier on the right took a step toward her. She turned and prepared herself for a fight.

Saddam raised a hand in the air. "Wait!" he commanded. The soldier stopped. "I changed my mind. I will send a verbal message after all."

The soldier resumed his position by the bookcase, but Jackie could sense that he was ready to spring.

She turned back to study the tyrant. Was the Butcher of Baghdad playing with her again? Had she really gotten a reprieve? She struggled to force breath into her lungs.

"Tell President Armstrong that I wish to avoid the war as well. Tell him that I do not have weapons of mass destruction as he has claimed on CNN. Also relay that I am sick of being treated like a dog. He will respect me and my sovereignty. I will no longer allow the U.N. inspectors to invade the privacy of my labs. If he can agree to those terms, then we can avoid the war that will devastate his army."

Jackie felt a hurricane of relief flood through her body. She was going to live through the day. She had to once again concentrate to keep her bladder from releasing onto the plush carpet.

"I need you to do one more thing for me, Ms. Saeed," the dictator said, his chest swelling with pride. "I need you to take my portrait. I need it published in your newspapers. I want the world to know that I am confident and unfearful of the Great White Satan."

Jackie had totally forgotten the camera under her arm. She composed herself enough to bring it from beneath the folds of her chador. The photojournalist instincts took over, and beat down the fear. She assessed the lighting with a practiced eye.

"The morning sun is better against the bookshelf," she nodded toward the wall where the soldier was standing—grateful that her voice worked under the stress. "And the books will make you look scholarly."

Saddam grunted his agreement and walked to the library wall. The soldier stepped aside, coming even closer—she could smell his body odor. Jackie ignored the flutter of fear in her chest at the soldier's presence and concentrated on her subject.

She stepped toward the dictator to position him, but the soldier placed a hand on her shoulder. The grip was pure steel—it felt as if he could have crushed her bone without effort.

"Sorry," she stammered. "I was just going to turn him."

She took a step back and the icy grip was released. "Turn a little more to your left," she instructed. "That's good, now lift your chin a little so the sun can catch you in the face."

Her shutter whirred a few frames. "Good," she said. "Do you want to do one with your cigar? Or perhaps a gun? It might make you look more masculine." Even in a pressure situation, she knew how to flatter a man.

Her charms were working. Saddam beamed. "The cigar is a nice touch." He retrieved a fresh one from his desk and posed again.

When they were done, Jackie slid her camera beneath her chador. "I will relay your message to President Armstrong," she promised. "I will let you know if he has a reply. I will also send your picture and your quote to the editor as you requested. I'll try all my contacts—the Washington Post, New York Times, and the Associated Press. I'm sure somebody will want to publish your story."

"If you come back," the Butcher of Baghdad demanded. "Leave your toy dagger at home."

She bowed deeply, and practically ran for the door. Outside, the diminutive servant waited.

"Take me out of here," she said between clenched teeth.

A knowing smile crossed the man's face. He turned and headed for the carpeting of the hallway. "You were so smug when you walked in, American Pig," he said over his shoulder. "What happened?"

She didn't dignify his barb with a reply. She followed him wordlessly past the art and the decadence. It took a full five minutes before she was on the street.

She tried to walk calmly, knowing that the palace guards were still watching, but her knocking knees caused her to stumble on the cobbled street. She melted herself into a stream of women who were heading toward the market.

Jackie followed the flow for a few blocks and turned right so that she was out of sight of the palace. She found the stoop of a shop and sat with her face in her hands to calm her beating heart.

Shaking hands reached into her pocket and pulled out her phone—it was a special unit given to her for this mission. She hit the speed dial and was instantly connected. She heard the tinny ring on the other end, then a voice answered. She was amazed how clear the words sounded through the encryption.

"Jackie Scott for President Armstrong," she said, proud that her voice didn't crack. She was calming down.

"One moment," the operator said. It was obvious that her call was expected.

Two clicks later and she heard the President's voice. "Go ahead, Jackie," he said. "I've got you on speaker with several of my generals. Speak freely."

Jackie relayed Saddam's message. "Then he threatened to skewer me and hang my body naked from the palace wall," she said. She noticed that her shaking had returned.

Stunned silence was the response. For a moment, Jackie thought the connection had been dropped. "Hello?" she asked. "Are you still there?"

"That son-of-a-bitch!" President Armstrong shouted. Venom coursed across the encrypted ether. "Jackie, you get yourself out of the country right now!"

She shook her head as if he could see the gesture. "No," she said softly. "I'm an American citizen, but these are my people too, Mr. President. I grew up in Iraq. War is about to break out, and I want to be here. I'll document the coming devastation for the world to see."

She took a shaky breath as horrible memories flooded her soul. "I've seen the ravages of war, sir. I know the hell that's about to be unleashed. The world needs to see. But more than that, I need to be here with my people."

Again, her words were greeted by silence.

"Do you want me to give him a reply?" she asked, dreading the thought of seeing the man again.

"No. Just get out of the country," the President answered. "Thanks Jackie, you've done your part. Please come home," he pleaded.

She clicked the off button and pocketed the phone. Belatedly, she realized that she had just hung up on the President of the United States. She had been so upset by the Saddam meeting that she'd forgotten all her decorum. She hoped that her friend would forgive her.

Still flooded with anxiety, Jackie decided to take a stroll through the market. The sounds and scents took her back to her childhood. She haggled with several merchants to buy enough food for supper, enjoying the press of unwashed bodies around her.

She was about to leave, heading back toward Aaeesha's flat when she saw him. He stood a head taller than everyone around him. She had to look twice to make sure it was him. There was no mistake.

CHAPTER ONE

PRESENT DAY

Jacqueline Saeed Scott sat at the bar and pressed the old-fashioned Bakelite rotary phone tightly against her ear. Her hand shook as she spoke: "Where am I? Well, I'll tell you. I'm... um... I'm in a bar."

"Okay, Mom. You've already told me that. But where exactly is this bar? What town are you in? You've been gone for hours, and I've been worried sick! I've even called the police, hoping they could find you."

Thoughts swirled through her head with such force that it made her dizzy. She tried to catch the tail of an idea, but it slipped through her fingers. Words tried to form, but fell flat before they could be spoken. She felt herself drifting. She couldn't help it. It was happening more frequently. She would relive moments of the past, blanking out from the current reality. The force was like the undertow at the beach, dragging her under.

She was an eight-year-old girl again. Her best friend in the whole world, Aaeesha, was giggling and shrieking with delight as Jackie pushed her higher on the swing set. Jackie was wearing a yellow dress and black patent leather shoes. Her jet black pigtails flopped wildly every time she pushed Aaeesha's swing. They were in the park across the street from their home in Basra, Iraq. Their mothers sat on a bench and talked in Arabic, discussing 1960 politics.

"Ma! Answer me!" Charles demanded. His voice bringing her back to the present. "Where are you? And why didn't you take your cell phone with you?"

Which question did he want her to answer?

"Um… I'm… uh…" Now, Jackie was sobbing so hard that she wouldn't have been able to answer, even if her brain hadn't been swirled in fog.

"Ma. Okay. Listen to me," her son's voice sounded exasperated. "Hand the phone back to the bartender."

Jackie hiccupped and handed the phone to the man who was helping her on the other side of the counter. She wanted to say, "My son would like to talk to you." But all she could manage was, "Here."

Jackie heard the click of pool balls on the green table behind her, and the deep rumble of men's course laughter. The acrid stench of cigarette smoke annoyed the heck out of her nose. Neon lights flickered in the bar's windows; the one that said, "Miller Light" buzzed loudly and flickered like a strobe light. She wondered why she had pulled into the bar—but lately, she did a lot of things that she couldn't explain.

Charles' voice was so loud that she could hear him through the earpiece: "Look man, Mom's been pretty loopy lately. I think she's got the onset of Alzheimer's or some sort of dementia. She's been gone for hours and… Oh God, man…" He paused. "Tell me where you are. Call the police if you have to, but whatever you do, don't let her leave."

The bartender looked like he was in his fifties, and was festooned in body art. His used-to-be-white, sleeveless shirt was decorated with grease stains. He was bald and had a huge beer gut, and Jackie figured he could hold off six or seven guys in a brawl.

"Take a deep breath," the guy said. "My name is Manny. I'm at the Hungry Horse Saloon, here in Harrisonburg, Virginia…."

He was cut short by Charles' yelling through the earpiece.

"Harrisonburg! That's at least two hours from here! Oh my God! How'd she get that far? Oh God! I hope she didn't hit anybody on the way!"

"Calm down, man," Manny said. "My ma went through the same thing. I'll keep her here and take care of her until you can come rescue her. Bring another driver who can drive her car back home. Don't worry. It'll be alright." His voice had a little bit of West Virginia twang.

Manny winked at Jackie. She realized that Manny might be a tough guy on the outside, but he was really a big teddy bear. She felt so out-of-control that it was a relief to have somebody help her.

After he hung up with Charles, Manny handed her some napkins to wipe her face and blow her nose. Then he whipped up a big burger and a mountain of fries. Jackie's favorite part was the huge, thick, strawberry shake to chase it all down.

"You're pretty fat, Manny," Jackie said.

Manny just patted her arm, and smiled at her inappropriate comment. He handed her a tall glass of Coke.

"Thanks for taking care of me. I have good days and bad days. Today was... um... it wasn't so good. When I have a good day, then I feel like my old self—I mean, the person I used to be—not an old person..." She realized that she was rambling again.

The fingers on her right hand seemed to have a mind of their own and were nervously groping a spoon on the worn Formica countertop. She had to grab them with her left hand in order to stop the fidgeting.

"How did you wind up here?" Manny asked, drying a glass on a worn, but clean towel.

She wrenched her gaze up from her intractable fingers to find his compassionate face. "I don't really remember... No, wait. I was going out to get my hair done. And then... um... I don't know, I was so confused. And I was driving and driving, and I didn't know where I was. And when I saw people in the parking lot, I thought I'd pull in to get some help." She was crying again.

"Don't cry. What's your name again?"

"It's um..." For a second she couldn't remember her own name. She felt lucky that she'd remembered Charles' phone number. She was having a really bad day. She slapped her forehead and that seemed to help.

"I'm Jackie." She looked down at herself and realized that she'd put on her shirt inside out this morning. She was grateful to Manny that he hadn't pointed out her faux pas.

"Well Jackie, I'm going to pretend that you're my mom. I'm going to take care of you until your son arrives. You pulled into the right place."

While Manny went to help another customer, Jackie began crying again. She was so angry with herself. What happened? She used to be a walking tape recorder. She had been a Pulitzer Prize winning photojournalist. Her stories and photos had been shown on every media outlet in the country. Now she was this... this thing that couldn't even find her way home. She felt helpless, useless.

But Jackie knew there was something important that she had to do before her memory was completely gone. Time was short—was it too late? What was that thing that was so important?

She was in a cave... No, not a cave. It was dark—she was hiding under a... under a truck. She smelled leaking oil and old diesel fuel. Was she in Iraq? Something bad—something very evil was happening, and she had to be quiet so the men wouldn't hear her. She raised her camera and began shooting with her long lens. Under a naked bulb, there was a man passing money in the puddle of light.

Did it have something to do with Aaeesha? She shook her head; that wasn't right. Aaeesha's treasure was very important too, but she was dead. Did Aaeesha die because of what Jackie was shooting that night? No, that wasn't right either. But the events were linked somehow.

She sucked in a deep breath, and forced herself to quit crying. When she wiped her face and calmed down, the revelation came to her: finding Aaeesha's treasure was the key. A box. Somewhere there was a box that held all the truth. It held Aaeesha's treasure and the important photos. And... and... some other very important things. If she could find Aaeesha's treasure, then she'd find the whole truth. The pictures that she had taken in the dark place many years ago would affect the whole country.

Manny stopped to see how she was doing. She dabbed at her eye, hoping her mascara hadn't streaked her face black.

"Aaeesha's treasure," Jackie said, grabbing his arm, trying to make him understand. "That's the key. I've got to find Aaeesha's treasure."

Manny nodded, but she saw that his eyes were full of pity, not comprehension.

CHAPTER TWO

Jackie sat on the chair in front of the mirror. The looking glass was about four feet in diameter and was attached to an antique vanity. Richard had bought it for her before the accident. It meant a lot to her.

The walls of her second-floor bedroom were a pleasant baby blue and covered with photos. Most of the pictures were of her family, but there were several landscapes. Her favorites were the black and whites of Rosalynn Carter and that other woman—she couldn't remember her name right now, but she was a First Lady too and had been Jackie's close friend.

Beneath her slippers was a thick, deep blue Persian rug—the real thing. It had belonged to her parents when they'd lived in Basra. Her father had it shipped with the rest of their belongings when they'd moved to Virginia.

Jackie's salt and pepper hair hung to the middle of her back. She was trying to brush it, but something was wrong with the brush. She looked at it curiously, realizing that she was holding the bristles the wrong way—away from her head. She flipped the brush and continued her grooming.

The 66-year-old who looked back at her was almost a stranger. She had never been stunningly beautiful like her daughter Abigail—may she rest in peace. But neither was she homely. There was an ethereal quality that spoke of grace, hidden beneath the skin.

Her hair had once been jet black, and her face molded from the sands of the Middle East. Her father had been an Iraqi with American citizenship and had taught her Arabic from the cradle. She got her facial features from his side of the family; she looked Arabic.

Jacqueline had graduated at the top of her class at Emerson. She had once been the most sought-after photojournalist of her time. Now, she sat here, a shell of her former self. Her deep brown, once intelligent eyes were now glazed and confused.

She looked at her thin frame. She knew that she was losing weight, but she didn't know how to stop it. Something was wrong; she was scared.

To her right sat the rocking chair that her mom had used back in Basra Iraq. The old thing had survived a two generations of children and a move across the Atlantic. She could almost feel her childish head on her mother's shoulder.

She double-checked her reflection to make sure her shirt was on correctly today and was relieved to see the buttons pointing in the right direction. The deep tan of the blouse complimented her dark brown eyes and olive colored skin. She liked the touch of white lace on the collar.

Downstairs, there was a knock at the front door. Jackie heard Charles' voice calling through the glass.

"Ma! It's me. Open up."

Jackie sighed. She loved her son, but lately he'd grown anxious. Every time he came over, he fussed about something that she wasn't doing right. The car incident the other night had driven the man practically nuclear. He'd yelled at her the whole way home. All she wanted was to sleep in the passenger seat; she'd been so exhausted. Even now, she still felt the remnants of fatigue from that horrible evening.

She placed her brush on the vanity, taking a moment to feel the familiarity of the wood grain beneath her fingers. She felt like she was touching the memory of Richard's soul.

It was December 24. Jackie was running toward the back door because her kids were at it again. Their pre-teen voices were shattering the tranquility of the neighborhood. It hadn't started snowing yet, but the forecasters were calling for it. Jackie had sent them to the back yard, so she could get some baking done.

"It's mine! Stay out of my stuff!" Charles shouted.

"I wasn't hurting it! I just wanted to play!" It was Abigail's younger voice.

"Give it back!" Charles yelled.

"Children! Stop it!" Jackie called as she ran.

Not yet having made it to the yard, Jackie heard the grunts of children scuffling over a toy. She heard the snap of plastic just as she burst through the back door.

"Mooooooom!" Charles held up his broken Teenage Mutant Ninja Turtle action figure. "She broke it! Make her stay out of my stuff!"

The joyful moment of familial discord was shattered by an even larger crash at the front of the house.

"What now?" Jackie shouted as she ran back into the house toward the sound of the larger crisis. As she passed the kitchen, she could smell something burning.

She rounded the hall corner to find Richard standing red-faced over a broken vase. Jackie screeched to a halt and stared in horror. The vase had been a gift from her mother.

"I… I'm sorry." Richard began. But when he saw Jackie's face, he must have realized his best recourse was to keep his mouth shut. She saw him biting his lip.

Jackie sensed her children at her sides. They were dumbfounded as they gaped at the mess. They knew how much that vase meant to Jackie. The silence was palpable.

Finally, Jackie found her voice. Her hands flailed wildly. "Richard, what are you doing? How did it get knocked down?"

It was then that she finally noticed the bulky item that Richard and his buddy Michael were trying to wrestle through the front door. It was about six feet tall and was covered in burlap.

"It's your Christmas present," Richard said sheepishly, laying his hand on the covered item. "We were trying to sneak it into the house. Um… I guess we weren't very stealthy."

The pressures of the day seemed to collapse in on her. Everything was going wrong. On top of it all, her mother's vase had just been smashed into a thousand pieces. Jackie was about to cry when the smoke alarm in the kitchen started screeching. Beep Beep Beep Beep Beep Beep!

Richard sprinted into action and burst past her and the kids. Jackie heard a fire extinguisher being deployed. A moment later, Richard emerged back into the hallway followed by a billow of smoke.

"It's okay Mom." It was Charles. She realized that the twelve-year-old was hugging her around her waist. Abigail joined in.

Jackie stood for a moment feeling the warmth of her children's bodies against hers. She thought of the priceless gift of love. These kids meant more to her than anything in the world. Richard, the love of her life, had gone to immense effort to try to surprise her with a wonderful Christmas present. How could she be angry over these other insignificant things?

Jackie felt a tear roll down her cheek. It was a teardrop of gratitude. This was one of those crazy family moments when life couldn't be any better—even through the chaos. Yes, it was a mess, but it was Jackie's mess and she cherished every second.

She leaned her cheek down on the lanky boy's head and ran her hand across his face. He was too young to be able to articulate his feelings, but Charles had known exactly what his mother needed—a hug.

Richard leaned across the kids and hugged her too.

For most people, that Christmas could have been called the worst of their lives. But for Jackie, the moment of bonding had been the most precious Christmas gift in history.

The vase didn't matter. The broken toy no longer was on anybody's mind. Dinner could be purchased from Safeway.

Jackie sniffed and indicated a finger at Richard's friend Michael, who pulled the burlap back to reveal a beautiful vanity with a four-foot circular mirror. She loved it instantly. To her, the vanity represented that moment of familial bonding that had happened in the midst of chaos.

The banging on the front door again echoed through the house, jerking Jackie back to the present. She sighed and stood, running her hand once again across the vanity's surface. She felt the presence of the past and the spirits of her departed loves. She looked in the large mirror and saw the old lady looking back at her. The woman in the looking glass was almost a stranger.

As she made her way down the stairs and toward the front door, she looked into the living room. Things were starting to get messy and she felt out of control about the disorder. There were a few stacks of boxes in the corner that held some very important items—not that she remembered what those things were. Nevertheless, they needed to be protected.

She was jarred by the thought that perhaps one of those boxes might hold Aaeesha's treasure. She stopped to look, but the knock was more insistent this time.

"Mom, it's me. Charles," her son called again. "Can I come in?"

She peeked through the window to see Charles standing on the front porch. He was in his early thirties. He had gotten his height from his father, but he had Jackie's nose. Today he had on a suit jacket, and she could see his hospital nametag peeking from behind it. His tie was a simple brown to match his hair.

Jackie saw the top of another head behind Charles, but didn't take the time to study the face. She opened the door.

"Mom, I'd like you to meet Marna Hunt..." Charles began as he pushed the young lady front and center by a gentle hand.

"Abigail!" Jackie shrieked and grabbed the girl in a bear hug.

"No, Ma. I know she looks a lot like Abigail, but Abigail and Dad died in that car accident back in '98. This is Marna…"

"Abigail! It's been so long!" Jackie said, holding the girl at arm's length and studying her.

The girl looked to be in her mid-twenties. She was as thin as a reed and only came to Jackie's chin. A pool of mirth hid in her coffee colored eyes. The young woman's jet black hair was pulled into a tight ponytail, and Jackie could see the end of a red bow tying it in place. Her arms were like sticks, and the legs showing from beneath the turquoise dress were spindly.

But none of that mattered. Abigail was home.

"Please, come in." Jackie turned and motioned the pair to follow. "Sorry about the mess," Jackie called over her shoulder. "The cleaning lady's been sick lately." She laughed at her own joke. "I'm the cleaning lady."

"Oh God, Ma. It stinks in here," Charles complained as he closed the front door. She saw him look into the living room. "And how do you find anything in this mess? Please, let me help you clean."

"You will not help me clean," Jackie said, turning on her son with fire in her eyes. She planted her hands on her hips. "Last time you tried to help me clean, you just started throwing things in the trash. You threw out valuable things—including photos from my stint at the White House. We'll never get that stuff back. You're too careless."

Charles rolled his eyes and threw his hands into the air: "You're impossible, Ma! You live like a pig!"

Marna turned to Charles. "It's okay Charles. I'm here now. I'll help Mom straighten things up." She turned to Jackie. "I'll help you, Ma. I'll be real careful, I promise. We'll go through each item, and you can tell me what you want to keep."

"She's not your…"

Marna cut Charles off with a furious look.

"No," Jackie said, waving her hand dismissively. "It'd be too much work. I wouldn't want to put you through all that."

"Look, Ma," Charles said forcefully, his finger pointing at the young woman. "Marna is a home helper, and I've hired her through a company that comes highly recommended..."

Marna cut Charles off with the palm of her hand, and she turned her face sweetly to Jackie. "Um... Mom?" she said, rubbing the back of her neck and looking sheepish. "I kinda... Well, do you think that I could stay here with you a little while if I helped you clean up? I really need a place to stay..." She looked at her tennis shoes. Jackie noticed that they looked a bit worn.

"Are you in trouble, Abigail?" Jackie asked, concerned. She put a finger under Marna's chin and raised it so she could look the girl in the eye.

"Well, um... sort of. I just need a place to stay until I can work things out. I'll help around the house a bit to pay for my rent. I can cook real good."

"Of course!" Jackie said. "I mean, your brother, Dr. Charles, has that huge mansion, but if you'd rather stay with me—I'd be delighted." She looked around tentatively. "But where will you sleep? Your room upstairs has a lot of boxes..."

"Thanks, Ma!" Marna said, bouncing and hugging the 66-year-old's neck. She pecked her on the cheek. "I left my suitcase in Charles' car. I'll be right back." She bounded past Charles and out the door.

"Look, Ma..." Charles began again.

"Save it, son," Jackie cut him off angrily. "Your sister needs a place to stay. It's my duty to take care of her."

"...but Ma. You don't understand. She's not Abigail. Her name's Marna Hunt, and she's a home helper, and she's here to take care of you."

"No, Charles. This time you're the one who doesn't understand. I don't know why you're trying to confuse me, but obviously you've got some sort of problem with your sister living here. But get over it, because I'm not changing my mind."

"Fine!" Charles shook his head angrily. "Have it your way. I gotta get back to work. You two have fun."

He whirled to go just as Marna bounced back in the door with her suitcase.

Charles looked at his mother who was tapping her toe in frustration. He turned back to Marna. "I think you're being unprofessional, but she obviously likes you." He ran his hand through his hair as if he was torn by a decision. "You need to stop pretending to be somebody you aren't."

He glanced at his watch. "I've got a surgery in an hour, and I don't have time for this. But when I'm done, you'd better believe I'm gonna have a chat with your boss."

Charles pulled a set of keys out of his pocket and handed them to the girl. "Here are the keys to Mom's car. Under no circumstances is she allowed to drive—last time she wound up in Harrisonburg. You've got her credit card, so you can buy food and cleaning supplies. You've also got my phone number if you need anything." He shook his head.

"Naw. We'll be fine, Charles. Us ladies are gonna have a great time." She patted his arm. "Now get out of here and get back to the hospital."

Jackie felt herself drifting again.

Abigail bounded down the stairs two steps at a time. Her teenage face had always been so fresh and innocent. Her hair was always flowing in the wind because she always ran—never walked. "Ma! Love you! I'm headed out with Gina! We'll be back before ten! Bye!"

"Ma?" Marna was shaking her arm and pulling her back to the present.

"Oh. I'm sorry. I drifted a little bit there. What were you saying?"

"I said, let's go get some lunch. Then, while we're out, we'll get some cleaning supplies so we can get started."

Jackie looked around her at the mess. "I dunno. Why don't we start tomorrow?"

"We'll see how we feel when we get back. Come on, I can't wait to hear what you've been up to lately."

The energy of the girl infected Jackie. She smiled. She kicked off her slippers and stepped into her shoes by the front door. She grabbed her sweater off a pile of boxes. "Okay, but you've gotta buy me ice cream for dessert."

CHAPTER THREE

They sat at a booth in Ledo Pizza. They were just off the Washington & Old Dominion trail, but on the other side of Maple Avenue—the main thoroughfare of Vienna, Virginia. Marna pulled a slice off the plate and caught the mozzarella strings with the index finger of her left hand.

Hanging from the ceiling, the dim lights couldn't keep up with the dazzling sunlight that was streaming into the pizza parlor. The pizza sat on an elevated platter with a pedestal. The scent of pizza grease saturated the walls and the cheap plastic seats of the booth.

"The world runs on secrets," Jackie told Marna. "My mother had secrets; I had secrets; you probably have some secrets too."

Marna didn't answer but smiled conspiratorially as she sprinkled hot pepper on her slice.

"I thought you hated hot pepper, Abby," Jackie said, puzzled.

Marna shrugged. "I guess we all grow up." She held the slice high in the air and bit off the pointy end.

"I've got to tell you some secrets. You're old enough now, and Lord knows I can't trust Charles—he's been so crazy lately."

"What are your secrets, Ma?" Marna asked as she wiped some grease off her lips with the back of her hand.

"I… um… Well, that's just the problem. I don't remember them anymore. They're very important. I need your help."

"How am I going to help you remember something that you can't remember?" Marna stopped chewing. She looked puzzled. "Come on, Ma, you've gotta eat more. You need to keep up your weight." She pushed another slice onto Jackie's plate.

Jackie pushed the slice around with her finger for a moment. "I hid the important stuff in a box somewhere. I've gotta figure out where I've hidden it." She tapped her temple with her index finger. "The clues are stuck in here, but my mind is all jumbled, and my memories are scrambled. Sometimes, I have thoughts and words that won't come out right. Then other times, I suddenly remember something, but a few minutes later I lose my thoughts again."

She looked up, appreciating how her only daughter was listening so intently. "I just thought that if I gave you clues when they come to me, that maybe you could remember them, and we could figure it out together."

Marna nodded. She picked up Jackie's slice and put it into the older woman's hand. Without thinking, Jackie took a bite and started chewing. "My Mom gave me a secret when I was a little girl. And then, Aaeesha, my best friend in the whole world—she had a secret. Well, really it wasn't Aaeesha's secret, it was... it was... I don't remember, but it was something that was related to her." She slapped herself in the forehead. "Maybe it was more of a treasure. Yes, that's it. It was Aaeesha's treasure. And then there's another secret that the whole world needs to hear—it's really important. But I can't remember any of it." She gritted her teeth in frustration.

Marna nodded. "We'll figure it out together, Ma. It'll come back to you when the time is right."

After the pizza was gone, Jackie ordered an ice cream cone. She sat, enjoying the sensation of cold on her tongue.

After lunch, as they were walking over to the Safeway, Jackie realized that she'd eaten almost half of the pizza pie. She rubbed her tummy. "I don't remember the last time I felt full." She gave Marna a side hug as they walked. "It's good to have you back, Abby."

Marna smiled up at her. "It's good to be back."

Scents of damp earth hung on the humid Virginia air. Somewhere above, a jet engine was roaring in delight as it gained altitude from Dulles airport, or maybe Reagan National.

Jackie got the uneasy feeling that Marna was hiding something. "Honey, you gotta tell me what's wrong. That's what mothers are for— we listen."

They walked in silence for a moment. Finally, Marna opened her mouth. "Not yet, Ma. I'll tell you later. I promise. But I'm not ready yet."

All of a sudden Jackie saw a guy with a dark suit and dark sunglasses. She hiccupped and darted behind Marna. "That guy over there," She whispered hoarsely. "He's one of them."

"One of who?" Marna asked. The man had a curly wire coming from his collar connected to an earpiece.

He stepped up to the ladies and looked around Marna at Jackie. "Good afternoon, Ms. Jacqueline Scott. Good to see you out and about on such a fine day."

Jackie didn't answer; she just kept her face hidden behind Marna.

"Hi, my name is Johnson." The man held out his hand, but Marna just left it hanging.

"What do you want with Jackie?" Marna asked, angrily.

"Well, your friend, Ms. Scott, is on the FBI watch list. We drop by occasionally and make sure that she's not selling any secrets to the Russians, or anything like that."

He laughed as if everyone knew the joke.

"Let me see your badge!" Marna demanded.

Jackie peeked over Marna's shoulder as the man produced a shiny shield in a wallet.

"Well, *this* woman's got dementia, and she's under my care. Why don't you go write some parking tickets, or go rescue a kitty from a tree, or find something constructive to do? If you've got nothing better to do than harassing senile old ladies, then you ought to just turn in your damned badge!"

"Naw, we just want Ms. Scott to know that we're still watching." The man shot a finger gun at Marna before turning to walk away.

Marna waited until the man got into his car and drove away. Reaching her hand behind her back she gently caught Jackie's. "Now what was that all about? And don't lie to me."

"It's them. Those agents. I know something, and they keep harassing me about it. The problem is that I don't remember what the information is. It's important, but I can't remember." Jackie was shaking.

Marna shook her head and walked angrily toward the supermarket. Jackie saw her head constantly swiveling, watching for the Feds. Jackie appreciated Marna's protection. She was pretty shaken up as well.

By the time they'd reached the store, the ladies had calmed down. Marna set about the task of shopping, and Jackie followed meekly.

It relieved Jackie that Marna seemed to know exactly what things to buy. She pushed the cart up and down the aisles, chatting ceaselessly about all the things she was going to make. The endless choices of shopping was something that drove Jackie insane. It was wonderful to have her daughter take charge.

At the checkout, Jackie gushed at the cashier. "Bob, you remember my daughter, Abigail? She's come back home to stay with me for a little while." She hadn't remembered Bob's name, but the little plastic tag on his shirt had helped.

Bob scowled at Marna. He looked flustered. "But Mrs. Scott, your daughter's…"

Marna cut him off with a shake of her head. She held out her hand. "Good to see you again, Bob. I know I've been away for a while."

Bob stuttered a moment before finding his composure. "Um… Good to see you too… um… Abby." He took the proffered hand gingerly. He had a confused look on his face.

As they were walking back home with their bags, Jackie started drifting again.

She was nine. Mom was downstairs talking on the phone with a neighbor, and Aaeesha's mother was cooking something on the stove that made Jackie's mouth water.

Upstairs and on the floor of Jackie's bedroom, the girls were playing. "Okay, your doll is the student, and mine is the teacher," she said to Aaeesha in Arabic, pushing the little furniture around to make a schoolhouse.

"Don't be so bossy, Jackie," Aaeesha said. "This time, I want my doll to be the teacher."

"No," Jackie said impatiently. "These are my dolls, and you have to do what I say!"

Jackie looked into her friend's eyes and saw the hurt.

"You're rich and spoiled!" Aaeesha said, getting up and stomping out of the room. A moment later, she poked her head around the door and yelled, "My Momma has to work for your mother and earn every penny, just so we can eat. Your Daddy works for the oil companies and is very rich. You're not special just because your Daddy's rich!" Aaeesha slammed the door and Jackie heard her little feet marching down the stairs.

Jackie was heartbroken. She knew her friend was right. Their economic disparity was something that she'd known for a while but she hadn't yet come to terms with the reality. She'd been to Aaeesha's house—it was clean, and tiny, and everything was worn. Aaeesha's clothes were always threadbare.

Jackie was suddenly embarrassed at her parents' wealth. Aaeesha was her best friend in the whole world. Jackie wanted to make things right. She needed to share.

Jackie found a box, and she began gathering her most treasured possessions: dolls, trinkets from the United States, her favorite book, and a little bottle of perfume. She took her favorite dress out of the closet and folded it neatly into the box.

She took the peace offering downstairs and found Aaeesha's face behind a book. But Jackie knew that Aaeesha was really just hiding her face. She was too mad to even look in Jackie's direction.

"Here," Jackie said, holding out the box. "This is for you. These are all my favorite things—I want you to have them. You were right. I'm sorry. You are my best friend and I don't want us to be mad at each other."

"No," Aaeesha said from behind her book. "I don't want your stupid stuff."

"Please. I don't want us to fight. My things mean nothing to me, but you're my friend."

Aaeesha threw down the book and grabbed Jackie's neck, sobbing. "I don't want to fight either."

Suddenly, Jackie realized that she was sitting in a chair in her kitchen in Vienna—thousands of miles from her Iraqi home. Marna was scrubbing out the refrigerator. There were groceries on the table, waiting to be put away.

Jackie wanted to reach out and clutch Aaeesha tight. She and Aaeesha had been through so much together. Memories and current reality swirled together in an inseparable maelstrom.

"Daddy will be home soon," she said to Marna. "Will supper be ready for him?"

Marna looked over her shoulder at the older woman. "We'll have supper ready in a few hours."

"Aaeesha's my best friend," Jackie said thoughtfully. "I was mean to her, but she forgave me."

"We all make mistakes," Marna said wisely. Her voice sounded muted, because her head was inside the fridge. "But a good friend is a person who knows all our faults and loves us anyway."

"How did you get to be so wise, young lady?"

"I guess I learned from the best," she said. The grin in her voice was evident, even though her head was buried in the big, white icebox.

Jackie came fully to the present. She suddenly realized how far she'd been gone. She knew now that Aaeesha was dead and so was Abigail and Richard. She wanted to cry. She didn't know if it was because she missed them so much or if it was because of embarrassment at her own mind.

"Probably some of both," she said out loud.

Her mind swirled a bit. There was something wrong but she couldn't put her finger on it. Abigail, Richard, and Aaeesha were dead. Yet Abigail was right here cleaning out the refrigerator. She felt confused and disconnected.

"I found some earrings in here," Marna said, pulling her head out of the icebox and jerking Jackie back to the present. She handed Jackie a pair of pearls.

"Oh," Jackie said, embarrassed. Her confusion was momentarily distracted by the cold pearls in her hand. She looked forlornly at them. The misplaced jewelry was just another reminder of her failing mind. "Sometimes, I put things in the wrong place," she said sadly.

After Marna had cleaned out the refrigerator, she scrubbed down the rest of the kitchen. The whole place smelled fresh and new. She cooked up some spaghetti and whipped together a nice salad.

"Let's get some wine to go with dinner," Jackie said.

"No!" Marna replied loudly. Her face was red, then turned sheepish. "I mean… um… No, I can't."

"Why?" Jackie asked.

"I... um... well, I guess I might as well tell you." She paused as if she was trying to find her words. Jackie knew what that was like, so she gave her a moment. "I'm a recovering alcoholic. If I were to get a taste, I'd fall off the wagon and crash my life again." She shook her head. "There. Now you know my secret."

Jackie was stunned. "How long has this been going on? I don't remember you having a drinking problem."

Marna looked embarrassed. "You never knew, Mom. But it mostly happened while I wasn't living here."

Jackie took the girl in her arms. "I love you anyway. It's okay. I'm glad you told me." She kissed the top of her head. "If you don't want wine, then I won't have any either."

Marna pulled away. "Thanks, Mom. Anyway, I'm going to have to go to an AA meeting on Tuesdays. Then I've gotta also go to a dementia caregiver's support group on Thursday evenings."

Marna picked up the dishes and started out of the kitchen. "Come on. Let's eat out back."

They spread the dishes on the picnic table that overlooked the Washington and Old Dominion Trail. Bikers and joggers passed on the blacktop ribbon. Jackie could smell the slow-moving water in Piney Branch Creek. In a thicket on the other side of the creek, she spotted a doe and fawn grazing.

"It's so peaceful out here," Jackie sighed, as Marna served the spaghetti.

"Who takes care of your yard?" Marna asked, sitting down and uncovering the hot garlic bread.

"Charles hires people to do it for me," Jackie answered.

They ate in silence for a moment before Jackie looked up, her eyes glittering with mischief. "You kissed Robbie Miller under that tree," she said, pointing.

"Mom!" Marna protested.

"What? Don't tell me you don't remember," Jackie laughed. "And people say *I'm* the one with the memory problem."

CHAPTER FOUR

They brought the dishes back in from the yard. Marna started washing up, and Jackie went into the living room and began moving boxes around.

"We'll tackle those tomorrow if you want, Ma," Marna called from the sink.

"No. Got to do it now," Jackie muttered. She opened the top box and began rummaging through it. "It's in here somewhere. I've just got to find it."

Jackie felt a tear rolling down her cheek—the loss, the frustration, her mind. *Everything was slipping away!* Anger surged through her. "I used to be so smart!" she growled at herself. "Now I'm turning into a senile old bitch!"

She took the box and furiously dumped it out into the middle of the floor—papers and photos strewn everywhere. She fell to her knees and savagely began rifling through the mess. Curses escaped her lips. The more she searched, the more frustrated she became.

Behind her, she heard Marna's tennis shoes on the wooden floor. "Oh Mom, what have you done?"

"This!" Jackie shouted, extending her hand at the mess. Why couldn't she see the problem? "I'm an old woman, and my mind is turning to shit, and I can't find shit, and I'm mad as hell. I've dumped this box out so that I can find the clue. *I've got to find the treasure!*" Jackie rarely cursed, but she was so frustrated.

"Oh, I see what's going on." Marna sat down in the middle of the mess and took both of Jackie's hands in her own. "I didn't think about this, but it's six o'clock. You're experiencing what's called, sundowning. You probably feel this way every day at six o'clock, but nobody's here to help you."

Jackie just looked with pleading in her eyes, so Marna continued. "It's okay. It's quite common among dementia patients. It'll pass in a couple of hours."

"I don't want dementia. I want it to go away," Jackie said sullenly. "I want to be smart again like I used to be."

Marna nodded sagely. "We all want that. But fighting that battle will get us nowhere. We have what we have; now we need to do the best we can."

She reached one of her hands up and smoothed Jackie's hair. "So, you need to tell me how you want me to help you. Do you want me to distract you with other activities, or do you want me to just let you handle it yourself?"

"Help me," Jackie begged through tears. "Please help me."

Marna took her cell phone out of her pocket to check the time. "Okay. I have to leave at 7:00 to go to my support meeting. But I'll help you until then."

She looked at the mess that she was sitting in. "Alright, we need something to keep your hands busy. We might as well start right here. I'm gonna get a little bossy, but we're doing it to keep your hands occupied. If you want to quit at any time, just say so."

"Okay," Jackie said meekly.

Marna held up a photo. "These look like photos you took when you were working at the White House. What are these papers?" She held up a fistful of typed sheets.

"Those are the reports and newspaper articles that I wrote. You'll find lots of handwritten notes too."

Marna stopped.

"The secret that the FBI man was worried about—is that in these boxes?"

Jackie shrugged. "I don't know. I don't remember. Maybe if I see a clue or a photograph, I might remember what it was."

Marna nodded. "Well, I guess we won't know until we figure it out."

The younger woman sifted the photos with her hands for a moment. "Maybe, we should sort them according to whomever the President was at the time. Can you recognize the people in the photos and know what administration they belong to?"

"Um… I can try."

"Okay. When did you start covering the White House?"

"1979. The year you were born. I wanted to be a good mother, so I quit the war correspondent gig."

"You were a great mom." Marna patted Jackie's arm and smiled. "So, um, let's see. In 1979, who was President? Nixon? Carter?"

"Jimmy Carter," Jackie said emphatically. "I was Rosalynn's personal photographer." She thought for a minute. "I think I was Laura Armstrong's ** personal photographer too. We were friends."

"Alright, let's find all the photos and all the reports that would have been submitted under the Carter administration."

Soon, Jackie was finding photographs and reports and telling the story of every shot. Marna began a stack of Carter admin pics and another of the reports of that era. Then they moved on to Ronald Reagan.

Suddenly, Marna slapped herself in the forehead. "I've gotta go Mom—I'm late. If you want to keep sorting, that's fine. Or you can do something else if you want. I'll be at the dementia support meeting. I'll tape my cell phone number to the phone, so you can call me if you need anything."

**Some names have been changed to allow the author literary freedom.*

"I'll be fine," Jackie said. "I've lived here by myself for years, so one night won't be any different. Go do what you need to do. Go get the support you need." She leaned over and kissed Marna's cheek. "And thanks for helping me through the sundowning. It was a lot better with you here."

Jackie watched Marna write her phone number on a piece of paper and tape it to the phone. Then she bounced out the door. Jackie sighed and hugged herself. She still felt anxious, but it was a lot better than when she'd dumped out the box.

She went to the kitchen and found a teacup. Marna had put all the cups into one organized cupboard.

She found the tea, filled the mug with water, and then put it into the microwave to heat. When it dinged, she took it out and sat at the kitchen table and began sipping the tea.

She was a girl again—maybe 10. She and Mom were walking along the pier. There were people bustling about, but everyone was engaged in their own business, so it felt like they were alone in a sea of busy souls.

"See those big ships?" her mother asked in English, pointing at the gigantic hulls that towered tall over the docks. "Your father is in charge of loading oil onto those boats. The oil is then hauled across the world to various refining factories. Without that oil, the world would grind to a halt."

"So, Daddy's really important?" Jackie asked.

Her mother nodded. "He is, but he can't do what he does without you and me. So, by extension, we're really important too."

"How do you mean?" Jackie asked.

"We keep his secrets," Mom smiled down on her daughter.

"I don't have any secrets," Jackie said.

"Not yet. But I have a very big secret, and since I think you're old enough, I'm going to share it with you."

Jackie blinked. She could tell that this was an important moment. She looked up at her mother expectantly.

"The secret I'm about to share, you have to promise that you will never tell a single soul. If you tell anyone, even Aaeesha, then we will have to move out of Iraq, and Daddy will no longer be allowed to be in charge of loading the boats. So, this is very serious."

Jackie nodded, feeling as if the entire fate of the world weighed on her shoulders.

Her mother continued. "I know this is a big burden, but if I don't tell you, then I'll be robbing you of the truth." She took a deep breath as if she was plunging into the deep end of the pool.

"People think that I am Muslim, like your father. But I'm not. I am Jewish. Nobody knows this, not even Aaeesha's mother, and she must never learn this secret. As you know, most Muslims hate Jews."

Jackie waited, sensing that her mother wanted to tell her more. "Your father and I are the modern-day version of Romeo and Juliet. I was the only one of my family to survive the Auschwitz concentration camp— I'll tell you about that someday. After Auschwitz, I emigrated to the U.S. It was there that I met your father, and we fell in love despite our differences. You were born in the U.S., so you are a citizen of that country, even though you may feel like Iraq is your home."

"So, your secret is that you are a Jew," Jackie recapped. "And because you keep that secret in your heart, Daddy gets to help load the oil on the tankers, and the whole world can function. And that's all because you keep your secret safe."

"Yes, that's the simple version," her mother said.

Jackie turned and looked her mother in the eye. "I promise you that I won't ever tell anyone. Not ever. This is our secret."

Jackie thought for a moment before speaking again. "And because you keep this secret, you can hire Aaeesha's mother, and that helps to keep a roof over their heads," the girl said, looking into her mother's face for confirmation.

"You're smarter than your years, child." Mom paused and looked into the distance. "This world is so full of evil. I try to find little ways of making a difference," she sighed. "It's a little thing compared to the whole world, but yes, we take care of Aaeesha's mother. Aaeesha doesn't know it, but we've also set aside a college fund for her."

Jackie was shocked and hugged her Mom. "You're trying to make the world a better place."

Jackie saw a tear in her mother's eye, as she bent down and kissed the top of her daughter's head. "I love you sweetie," she said, hugging the girl close.

Jackie found herself sitting at the table in a strange kitchen. It was not the kitchen of her childhood. It took her a moment to remember it was her own house in Vienna, Virginia. In front of her sat a teacup that was half empty, and cold.

She heard the front door slam and fear shot through her heart. "Hello?" she called with a quaking voice.

"It's me, Mom. Abby," the young voice called. Then the woman stepped into the room.

"Who are you?" Jackie pushed her chair away from the girl, frightened. Her eyes darted about, looking for a place to run. But terror stole all the strength from her legs and rooted her to her seat.

"It's me, Abigail. Don't you remember? Earlier today, Charles brought me over. Then we had pizza, we cleaned the kitchen, and cooked spaghetti for supper."

Jackie looked around. The kitchen did seem a lot cleaner than usual. She shook her head. "But you're dead. You died in the car accident with your father."

The girl kneeled in front of her ward and took her hands. "My real name is Marna Hunt. I'm a home helper. But when you first saw me, you thought I was Abigail, so I just went with it. Your son, Charles, hired me to help you. I don't care if you call me Marna, or Abigail. But I'm here to help you with whatever you need."

Jackie looked at the young lady that was on her knees in front of her. She seemed to remember something about a kind person helping her this afternoon. She figured that if the girl meant her harm, that she'd probably have done it by now.

"You say that Charles hired you?"

"Yes. Do you want to call him to verify?"

She slowly shook her head. "No. It's too late to wake him. I remember you, now. But you shouldn't play a trick on an old lady, that's not nice."

Jackie saw color running up her neck. "You were convinced I was Abigail, and Charles couldn't convince you otherwise. So, I just went with it."

"Yeah, I get confused sometimes." Jackie looked at her hands, ashamed. She remembered the girl now—she had helped her with the sundowning. She had left to go to a meeting. Now, she was back.

"It's okay. That's why I'm here."

"I remembered something while you were gone," Jackie finally said. "My mother was a Jew, but she pretended to be a Muslim so that my Daddy could ship oil to the rest of the world. Daddy really was a Muslim—our surname was Saeed."

Marna nodded and stood. She took a notepad from the cupboard over the sink and began writing. "Your mother was a Jew, and your father was Muslim. What else?"

"Mom paid for Aaeesha's college—Aaeesha was my best friend," Jackie said, remembering.

Marna wrote this down and looked up. "Anything else?"

Jackie sat for a moment. "I don't think so. Did I do good, Abigail? Did I remember something important?"

"It was very important," Marna said with certainty. She kissed the top of Jackie's head. "Anything that you remember is monumental."

"I want to go to bed. I'm tired," Jackie said, stretching out her hand so that Marna could help her to her feet.

CHAPTER FIVE

Jackie woke to the smell of coffee. It took her a moment to remember that she wasn't in Basra, but in Vienna—in America. She walked downstairs, and heard the sound of a scrub brush coming from the bathroom. There was a young woman who was on her knees scrubbing behind the toilet.

"Who are you?" Jackie demanded.

The young woman stood up and pulled off her huge rubber gloves. She stroked a stray hair behind her ear. "Oh good, you're up. I made coffee. Would you like some bacon and eggs?"

"Um, sure," Jackie said, and then it came back to her. "You're the woman that came by yesterday. What's your name again?"

"Marna," she said as she led the way to the kitchen. "But yesterday you called me Abigail."

"Abigail's dead," Jackie said, flopping down into a kitchen chair. "She and her daddy—that would be my husband, Richard Scott. Anyway, he was taking her to the University of Virginia—UVA. I was just ending my White House gig and occasionally going back into the field. I was following the President on a European tour. I was in Germany when I got the call."

She looked at the ceiling, her eyes going glassy. "I remember... it was like I had been punched in the stomach. I was sitting on my bed in the hotel. I remember wishing that I had been the one driving that day."

Jackie looked across the kitchen table at Marna, who had now gotten a cup of coffee and was sitting to listen. "You died," she said to the woman she thought was her daughter. "And I wasn't there. I felt so guilty."

"It's okay, Jackie," the girl reached across the table and patted her arm. "You did the best you could. Abby knew that."

"You're a good daughter, Abigail," Jackie said. She was having trouble remembering that the young woman in front of her wasn't her daughter.

Marna stood. "Eat your breakfast. We've got a big day ahead of us."

Jackie ate her eggs while Marna went back to scrubbing in the bathroom. When Jackie was done, she went to the door of the water closet and watched the girl work. Her ponytail bobbed as she scrubbed the brush over the ring that was around the tub.

"I called my supervisor this morning," she said, not looking at Jackie. "I told him how you called me Abigail yesterday… and how I'd just gone with it. He was very angry with me. I'm on probation. He said that you could call me anything you want, but that I'm never supposed to pretend to be someone that I'm not."

She straightened up on her knees and looked at Jackie. "I'm sorry; I was unprofessional. I shouldn't have deceived you. That was wrong of me."

Jackie didn't answer so she went back to scrubbing. "But when I walked in, you reminded me so much of my grandmother—she's the only family member that ever really loved me. Then you started calling me Abigail, and I wanted to be what you wanted me to be…" Her voice trailed off. "I'm sorry." She bit her lower lip. "Grandma had dementia, and I loved her so much. She's the reason I became a home helper."

"It's okay, Abby," Jackie said. "Compared to the mistakes I make, yours are insignificant."

"Marna," the girl corrected.

Jackie waved her hand dismissively. "You said we have a busy day today. What are we going to do?"

Marna filled the bottom of a bucket and swished the water up the sides of the tub to rinse away the dirty suds. "Well, it's up to you. We can go through more boxes, or we can go visit the Humane Society of Fairfax."

"Why would we go to the Humane Society? Do you think it's inhumane to live here? Does it stink too much?" she laughed.

Marna laughed too. "No, it's a place that rescues pets. Kind of like a used pet store. You get a pet that's already trained and knows how to love."

"I don't want a pet," Jackie said. "I've never been a pet person."

Marna shrugged and continued cleaning. "We don't have to adopt a pet; we can just go there and cuddle them. It's so much fun just to play with the animals."

Jackie looked over her shoulder at the mess in the living room. "So, you're saying this would be a good excuse to avoid cleaning?"

Marna laughed. "Sure. If that's what you want to do."

Thirty minutes later, Jackie was strapping herself into the passenger seat of the Mercedes. "You know, I got myself in trouble with this car last week."

"I heard about that," Marna said smiling. "You drove all the way to Harrisonburg. You had Charles so upset he was about to call the National Guard."

"Not my finest moment," Jackie answered.

"Oh, I don't know about that," Marna said. "Everything has an upside. If that incident hadn't happened, Charles wouldn't have hired me. So, see? It all works out."

Jackie tapped her finger on her knee. "That's right, you're not Abigail. I keep forgetting. What's your real name?"

"Marna," she said, putting the car into gear and pulling onto the street.

"And you have a drinking problem?"

"Good memory. I'm a recovering alcoholic. And I have a boyfriend that is probably bad company." Marna merged onto I-66, heading west.

"How old are you, Abigail?"

"Marna," she corrected. "I'm 26. I grew up in a bad home where my mother was a junkie and a whore. By the time I was 12, I was out on the street doing things I ain't proud of. But when I turned 18, I got into a program that changed my life. I got clean, and later on I took courses to learn how to be a home helper, with a specialization in dementia care."

"Where's your mother?" Jackie asked.

"Same place as Abigail," Marna answered. "In the graveyard. But the difference is that my mom drugged herself into the grave. Abigail was loved her whole life. Frankly, I'm jealous of Abigail."

Jackie watched Marna pull the big machine into a parking lot. They went inside, where they were accosted by a cacophony of barking and mewing.

"Can we visit with one of your pets?" Marna shouted over the din to the woman at the counter.

The woman led Jackie and Marna to the cages in the back. "Ooooh, can we hold that one?" Marna pointed to the cage of a small Rat Terrier.

The volunteer opened the cage and took out the little dog. "Good choice. This is Cassie. She's five years old. Her previous owner was a retired woman who… Well, she passed. But all that's to say that Cassie knows how to take care of an older lady. She's already house broken, and a small dog like this will probably live to be fifteen or seventeen."

The lady handed the dog over to Marna. Cassie immediately wiggled in Marna's arms, stretching as far as she could and licking Jackie's face.

Jackie squealed with surprise, and then with delight. She took a step backwards and began petting the dog's head. But Cassie was having none of that; she twisted around to lick Jackie's hand.

"She likes you," the volunteer beamed. "You must remind her of her previous owner."

"Can you hand me that leash?" Marna asked, pointing at one that hung by the cage. "Maybe we can take her outside for a little bit."

The volunteer clipped the pink leash onto Cassie's harness. "I've got to get back to my desk, but you can take her out to the yard. She probably needs to go out anyway." She handed Marna a plastic bag. "Here, you'll probably need this."

As soon as Marna set the eight-pound dog on the floor, she began straining at her leash for the exit. They led Cassie out to a small patch of yard where she did her business.

Jackie and Marna sat in a pair of lawn chairs, and Cassie quickly jumped into Jackie's lap. She licked Jackie's chin for a few moments, then curled up into the woman's lap and fell asleep with a contented sigh. Jackie petted the dog's head.

"Jackie, I'm concerned about this FBI watch list thing," Marna said. "What did you do, or what do you know that they're so concerned about?"

Jackie felt like she was about to cry. "I don't remember," she managed to choke out. "I used to have an eidetic memory—I never forgot anything. Then one day I woke up, and pieces were missing."

She looked down at the contented dog in her lap, remembering when she was razor sharp. "I witnessed a lot of things when I covered the White House. I got to know the families of several of the Presidents. Several times, I was invited to join Presidents for their family dinners. I was the photographer in the Oval Office more times than I can count. I observed Presidential meetings, and I heard them speak with other national and foreign leaders. I am friends with former First Lady Laura Armstrong. I also saw a lot of horrors when I was a war correspondent. Maybe I saw something in the White House, but who knows..." She shrugged.

She stopped, remembering something. "In 1982, Ronald Reagan was doing a Middle East tour. I didn't want to go on the tour because I had children at home. But Nancy Reagan liked me a lot, and pressured my editor, so I was sent. While in Egypt, the President disappeared for a little while. Because I could speak Arabic, I was able to track him through the streets to find his meeting location. With my long lens, I was able to photograph him at a meeting. I later learned that the identity of the other man was Saddam Hussein.

"When the Secret Service learned what I had on my camera, they confiscated my film," she grinned slyly at Marna. "However, they didn't know that I'd taken three rolls, and not just two."

Jackie petted the dog's ears. The dog quivered and sighed, licked Jackie's hand and fell back to sleep.

For some reason that Jackie couldn't explain, the dog felt as if it were a part of her soul. She watched her fingers trail through the short fur. Her fingers were no longer fidgeting, but connecting to the little dog's heart.

She felt Cassie's trust. There was an inexplicable connection between human and canine: a harmony that transcended the boundaries of species. It was as if a deity had proclaimed that the two should become one.

Jackie tried to wrestle her sluggish mind back to the conversation. Memories swirled, tangled together and all clumped up. But today, one was clear. "They swore me to secrecy and I never told anyone about the incident, until today," she smiled at her young charge. "And today, I told my daughter."

"Marna," the girl corrected.

"Yeah, I know you're not Abigail," Jackie nodded. "But it's easier to think of you as my daughter, may she rest in peace."

"What else do you remember?" Marna prodded.

"I have a photo of George Armstrong—the senior one—throwing an ashtray against the wall in anger," Jackie laughed. "He was really pissed, and I can't remember why."

"So, you know lots of Presidential secrets; that's why you're on the watchlist?"

"No. I think, maybe I made somebody angry," Jackie said, staring out into space.

"And you don't remember who?" Marna prompted.

"No," Jackie said sadly.

"Do you still have your photography equipment?" Marna asked.

Jackie snapped out of her reverie. "What was that, sweetie?"

"Your cameras, do you still have them?"

"Um… Sure. I think so. They're probably in that mess in the basement somewhere. Why?"

Marna touched a hand to her hair. "I've never had anybody take professional shots of me. You think you could do that?"

"Of course, you have!" Jackie said vehemently. "I took lots of photos of you when you were… Oh. Right. Sorry, you're that other girl."

"Marna," she said.

"Yeah. Um… Sure, I'd be happy to take some photos. My equipment is old, but…" She stopped. "I don't know if I remember how to work my camera. By the time I had retired, the digital cameras were pretty good. But I was an old stick-in-the-mud and never really made the switch. I've used digitals, but I never owned one. My old 35mm was pretty complex to operate…" Her voice trailed off in nostalgia, thinking of the old days.

Marna smiled and patted her hand. Cassie took the opportunity to lick it. "I'm betting that it will all come back. Things that you did your whole life are generally stored in your long-term memory."

"We'll see," Jackie said doubtfully. "But we've got to find those cameras first."

"Then that will give us an excuse to clean out the basement," Marna smiled broadly.

But Jackie was no longer listening. She was back in the hallways of the White House. She'd seen many of the rooms—at least the ones above ground. Her mind was sniffing along the hallways, just like little Cassie, sniffing for clues. Was she on the FBI watchlist because of one of the Presidents? Had she heard something, or seen something that she wasn't supposed to have seen? Had she done something or published something unintentionally?

The little dog licking her chin brought her back to the moment. "I don't know what it was—or is," Jackie said.

She looked at the young woman sitting beside her. "I was drifting for a little bit, wasn't I, Abigail?"

"Just a little. Not too long," Marna said. "It's fine. Nobody's in a hurry. I can wait."

Jackie reached over and patted the young woman's arm. "Thanks. Everyone else is in such a rush—I can't keep up anymore," she sighed. "I can't do a lot of things anymore."

"Are you hungry?" Marna asked.

Jackie thought for a moment. "Actually, I am a little hungry. Is it suppertime?"

Marna grinned. "No. Lunchtime." She stood and reached for the little dog. "Well, we'd better turn Cassie back over to the shelter people. We can't take her with us."

"No!" Jackie said, clutching the dog to her chest. "We can't send her back to her cage!" For some reason, the thought of the loving little dog in the shelter caused her heart to panic. "We have to save her! Please don't make her go back!"

Marna stepped back. "You're sure? You want to take Cassie home? That means that she'll be your dog, and pets are a lot of responsibility."

"We can't send her back!" Panic etched Jackie's voice. "We have to make the world a better place, even if it's just for one little dog. It's what Mom would have done." Her voice got quiet. "It's what I promised Aaeesha."

Jackie could see Marna lost in thought. "Charles is going to think this was my idea. He might be mad."

"No, this is my idea," Jackie said emphatically. "Let me tell him."

Marna took her phone out of her pocket and hit a speed dial. "Hello? Charles? This is Marna. I... um, well, I took your Mom over to the shelter because they taught me that pet therapy is good for dementia patients." She paused listening. "Well, what's happened is that Jackie refuses to leave unless we adopt this little dog." She listened for a moment. "Uh-huh.... Uh-huh.... No, this wasn't my idea, but I really do think it's a good thing." Then her face turned red. "Okay, just a sec."

Marna held out the phone for Jackie. "Hi Charles," she said as she took the iPhone. "No, this was not her idea; it was all mine."

"Ma, I'm not so sure this is such a good plan," Charles complained. "You need less responsibility, not more."

"Abigail—um, I mean... um, Marna will help me. But the important thing is that I can't let this little dog go back to the shelter. Her mother—I mean—her human died, and she needs somebody."

On the other end, she could hear her son growling. "I don't care what you say, Mom. This is Marna's idea, and I think it's a bad one. I think it was a bad idea to hire her. First, she was pretending to be Abigail, and now she's deceiving you and talking you into buying a dog. I think we need to let her go. We need to get things back to the way they were before!"

"*No!*" Jackie said vehemently. "You will not fire her. This is my decision and you have nothing to say in the matter. She's not deceiving me. Ab... I mean, the girl stays and so does the dog." She was mad enough to spit nails. "I'm hungry, and she is going to take me and the dog home to make us some lunch!"

She angrily held out the phone to Marna. "Hang up this phone, because I don't want to talk to him anymore!"

Marna looked at the phone as if it was a live hand grenade. She gingerly reached out and took the iPhone. "Um, Mr. Scott, um…" She listened for a moment, and nodded. Before she could even say goodbye, Charles had ended the call.

Marna looked at Jackie with fear in her eyes. "I need this job, Mrs. Scott. Charles is gonna try to get me fired."

Jackie smiled. "Do you know how many people tried to get me fired over the years? Let me handle this. Dial your boss and hand me the phone."

Marna started dialing, and held the phone to her ear. "May I please speak to Dr. Canfield?" Marna said into the iPhone. She waited a beat until the man answered. "Dr. Canfield, this is Marna Hunt… Yes, sir… um, Mrs. Scott would like to speak with you. See, her son is upset because she wants to adopt a pet from the shelter… Yes sir, I agree with you; I think it's a terrific idea too. But, Mrs. Scott would like to speak with you. Hold on, one moment, sir."

She handed the phone over to Jackie. "Dr. Canfield," Jackie purred. "I'm so glad to make your acquaintance over the phone. Abigail—I mean, um, Marna explained the situation to you."

"Yes, Ma'am. We find that pet therapy is often helpful with dementia patients."

"Well, sir. My son doesn't share your perspective. And when he heard that I wanted to adopt this cute little dog, he flew into a rage. He's threatening to fire Ab… I mean, um Marna, and I just wanted you to know that I will not tolerate Ab… Marna's removal. She has been very helpful, and I would like a commendation placed in her HR file—if you would please."

"Well, Mrs. Scott, I'm glad to hear that her work has been satisfactory. I will add that commendation to her file. And Mrs. Scott, if you could do me one favor…"

"Yes sir?" Jackie asked.

"Give your son some grace. This transition is very difficult for him. From his perspective, he feels like he's losing his mother. He probably wants things to go back to the way they were before. But you've changed, and you will continue to change. Marna is trained to deal with these progressions, but family members generally find the transitions very difficult."

Jackie paused. "I, um, hadn't thought of it like that. I've been so busy trying to survive that I hadn't thought about how Charles is feeling."

Dr. Canfield laughed. "That's perfectly normal. I'll tell you what, if Charles doesn't call me, then I'll reach out to him. We'll all work our way through these changes together." He paused, and Jackie could hear the scratching of a pen as he made notes on the other end of the phone call. "While I have you on the line, I'd like you to tell me about the name confusion, Mrs. Scott."

"Well, I… um, sometimes get confused about Ab… Marna's name. I now know her name's Marna, but it's easier for me to call her Abigail. Will that hurt anything, sir?"

He sighed. "Well, it'd be better to call her by her given name, but no, you're not hurting anyone if you get confused. She didn't try to deceive you, did she?"

"She didn't mean anything bad, sir," Jackie said adamantly. "I was confused and she was just trying to help." She winked at Marna.

"Do you like the dog, Mrs. Scott?" Dr. Canfield asked, changing the subject.

"She needs me, sir." She had forgotten the man's name. "I need to take care of her."

"Well, you have a great day, Mrs. Scott. Enjoy that dog. Let me speak to Marna before you hang up."

Jackie handed the phone to Marna. The young woman and the man spoke for a little bit, then Marna took them inside to do the paperwork for Cassie.

On the way home with the dog in her lap, Jackie began drifting again.

It was a sad day in her memory. She and Aaeesha were in the upstairs bedroom in Basra. The girls were thirteen. Aaeesha was crying, and Jackie was biting her lower lip. "I'll miss you terribly," Aaeesha said in Arabic.

A large stack of boxes stood in the middle of the floor, waiting for the moving men. The boxes would be loaded onto trucks, then eventually into the hold of one of her father's ships. They held Jackie's possessions, but not the contents of her heart.

"I'll visit," Jackie answered.

Aaeesha held out a curled pinky finger. Jackie reached out and hooked her own little finger around her best friend's. "Make the world a better place," the girls said in unison, leaning into each other's foreheads—eyes inches apart, noses touching.

"I'll write," Jackie said as she pulled back.

"You'd better," Aaeesha said, trying to grin through the tears.

Jackie was brought back to the present as the Mercedes bumped into Jackie's driveway. "Who's that man on the porch?" Jackie asked.

"Oh no," Marna said.

Cassie stood on Jackie's lap with her front paws on the door handle. She saw the man and began growling.

CHAPTER SIX

The man wasn't all that tall—maybe 5'10"— but he was certainly bigger than either of the women. His watermelon-sized beer gut spilled over his belt. He was wearing a black, leather jacket and had slicked-back hair. Studs protruded from his nose and his ears. His skin looked unnaturally white.

Jackie looked around to see if there was a Harley parked on the curb. Seeing none, she figured that the guy must have walked from the Vienna Metro station.

She tried to contain the growling, snarling eight-pound dog as she opened the passenger door and stepped out into her yard, but Cassie wriggled out of her arms. The fur ball ran at the man barking wildly as if she could sense he was a criminal. Cassie obviously had no sense of her own size, and she was attacking as if she thought she was a pit bull.

The man launched himself off of Jackie's porch swing and was now standing at the top of the stairs. He shook a finger at Marna. "Where have you been? You get your stuff and move back home with me!"

Jackie's small house was white with green trim. A cherry tree shaded the front yard. There were ornamental bushes on each side of a brick walk that lead to the front steps. The floor of the wooden porch was painted gray. The porch swing was swaying in the breeze because of his sudden departure. But the beauty of Jackie's quaint house was marred by the cretin in leather. He looked like a pile of dog poo on a manicured lawn.

"Rodney, you're drunk! What are you doing here?" Marna shouted angrily.

"I came to get you. I'm moving you back home!" The man's emotions were running up his neck in streaks of red contrasting starkly with his white skin.

He kicked at Cassie who was running circles around him, barking at the top of her lungs. Fortunately, Cassie was faster than his size ten clodhoppers.

"I'm not moving!" Marna stomped her foot. "I live here now. I take care of Jackie."

"Well, we'll see about that!"

The man came off the porch and roughly pushed Jackie aside. Jackie flew into the grass and landed on her butt. She rolled over and saw Rodney grab both of Marna's flying fists in one of his dinner plate-sized hands before lifting the girl's small body over his shoulder. Marna, barely five feet tall and almost a hundred pounds, was no match for the 200-pound ape.

Cassie jumped into the fray and started biting Rodney on the ankle—growling and pulling on his pants for all she was worth. Rodney kicked at the dog again, but the little canine was tenacious.

Jackie's self-defense training quickly took over. "Hey!" she shouted, as she recovered to her feet. The man turned to assess the new threat, and Jackie stepped forward and stomped hard on the instep of his foot. Rodney's hands were occupied, trying to contain Marna, who was flailing at his back with her tiny fists.

Rodney howled from the pain in his foot. While he was distracted, Jackie took a step back and punted the man in the groin. The kick carried enough force to lift the man off his feet an inch. It was a good kick—the Redskins might have hired her for field goals if a scouting agent had been watching.

Rodney bent over and screamed, throwing Marna off his shoulder and right into Jackie. Both women tumbled to the ground bum-over-teakettle as a siren whooped loudly in the street.

"Hey! Stop right there!" A police officer jumped from his patrol car and ran toward the fight.

Rodney stumbled to his feet and ran around the house toward the park and the woods beyond. He was still groaning in pain as he escaped.

Cassie came running over to Jackie, whining and trying to crawl into Jackie's arms.

The officer helped the women to their feet, and checked to see if they were all right. "Wow, it's a good thing that I happened along at that moment. I was just making my patrol rounds."

Jackie scooped the little dog into her arms. The officer began speaking into the microphone that was attached to his shoulder: he needed help tracking down the attacker.

Then he turned to the women. "Let's get an ambulance over here to check you two out and make sure you're okay."

"I'm fine," Jackie said. "I don't want an ambulance."

"I'm fine too," Marna said angrily. Then she paused, looking at Jackie. "It's my duty to convince you to take the ambulance."

"No," she said stubbornly. "I don't want Charles to find out about this little incident, and if I go to the hospital, then he'll know." She looked Marna in the eye. "This will be our secret." It was a command, not an invitation to conspiracy.

Marna looked angry, but she nodded once. "You're a stubborn woman, Mrs. Scott."

Jackie smiled in spite of her rage. "Then it's a good thing I've got a stubborn nurse." She kissed the dog's head and scratched her ears, trying to calm the furball.

"Alright," the officer said resolutely. "No ambulances. Can you give me a description or name of your attacker?"

"He wasn't just an attacker, he was trying to take, um... Marna by force against her will."

The cop raised his eyebrow. "A kidnapping attempt?"

"No!" Marna said, hugging her torso as if she could constrain the cop by embracing herself. "He's my boyfriend. He just wanted me to come back home! Don't put an attempted kidnapping charge on him! He was just drunk!"

The cop and Jackie looked at each other. "Well, I never want to see him again—at least not at my house." Jackie looked back at Marna. "He's bad news. You even told me that yourself. You are a recovering alcoholic. You don't need drunks in your life, and this guy showed up at my door drunk as a skunk and assaulted us and tried to kidnap you." Jackie realized that she was yelling loudly.

"Rodney huh?" the officer said scratching in his notebook. "Does he have a last name? I can issue a restraining order."

Marna's "No" and Jackie's "Yes" were said at the same time.

"I'm the homeowner, and I say that he can't come here!" Jackie said angrily.

"No problem," the officer answered. "I'll file the order under your name."

Other cop cars started showing up, and the officer who had rescued them directed the police into the woods behind the house. At the officer's prodding, Marna reluctantly gave up Rodney's last name.

The cop wrote down their information, as well as the name and description of Rodney. "He'll be easy to recognize," Jackie said proudly. "He's the guy with testicles the size of grapefruits."

After the officers left, the two women went into the house. The tension between them was thick as smoke. Cassie, on the other hand, dashed through every room, sniffing excitedly at every corner. She bounced her front feet up on Jackie's leg before exploring again.

"We need to go buy her some things," Marna said, still clenching her teeth. "We need a cage, a leash, a bowl for her food and water… Probably some other stuff too, but right now I'm too angry to think."

"We need to eat lunch," Jackie said through her gritted molars.

Marna started making lunch, slamming plates down on the counter.

"Why do you say you still love him if he's treating you so badly?" Jackie demanded. "He's bad for you!"

"How come you're afraid of the FBI agent who's just watching you, and then when Rodney comes around, you kick his ass?" Marna retorted.

"I… I don't know," Jackie said tentatively. "Sometimes things in my head just don't make sense." She paused, thinking. "When that guy grabbed you, my training took over—you know I used to work in war zones, so I learned some self-defense… Learned about guns…" She started drifting and pulled herself back. "Then, when he threw you over his shoulder, I panicked. Abby… I love you!" Jackie said.

"I'm Marna," she answered sullenly.

"Doesn't matter. I love you, and I didn't want to see you hurt. That idiot doesn't deserve someone as sweet as you. You deserve better."

The two women were silent for a moment, only hearing the sound of Marna's cooking, and Cassie's toenails clicking on the wooden floor as the dog explored her new territory.

"You're right," Marna said softly. "Now what do we do?"

"I'm gonna find my .45 in case that idiot comes back," Jackie said.

"No!" Then apparently realizing how loudly she had just yelled, Marna composed herself. "I mean, no, don't do that. You shouldn't handle a weapon. You'll think I'm a stranger and shoot me."

"Oh, honey. I'd never hurt you."

"You didn't know who I was this morning."

"Really?" she sighed loudly. "I don't remember that," Jackie said sadly. She flopped into a kitchen chair and buried her face in her hands. "This stupid disease is taking everything away from me. Now, I can't even defend my own home."

"Where's your gun?" Marna asked.

"I don't remember," Jackie said sadly. "Go ahead and ask me my name. I don't remember that either." She bit her lip, trying not to cry.

Tension hung in the kitchen for a few minutes as the only sound was the clanging of pots on the stove. Jackie stewed in her self-pity while Marna was upset over the encounter in the yard.

Marna cursed under her breath as the box of macaroni spilled onto the counter. "Thanks for defending me," Marna said sullenly as she scooped up the mess. "I've never had anybody come to my defense."

The mood in the room began to melt. Jackie could tell that in spite of her anger, Marna was grateful to have an ally.

Jackie knew that human emotions were complex like that. A person could be furious and grateful at the same time.

"You shouldn't say never," Jackie answered. "You said that your grandma loved you, and there were people who helped you get into that rehabilitation program. I'm sure you had teachers who took an interest in you. You have your AA sponsor…"

"It's been a long time since I had a female friend who had my back," Marna cut Jackie off as if she hadn't heard Jackie's answer.

Seeing an opportunity, Cassie leapt into Jackie's lap and started nuzzling against her bosom. Jackie hugged the dog and kissed the top of her head. "You love me, even if I'm losing my mind," she said to the dog.

"And you love me, even if I don't deserve it," Marna said, hugging Jackie from behind.

CHAPTER SEVEN

After lunch, the two humans and the canine raided a pet store. They came back into the house with several hundred dollars' worth of dog paraphernalia—including a pink, rhinestone studded collar for the furry princess.

That evening, when Jackie started sundowning, they decided to tackle the basement to keep her hands busy.

"Oh my!" Marna said as Jackie flipped on the basement light. "You weren't kidding! This is a mess!"

"Yeah, but Aaeesha's treasure is hidden somewhere in here," Jackie said, grimacing. "Or at least I think it is."

"It stinks," Marna said, wrinkling her nose. "Some of this is just plain garbage." She held up a white trash bag. Its contents had obviously been petrified over time. "How long has this been down here? It looks like you intended to take this out to the curb, but brought it down here instead."

"I... um, I guess I got confused," Jackie said. "I hope I didn't get mixed up; bringing my trash down here and taking important boxes out for the garbage man."

Now that Marna mentioned it, she could see that there were mounds of dirt and trash stacked among the boxes. "No wonder my house stinks," she said. "I'm so embarrassed."

Her hands were thrashing as if she was washing them under a faucet. "I gotta do something. Help me, Abigail." Anxiety filled her voice.

"Okay. Go upstairs and get the box of trash bags. We'll need the broom and dust pan too."

A moment later, Jackie was back downstairs with the garbage bags. "Here," she held the box out with a shaking hand. "I couldn't remember what else you wanted."

"Alright, no problem. You start sorting while I go up and get the broom."

Marna shook out an empty garbage bag and handed it over. Marna headed for the stairs but stopped when she saw what Jackie was doing.

"Okay," Marna said, coming back and holding Jackie's hands. "This isn't working. You're throwing away everything."

"I am?"

"Yes. See, you didn't even look through this stuff."

"Oh. I threw out Abigail's high school diploma. *Argh!*" She slapped herself in the forehead.

"It's okay. You're sundowning, so you're hyper and anxious. We'll get through this. I'll hand stuff to you, and you decide to *keep* or *throw*. You want to keep the diploma, so put it in this box. Put the taco wrapper and the rotten apple into the trash bag, because that's garbage."

Jackie nodded and did as she was told. Marna handed her another item. "This is Abigail's soccer trophy. I want to keep that." She placed it into the correct box. Jackie was on her knees, and Cassie tried to crowd in to get some attention.

Upstairs, they heard footsteps and a voice call out. "Ma? You home?" It was Charles. "I stopped off on my way home from the hospital to see how you're doing."

Cassie ran to the foot of the basement stairs, barking.

"We're in the basement, Charles!" Jackie called loudly.

A moment later feet appeared on the stairs. "We're down here," Marna said. "Your Mom is sundowning, so we're keeping her hands busy."

"What's sundowning?" Charles asked as he reached the bottom of the stairs.

He sat on the bottom step as Marna explained it to him.

He nodded and reached out to pet Cassie. "Looks like I need to do some studying on dementia." He paused. "I had a nice chat with your boss today, Marna. Ma, I'm sorry if I've been too hard on you. This transition is tough on all of us. And I'm sorry about the dog—if you want her, then you can keep her."

"Don't stop, Abby," Jackie said, anxiously. "Keep handing me things, or I'm gonna explode." She sorted for a moment. "The dog isn't your decision, Charles. She's mine."

Marna handed over some more items, and Jackie sorted them.

"You're still calling her Abigail, Ma," Charles said.

Jackie didn't even answer but kept frantically sorting her stuff. Even through her anxiety, she could feel the tension between her two children—no that wasn't right. One was her child, and the other one was a girl who she wanted to adopt. She could tell that Marna was afraid that Charles would get her fired.

"I've gotta find Aaeesha's treasure," Jackie said, trying to focus her stubborn brain on the task at hand. Her knees were hurting from the hard cement.

"That again?" Charles rolled his eyes. "Last year, we went through this whole house looking for Aaeesha's treasure. I think it's something you made up, Ma. You don't even remember what you're looking for."

"I'll know it when I see it. It's here," she said resolutely.

"Look, Ma, I came over to invite you to dinner after church on Sunday—if you'd like to come, that is."

Jackie accidentally tore a photo. "Damn it!" She rarely cursed, but her agitation was piercing. She stood, ready to stomp up the stairs, but then forced herself to sit back down on the cold cement. She stretched out her hands to Marna. "Faster!" she demanded.

Marna grinned and shoveled things as fast as Jackie could sort.

"Man, she's really upset, isn't she?" Charles asked, sitting on the stairs, watching the two women work.

"Yeah," Marna answered. "She'll be okay in a little bit. It's just part of the sundowning process."

Charles held his head in his hands. "I'm supposed to be the doctor. I'm supposed to know what's going on with my mother. Not some thirteen-year-old kid who my Mom keeps calling Abigail."

"Stow it, Charles," Jackie snapped. "She's not thirteen. She's... um..."

"Twenty-six," Marna said helpfully.

"Yeah that," Jackie said hotly. "Sometimes you think that your doctorate degree makes you the smartest thing on the planet. You're very smart, but if your ego fell out of your pants, somebody would step on your dick. You don't have to be the expert on everything. Abby is an expert on senile old farts like me, and you are an expert surgeon."

Charles growled at his mother and Marna snickered, biting her lip to keep from bursting out with laughter.

"What about dinner on Sunday?" Charles asked again. His face glowed red, but recently he had stopped reacting to his mother's barbs.

"Can we see how she's feeling?" Marna asked. "She's going through a lot of changes. And sometimes it's best just to see how she's doing."

Charles nodded. "That how you want to do it, Mom? The kids would love to see you."

"Don't talk to me right now," Jackie said through clenched teeth. "It's not a good time."

"Did you have a good day?" Marna asked Charles.

"I guess. I did two appendectomies and an ovarian cyst. I had to refer another case to a cardiologist," he said absentmindedly.

He stood. "Okay I'm late to Chucky's Little League game. I'll get out of this little tension factory and get home to my own zoo. You ladies have a great evening."

He stood to go, then turned back. "I just stopped by to see how you two were getting along," he repeated. "And to apologize about the dog."

After Charles left, the women sorted for another hour. Finally, Jackie calmed down enough that they decided to quit for the evening. They stood and surveyed their work.

"Look at you!" Marna said, putting her arm around Jackie. "You knocked out a big chunk of the mess. Great job!"

To Jackie's eye, it looked like she hadn't even made a dent in the pile. But she knew that Marna was trying to encourage her. She leaned down and kissed the top of the short woman's head. "I couldn't have done it without you."

"Are you ready to go upstairs again? Would you like some tea?"

Jackie nodded and followed Marna up the stairs to the living room. Before flipping out the light, she looked back down into the basement mess.

"I've got to find that box," she said. The impending gloom of losing her treasure forever overwhelmed her.

As they walked through the living room, Jackie was suddenly embarrassed by the stack of boxes that was still there. But she was too tired to do anything about it at the moment. Too exhausted to think, she turned her back on the problem and meekly followed Marna to the kitchen.

A few minutes later Jackie sat with her hands around a hot teacup, and her new dog in her lap. She felt a bit better and was grateful for Marna's help with the sundowning.

"You need to call your… um… what do you call the guy in charge of your AA?"

"You mean my sponsor?" Marna asked.

"Yeah, that guy. Ask him what he thinks about Rodney."

Marna shook her head and wouldn't look Jackie in the eye. "I already know what she thinks of Rodney. She says that if I don't get rid of him, then I'm going to crash my life."

"So, what are you going to do about him?" Jackie asked.

Marna didn't answer. She just shook her head and looked longingly out the kitchen window into the fading dusk.

CHAPTER EIGHT

Jackie awoke to the sound of rain pattering against her bedroom window. She remembered it was Saturday, and the smell of coffee wafted up from the kitchen below. Beside her, a warm ball of fur snuggled under the blankets. Through the second-floor bedroom window, the sky was gray and angry. The moment she opened her eyes, Jackie could tell that it was going to be a bad day. She sighed heavily and gritted her teeth—some days weren't even worth getting out of bed.

Cassie must have sensed that Jackie was awake because she began licking Jackie's hand.

Under the covers, Jackie smoothed the dog's ears. In spite of her gloom, she had to admit, the dog made her happy.

"I am so glad you agreed to come home with me." She gathered the fur ball into her arms and kissed the dog's head. She wrinkled her nose. "You need a bath."

She found her robe, and Cassie clicked her toenails down the wooden stairs behind her. Jackie paused in the living room. While she had been in bed, Marna had apparently taken the living room boxes to the basement with the others, and the furniture had all been dusted—the air smelled of lemon-scented furniture polish.

"There you are. Good morning, Jackie. Good morning, Cassie," Marna said brightly. She clipped the leash onto Cassie's rhinestone studded collar, and took her out in the rain to do her business.

Jackie shuffled her way to the kitchen. She found her favorite coffee cup and filled it from the pot that Marna had brewed. She added sugar and wearily sat at the table—even the white cup looked sad and gray. She took a strong whiff of the coffee and sat back.

Her daddy's office was high in a tall building. He had a corner office that overlooked the harbor. From the chair that he'd set by the window for her, she could see the men looking like ants crawling over the ships.

Father had stepped out of the office to confer with a coworker, leaving the office door open. There were two men standing outside by the strong-smelling coffee pot. They spoke loudly in Arabic.

"I wish Hitler would have done his job properly and killed off all the Jews. The vermin should have been wiped from the planet."

"They're like rats," the other man agreed. "The more you kill, the more that crawl out from under the rocks."

Jackie wanted to run out to that coffee pot and kick the men in the shins. They didn't know that they were talking about the boss's wife. And by extension, they were also talking about Jackie. Her young heart was broken. Jackie loved Iraq, but she also loved her mother.

To drown out the men's coarse talk, Jackie began chanting to herself. "Make the world a better place. Make the world a better place."

"Whew!" Marna laughed as she came in from the rain, jerking Jackie out of her reverie. "It's a soaker out there today!"

Cassie skittered into the kitchen and skidded to a halt by her bowl. She sat primly waiting for her breakfast.

"You want toast and eggs this morning?" Marna asked as she scooped out Cassie's food.

"No, I just want Cornflakes," Jackie answered tiredly. She got up and started looking for a cereal bowl. "What are we going to do today?" Her mind was fighting against the undertow of memories.

"What do you want to do? It's kind of nasty outside."

Jackie was pulled under again.

She stood in a small dress shop in the markets of Basra. The shop sold very expensive dresses for the wives and daughters of the wealthy. When Mom had taken Jackie and Aaeesha, the girls' mouths hung open as they fingered the fine silk and lace.

The girls decided to purchase identical, flowered dresses. Jackie still remembered the feel of the silk on her skin. Aaeesha absolutely beamed as they stood arm-in-arm, looking in the mirror.

"Jackie?" She felt a small hand shaking her arm, and she snapped back to the present.

"I want to go shopping. I want to buy us both new dresses for Sunday church," Jackie said. She really wanted to curl up in bed, but she was angry at her disease—she didn't want to admit defeat. Not yet. Not today.

"Really?" The young lady asked sheepishly. "Nobody has ever bought me a new dress before."

"I know, Aaeesha," Jackie answered. "But I want to help make the world a better place. And you need a dress—pure silk."

The woman didn't say anything for a moment. She just bit her lip and looked like she was going to cry.

"You called me Aaeesha," she said. "That was your best friend's name."

Jackie laughed. "I know you're not Aaeesha. You're… um…" She paused. Her brain couldn't grind through the sludge. "We need to give Cassie a bath, she stinks."

"Uh-hmm," the short woman agreed. She sniffed Jackie's hair. "And the dog isn't the only one that needs a bath."

"I don't like baths, and I hate how the shower water pounds the top of my head," she sighed, knowing that Marna was right. "Fine," she said, defeated. "Abigail. You're name's Abigail, not Aaeesha."

"It's Marna," the girl answered. She had a concerned look in her eye.

They sat in silence for a moment. "If you are going to give me a gift, then I need to clear it with Dr. Canfield and also make sure Charles is okay with it."

Jackie waved her hand dismissively. "I'll handle those two. It's just me and my stupid brain that's my big concern." She sighed.

"I've only been helping you for a few days," Marna said softly. "You must have really struggled before I came."

"I spent a lot of days in bed," Jackie admitted.

"I gotta ask you," Marna sat down at the table with her own bowl of Cornflakes. "Your mom was Jewish, and your dad was Muslim. Why are you Presbyterian?"

Jackie laughed. "I did it partly to spite my parents. The other reason was a boy. We were in love—or at least we thought we were. If we can make it to church, you'll get to meet him."

Suddenly, Jackie was a girl again.

She was yelling at her mother. "I can't believe you made me leave Iraq and come to live here! I hate the United States!" She stamped her foot angrily. She was speaking Arabic because she was so mad at the US: she didn't even want to speak its language.

"All the people here are weird, and they do things funny!" she said. "I want to go back home to Basra! I miss Aaeesha!"

Her mother looked like she was about to cry. "I know it's hard, honey. It's just culture shock. Your first day at a new school in a new country is going to be difficult. Someday you'll think of Virginia as your home, but right now everything feels bad." Her mother spoke in English. Her father had told them that they must always speak English in the US.

"I will never have any friends here," Jackie promised in Arabic. "I will never like anybody, or love anybody. As soon as I'm sixteen, I'm going to run away from home." Jackie felt the hollow place in the pit of her stomach.

Jackie felt a light touch on her arm. She snapped back to the present. "You're having a bad day, aren't you?" Marna asked.

Jackie nodded. "I was thirteen when we moved to the US. It took so long to become accustomed to the new culture." She sighed and looked at Marna. "I've been drifting a lot this morning. I'm a mess."

"You were pretty sharp yesterday; I was impressed. You even gave Charles a good zinger," Marna laughed.

Jackie sadly pushed back the bowl of Cornflakes. "I'm not hungry anymore."

Marna pushed it back in front of her. "Battling dementia takes a lot of calories—some people need as much as 4,000 calories a day. You've lost too much weight already. If you don't want the Cornflakes, I'll make you something else."

Jackie shook her head. "Give it to the dog… um… What's-her-name. The one with the fancy collar."

"Cassie. Her name is Cassie. She already ate her breakfast. If she eats your breakfast, she'll get fat."

For some reason, gloom was sweeping her under. "Is it bedtime yet? I want to go to bed."

"Okay. Why don't you go take a little nap? Then when you get up, we'll see what you want to do with the rest of the day." Marna helped Jackie to her feet.

Cassie was happy to jump under the covers again with her new mistress.

Jackie drifted again, but this time it was dreams and not memories. Rodney stood in the front yard, drinking booze straight from the bottle. All of a sudden, he turned into an FBI agent, and pulled out his gun. Jackie tried to run, but the yard turned into quicksand, and the more she struggled, the deeper she sank.

CHAPTER NINE

Lunch hadn't helped. Jackie still felt loopy. She kept getting pulled under by memories, and she felt like she was about to drown. One moment, she was in Lebanon, dodging bomb shrapnel, and the next she was sipping tea with Rosalynn Carter.

Right now, she needed to get away from the house—maybe all the photos and the memories in the boxes were haunting her.

She tried to get dressed for their shopping trip, but her stupid pants wouldn't act right—she tried putting both legs into the same hole. Once she got that figured out, she couldn't get the zipper to work. She wound up with a sock on her hand instead of her foot, and she discovered that her blouse was on inside out. She started crying because of her frustration.

"Help me, Aaeesha," she called to Marna through her tears.

Marna came into the room and saw the predicament. "It's okay," she said, wiping a finger under Jackie's eye. "Today you might be having a bad day, but tomorrow will most likely be better."

Jackie was really mad that somebody had to dress her. She felt like a child.

"What's your name again?" Jackie knew she was doing the wrong thing to call the woman Aaeesha, but she just couldn't remember the girl's name. And she looked so much like Aaeesha when she was young—it just kept slipping out.

"I know I look a lot like your daughter Abby, and apparently I hold some resemblance to your childhood friend, Aaeesha. But my name is

Marna," she said, patting Jackie's hand. "With your normal confusion, you call me Abigail. But you must really be struggling today. You're calling me Aaeesha."

Jackie bit her lip and blinked back a tear. She was so angry at her dementia.

"Are you sure you want to do this? We don't have to go shopping," Marna suggested as she finished the top button on Jackie's blouse. "We can go shopping another day."

Jackie shook her head stubbornly. "We're going dress shopping. I don't care if you have to wrap me in bubble wrap and put me in a wheelbarrow. I'm not going to let this disease beat me."

It took a while, but they finally were able to wrestle Jackie's stubborn body into the passenger seat of the car. Cassie had been none too pleased when they'd shut the door of her cage, but she settled down politely to await the women's return.

"Where are we going?" Marna asked, putting the car into reverse. Her foot was still resting on the brake.

"Washington," Jackie said sullenly. "There's a custom shop down on G Street."

Marna nodded and backed out of the drive. She made her way to I-66 and headed east into the city.

Jackie was eighteen. They were only months away from graduation. She was sitting in Monroe Turner's red Corvette convertible at the drive-in. Jackie wanted to watch the movie, but Monroe wanted to talk.

"I signed up," he told Jackie.

"Signed up for what? The circus?" she laughed.

In the car next to them, Jackie saw Reginald Williams. Reginald always played second fiddle to Monroe. Monroe was first string quarterback, and Reginald was his backup. Interestingly, they always seemed to get along. But when Jackie decided to date Monroe instead of Reginald, she could see the envy shimmer in his eyes.

Right now, Reginald was kissing Amy. But his eyes were open, and he was watching Jackie. He wanted her. She knew. It wasn't because she was the prettiest girl in school—far from it. Reginald wanted her only because she belonged to Monroe.

Rumor was that Monroe and Reginald had a fist fight over her, and Monroe had won. Both guys sported shiners for several weeks, but Monroe refused to talk about it. Somehow, the two remained friends in spite of the fight. Even though she still dated Monroe, Jackie was disgusted by the violence. She would never understand guys.

"The Army. I'm going to Vietnam." Monroe's statement shocked Jackie's mind back to her own car.

Her eyes flashed wide. "Are you insane?"

"I gotta go. Our boys are gettin' slaughtered by the Commies, and I'm gonna make a difference. Me and Reginald signed up together. We're gonna try to be in the same unit."

She was so stunned that she couldn't speak.

"I know we're both young, but I want to marry you before I go," he said, pulling a little box out of his pocket.

She wanted to crawl out of her skin and hide under a rock. "I mean... I love you, Monroe, but..." She realized she was shrieking. "I don't want to marry a soldier. I want the world to be filled with love, not hate!"

"Baby, don't be like that. I love you, but the army is something I just gotta do!"

Jackie was so angry that she got out of the car. She slammed the door. She leaned back over the car door of the little coup. "I don't want to marry a killer, Monroe. I want to marry a man who will love the whole world the way that he loves me."

She was seeing red. Logic had flown the coop. She stomped toward the exit of the theater, fully intending to walk all the way home.

A head popped out of a driver's window from a car in the back row. "Jackie? What's wrong? Where are you going?" It was Richard Scott. Stephie Miller was in the passenger seat.

"I'm walking home!" Jackie snarled. "I wouldn't allow that blockhead to drive me home if he owned the last car in the world."

"Don't do that," Stephie said from the passenger seat. "It's too far. We'll take you home."

Jackie could see that Richard wasn't pleased at the idea, but he pasted a smile on his face. "Sure," he said. "Hop in."

Jackie stood for a moment, considering her options. She realized that Stephie was right. She sighed.

"Okay, thanks," she said meekly. She waited while Richard got out and folded the driver's seat down, so that she could slide into the back.

She cried for days. When Monroe and Reginald shipped out, three weeks later, she didn't even bother to say goodbye.

Now, Marna was shaking her and bringing her back to the present. "We're here Jackie. You look so tired; we can go home and sleep if you want."

"No. I want to do this, Aaeesha," Jackie said. "I need to buy my best friend a silk dress."

Marna ran around to Jackie's side of the car with an umbrella and helped her out. Concern was etched in the young woman's face.

"Thank you," Jackie said, taking her hand.

When they stepped into the little shop, Jackie heard Marna take in a sharp breath. Jackie saw the girl's fingers reach out to touch the gentle cloth, then she rubbed it against her face. "This is wonderful," she whispered.

The shop was warm and cozy. There was a thick, oriental rug under their feet. There were several rows of dresses along each of the walls, hung from silver racks—the styles ranged from formal ball gowns to everyday wear. The walls were covered in rich red oak paneling.

The short, balding shop owner came from behind the counter. "Jackie?" he asked. "Is that you? It's been so long. How are you doing?" He had a yellow tape measure around his neck with a few flecks of colored cloth on his shirt. His teeth were a bit yellowed behind his smile, but his generation hadn't caught on to the modern teeth whitening fad.

"Um... Mr. um..." She couldn't remember his name.

"Sinclair. Gabriel Sinclair. And you are?" He held his hand out to Marna. He took her proffered hand and kissed it. "My, you're lovely." He oozed old-world charm.

"This is Aaeesha." Jackie introduced her.

"Actually, the name is Marna," the girl said.

"I get confused a lot lately," Jackie explained. "Sorry." Her day felt like it was getting worse.

"Well, what can I do for you lovely ladies?" he asked. Jackie thought she heard a tint of London in his voice.

"Silk. I want to buy each of us a dress that we can wear to church tomorrow."

"I think I can arrange that," the man purred. "Of course, I know your size Jackie. And you, young lady, I'm going to guess you're a size four— or maybe a size two." His eyes reappraised Marna's tiny form. "Is that, right? Do you see anything here that strikes your fancy?"

The women sorted through the racks looking at dress after dress. "There are no price tags," Marna whispered.

"That's because if you have to ask, then you can't afford it," Jackie whispered back.

The shop owner—Jackie had lost his name again—told his assistant to fire up the espresso machine. And for a little bit, Jackie felt good again. She picked out a sky-blue dress, and Marna chose a deep chocolate brown silk that matched her eyes.

They had their measurements taken—or in Jackie's case, verified—then went next door to the shoe shop while the adjustments were made on their garments.

Marna was giddy shopping for shoes. She told Jackie that she had never owned a pair that cost more than thirty dollars. In this store, the prices started at three hundred and kept going up from there.

"These would be perfect!" she squealed.

Jackie, who had been drifting again, jerked back to the present and tried to paste a tired smile on her face. "That's nice, dear," she said, not remembering any name she could call the girl.

Marna sighed and hugged Jackie. "We need to get you home," she said. Jackie could see that, in spite of her excitement over the new clothes, she was more concerned about the condition of her charge.

With their dresses and new shoes in the trunk, Marna drove the car back home through the thick traffic, where the normally 45-minute drive took two hours. Jackie slept the whole way.

When they got home, Jackie went straight to bed, bypassing her sundowning phase with sleep. She didn't even bother with supper.

Jackie's dreams were vivid and disturbing. She found herself standing naked on the steps of the White House while flash bulbs popped as reporters captured her nudity for the world to see. Suddenly, somebody started shooting at her. It was a fully automatic rifle. By the bark of the gun, she could tell that it was an AK-47. Jackie screamed and sat straight up in bed.

She was pretty sure she was awake, but the room swirled around her. She knew she wasn't in Basra, but she couldn't remember where she was. Her breathing came in short gasps as she hyperventilated in fear.

The red readout on the digital clock said, 11:53. "Where am I?" she called loudly, but nobody answered.

"Help me!" she called again. Under the covers beside her a wiggling ball of fur nuzzled against her leg. Somehow, she knew it was her canine friend. But the dog was snoozing happily unaware of the terror that Jackie felt.

She slid from under the covers and padded her bare feet to the door of her bedroom. She walked into the hallway looking around. Everything seemed unfamiliar and foreign. She grasped the wall and forced her breath under control.

Jackie pushed open a door. The room should belong to Aaeesha. No. That wasn't right. It belonged to... but it didn't matter: the bed was empty. Covers were disheveled and rumpled.

Panic drove through her. Did the soldiers come and take Aaeesha while she slept? No. Aaeesha was dead. Or was she? Who was supposed to be in that bed? Jackie began to call Aaeesha's name as she went down the stairs.

She felt so alone. So vulnerable. Tears streamed down her face and dripped onto her nightgown. She knew she shouldn't have been alone. There was a woman—she was supposed to have been in that bed. But Jackie couldn't find anybody.

For a moment, she saw the face of a soldier as he ran up the stairs at her. She saw the pistol in her own hand and felt it buck as she fired. She watched as the back of the young man's head blew out, at the look of pain on his face as his body toppled backwards.

She grabbed the handrail as her heart thundered. It was just a memory that had come back to haunt her. She double checked the dark staircase and there was no blood and no body, and no .45 caliber pistol in her hand. Her memory was playing evil tricks on her.

"Aaeesha!" She called at the top of her trembling voice. She made her way down the stairs, jumping at every shadow. She shivered as she peered through the window into the driveway. The Mercedes was gone. Had Aaeesha escaped? Had the soldiers found her? Maybe she'd made it this time. Maybe Aaeesha was still alive.

With no other options, Jackie climbed the stairs. She crawled into bed and pulled the covers over her head, crying inconsolably. She cuddled Cassie so hard that the dog squeaked. Finally, she fell into a fitful sleep, dreaming of exploding heads and splattering brains.

CHAPTER TEN

Jackie woke and stretched luxuriously. She felt sharp and alert. As she stepped into her slippers, vestiges of last night's fiasco filtered through her mind. She shook her head at how far she'd been gone. She remembered her hallucination of the soldier coming up the stairs. No. That had only been a distant memory that had come back to haunt her. That event had been years ago and thousands of miles from Virginia.

She stepped into the hallway. She remembered her confusion of the night before. Through the crack in the doorway, she saw Marna's mussed hair covering the pillow. That's who the room belonged to—Marna.

Jackie remembered that it was Sunday morning. When she arrived in the kitchen, she saw that the stove clock said 5:07. She clipped the leash onto Cassie's collar and took her outside in the glowing dawn. She picked up Cassie's stinky landmine in a plastic bag and tossed it into the garbage can. The Mercedes was parked in the driveway where it was supposed to be.

Ten minutes later, she had the coffee perking, and the eggs sizzling happily on the stove. Jackie smiled at the strips of bacon—both of her parents would have been aghast to find her eating such sacrilege.

"Good morning Marna," she said as the yawning, young woman finally stumbled into the kitchen at 8:30.

Marna stopped and rubbed her eyes. "You called me by my correct name," she said in amazement.

"I seem to be having a good day. I guess my brain is trying to make up for yesterday's disaster," Jackie said, sliding a plate of breakfast in front of her young friend. Fresh strawberries lined the back of the plate. "Do you want juice with that?" she asked.

"Um, sure. Thanks," Marna answered.

The two sat down as Marna ate. Cassie was curled in Jackie's lap. "I called Charles this morning and said that we'd be happy to come to lunch after church. I hope that's okay with you."

"Yeah, that's great. I'd like to meet his wife and your grandchildren."

Jackie smiled. "Charles' wife's name is Katrice—she's a gold digger. The children's names are Chucky, who's eight, and Milly, who's five."

"Are we going to wear our new dresses to church?" Marna asked.

"How is Rodney doing?" Jackie asked, ignoring the question about the dress.

Marna looked like she'd been slapped. "I... um... How'd you know?"

"I didn't really know, until you just now told me. I woke up in the middle of the night, and you were gone—you took the car. It was pretty easy to guess where you went."

They sat in silence for a moment, while Marna ate.

"Did you drink last night?" Jackie asked.

"What is this? An inquisition?" Marna asked petulantly. "I'm an adult! I don't have to answer to you!" She shoveled a forkful of eggs into her mouth.

"Was he drinking?"

Marna didn't answer. Her face was flushed. Jackie knew the answer was yes.

"You say you're an adult, so why don't you act like one? You took my car without asking me," Jackie said. "And you went to hang out with a man that you know is bad for you. He was drinking, and you told me that if you took a drink it would crash your life."

"I didn't drink!" Marna finally said loudly. She lowered her voice. "I wanted to, but I didn't."

"Marna." Jackie sat down and reached across the table. She touched the young woman on the chin lifting her face to meet her eyes.

"Marna, I don't care what your past is. I've only known you for a few days, but I know you've got a good heart. You are kind and caring. I promise you that I will love you like my own daughter..."

She paused, considering how to put into words what needed to be said. She was so grateful that her brain seemed to be working this morning. "You told me that Rodney was bad for you. I'm going to help you out. If I find out that you are running out to Rodney again, I'll fire you on the spot."

She knew she was meddling, but she didn't want to lose Marna to the bottle.

Marna didn't answer, but she looked like she was about to cry.

"I know you've had a lousy childhood, so you really don't know what true love is when you see it. But I'm here to tell you that I love you, and Rodney doesn't."

Jackie got up from the table and began washing the dishes. Neither woman spoke until they were at the front door ready for church. Jackie was quite proud that she'd given herself a bath.

"Did you put Cassie in her cage?" Jackie asked.

Marna nodded. She was apparently still smarting from being called out on her rendezvous with Rodney.

Jackie stepped out into the Sunday morning sunshine. The late September air felt delicious. She guessed that the temperature must have been in the upper sixties, and the sweet songs of birds floated among the trees.

"You look quite beautiful this morning," Jackie said. "I don't think I've seen you with your hair down. You always wear it in that tight ponytail." With just a hint of makeup, the little woman was stunning.

"You have the kind of face that always makes other women jealous," she said smiling. She extended her arm to her young charge, and Marna took it.

Jackie saw an FBI agent in a parked, black SUV. He was a half block away where he could see the front door of her house. She waved at him and smiled as they walked past. She was amazed that she wasn't afraid. It really was a good day.

As they approached the Vienna Presbyterian Church, Jackie clutched Marna's arm and said, "I really appreciate you coming with me. I haven't been to church in a while. The crowds... they, um, they make me nervous and overwhelmed."

In spite of the clarity that she'd felt earlier in the morning, she began to feel the brain fog rolling in. She didn't know if it was because of the confusing social environment, or if it was just a wave in the ebb and flow of the dementia. "It's probably both," she said.

"What's both? What are you talking about?" Marna asked.

"Oh, sorry. I didn't realize I spoke out loud," Jackie said.

They each took a bulletin from the greeter, then pushed through the crowd. "Let's sit toward the back," Jackie said. "Then if we need to, we can escape."

It turned out that other people had the same idea. The back row was already full, so they had to sit three rows up.

"Grandma!" a tiny voice cried with glee. A little blonde-haired girl bounced at Jackie's feet. She was all bows and curls. She was wearing a dress that looked like it was straight out of a dollhouse.

"Milly!" Jackie said, bending down to her level. "Are you going to sit with me?"

"No. I hafta go to kid's church, but Daddy says you're coming over for dinner. Is that true?" She was bouncing and twisting her hair on her finger.

"It sure is," Jackie gushed. "And I'd like you to meet my friend, Marna. She's living with me now to help when I get confused."

Milly blushed and clasped her hands behind her back. Her chin dipped to her shoulder and she tried to hide behind Jackie's silk dress. "You're pretty," Milly said shyly from behind Jackie.

"Why thank you," Marna replied. "And you're quite beautiful yourself. You have such pretty eyes."

Milly hid her face in her hands.

"Tell her, 'thank you,'" Jackie prompted.

"Thank you," Milly managed from behind her five-year-old fingers. Then she turned, ran out of the sanctuary, and headed for kid's church downstairs.

"She's adorable," Marna said.

Jackie smiled. "She really is, isn't she?"

Marna and Jackie settled into the pew. Several people stopped by and said how wonderful it was to see Jackie again. Jackie shook their hand and introduced all of them to Marna—calling her Abigail most of the time. Charles came in with a pencil thin blonde on his arm. Jackie introduced Katrice to Marna.

Katrice was wearing a royal blue, custom tailored dress that showed just enough cleavage to keep her on the naughty side of propriety. She looked like she had just stepped off of a French runway—her hair and makeup were perfect.

"Good to meet you, Marna," she said, holding out a perfectly manicured set of nails. "I look forward to having you at dinner today."

Marna graciously smiled. "I look forward to visiting your home," she answered. A color of red rose up her cheeks.

"You blushed because you thought Katrice is pretty," Jackie whispered to Marna as Katrice walked away. "But what you don't realize is that your simple beauty puts her to shame."

Marna looked at Jackie as if she'd lost her marbles.

As they were singing the first hymn, Jackie pointed a man out to Marna. "See that man?" she whispered. "He took our football team to state in high school."

"Really?" Marna asked. Jackie could tell that Marna wasn't impressed.

"I'll introduce you after the service," Jackie promised. She hoped that the brain-fog wouldn't roll in too thickly by then.

Jackie pointed to a prim looking woman in her 50's. "That lady is a State Supreme Court Justice."

After the service, Jackie and Marna sat and waited as waves of people exited. As they waited, the woman that Jackie had pointed out as the judge stopped by their pew. Jackie couldn't remember her name.

"Jackie," the woman greeted in a cold voice. "I see you've made it out to church this week."

"You still don't like me, do you?" Jackie said, shocked that the thought had popped out of her mouth. "What did I do to upset you so much?"

The woman looked as if Jackie had just farted at a formal ball. "You know very well why I'm mad at you!" She was visibly shaking.

"Hi, I'm Marna Hunt." Marna extended her hand to the furious judge.

The judge just sniffed and walked away, leaving Marna's hand hanging in the air.

"Well, that was interesting," Marna laughed.

"Monroe," Jackie called out to the gentleman that she had indicated earlier. The man turned and found Jackie with his eyes.

He smiled. "Jackie, how are you?" He kissed her hand. "My, don't you look beautiful in that dress? And who is this lovely young lady?"

"Senator Monroe Turner, this is Marna... um... What's your last name, dear?"

"Hunt," Marna said. "My name is Marna Hunt, sir. It's an honor to meet you."

Senator Turner introduced his wife.

Jackie nodded.

"Marna is my nurse. She's helping me because of my dementia," Jackie told the senator and his wife.

"Really?" Monroe asked. Jackie saw many things going through the senator's mind at the mention of her disease. She thought she saw a flash of relief.

Charles pushed his way through the crowd to Jackie and Marna's bench. "We're going to head on home and get dinner ready. Just come in your own car when you're ready." He turned, noticing the senator. "Oh, Senator Turner. Sorry, I didn't see you standing there. I hope I didn't interrupt."

"No, it's fine," the senator said. "A mother's son is her top priority." He turned back to Jackie. "I'm so sorry to hear about your dementia. But I'm glad to see that you are in capable hands."

"May I bring Cassie this afternoon?" Jackie asked her son.

"Sure," Charles said. "The kids will love her."

"Well, I've got to get going." The Senator extended his hand to Marna. "It was good to meet you ma'am. And thanks for taking care of Jackie; she means a lot to me." He leaned in close so his wife couldn't hear. "We were high school sweethearts. Did she tell you that?" He grinned conspiratorially.

"Good to meet you too, sir." Marna batted her eyes and her smile showed all her teeth.

"Be careful, Abigail," Jackie said. "I… I mean, Marna. He'll charm the pants off of you." Jackie felt herself slipping a little more into the fog of dementia.

The senator patted Jackie's shoulder and grinned at the inappropriate comment. He allowed himself to be swept away by the crowd. Jackie turned to watch the man glad-hand his way out of the church.

"He's sure got a lot of charisma," Marna said, watching him too.

"Yeah," Jackie sighed. "He sure does." She glanced at Marna, hoping that she hadn't let too much slip. But the young woman apparently hadn't caught the words Jackie had said.

Jackie and Marna walked back to the house. When they got home, Cassie was overjoyed to see them. Marna opened the cage door, and Cassie shot out into the yard. She did five laps out of sheer joy before attending to her business. When Jackie opened the passenger door to the car, she bounded inside, excited for a new adventure.

"Here Abigail," Jackie said, handing over Charles' address.

"You're calling me Abigail again," she said. "Are you feeling okay?" Marna punched the address into the Mercedes' navigation system, and they headed out for Great Falls.

Jackie chose not to answer the question. She was determined to keep her dementia at bay—at least for today. It was illogical, but she didn't want to give the disease lip service. Not now. Not when the day had started out so wonderfully.

"The senator lives only a mile or two from my son," Jackie said. "His house is huge."

"What's with the judge? She sure was chilly. You must have done something real good to hack her off like that," Marna asked.

"I don't remember," Jackie replied. "I have no clue."

They rode in silence for a few minutes. "Senator Turner said that you two were high school sweethearts," Marna observed.

Jackie sighed. "He asked me to marry him before he went off to Vietnam in '70. But I didn't want to marry a soldier." She paused, wondering if she should tell more. She had tried to hide it earlier in church, but she changed her mind now and decided to tell Marna, "I had an affair with him after my husband died. It only lasted for a few months." She looked at Marna. "But that part is a secret, and Charles doesn't need to know."

"You keep a lot of secrets from Charles, don't you?" Marna asked.

Jackie sighed. "Charles gets too anxious about things. Anytime he has intel, he feels the need to act. Sometimes, secrets are just meant to be kept. You and I are different. We know how to hold things in our hearts until the time is right."

"You say that as if you know me," Marna said. It was almost a question.

"I know you better than you think," Jackie said. "I've rubbed shoulders with the movers and shakers of our nation. I've been in war and know the horrors. I've learned to read people like a book. You, young lady, have a heart that can be trusted—as long as we can keep bad men out of your pants."

Marna blushed at Jackie's inappropriate comment. She put on her signal and turned into the driveway of Charles' estate. The twenty acres of Charles' property was filled with mature hardwoods. Down the driveway, a huge mansion could be seen.

Off to the left, a magnificent buck lifted his head to look at the car. Behind him, a doe and fawn continued grazing, ignoring the intrusion.

"This was all Katrice's idea," Jackie said, waving her hand around the opulence. "One can have money and not make a spectacle. But Katrice always wanted to be rich, and now that she has money, she wants the world to know."

Jackie saw the look of shock on Marna's face. She'd seen it before when people first stepped into the world of the wealthy. She reached over and patted Marna's hand. "Take a moment to let it sink in. The affluence can be overwhelming. The truth is that I'm much wealthier than Charles—I inherited it from my father. But I just don't flaunt it like he does."

At the center of the circular driveway was a fountain featuring a marble statue of a woman in flowing robes carrying a basket of fruit on her shoulder.

Jackie saw Marna studying the statue. "She looks familiar…"

Jackie sighed. "That's me when I was younger. It was the one concession that Katrice made when they had the place built. Charles really does love me, you know," she smiled. "The artist was… um… generous with my beauty. I was never that pretty."

"Yes," Marna said, studying the statue. "Charles really loves you."

Marna turned off the car, just as the front door opened. Jackie's grandchildren ran shrieking out of the house. "Grandma!" they cried.

Jackie opened her car door, and Cassie bounded out to greet the children. The kids were sidetracked by the dog, and soon they were all playing chase in the grass.

"What's the dog's name?" Chucky asked, then giggled as Cassie jumped up on his leg.

"Kids, meet Cassie," Jackie said, joining in the laughter.

Jackie scooped Cassie up as she ran past. "Chucky, you're the only one who hasn't met Abigail… I mean…" She stopped, not remembering Marna's real name.

"Marna," the young lady said. "I'm Marna Hunt."

Chuck shook her hand like he was a grownup. "Good to meet you, ma'am," he said.

"He'll be our senator once Monroe retires," Jackie gushed as she observed the same charisma in the child that she'd seen in Senator Turner.

The group went up the front steps to the mansion and stepped into the lobby. Jackie heard Marna suck in her breath again.

The lobby floor was white marble—not the cheap stuff, but the expensive kind that had veins of black meandering its way through the rock. The surface was polished to a mirror shine. The dual curved staircases formed a pocket in the middle of the foyer, where there stood a grand piano. On music stands behind the piano were various stringed instruments. Jackie could see a double bass, a cello, a violin, and a viola.

Cassie squirted through the door and began sniffing her way excitedly around her new environment. The children ran after the dog, trying to pet and play.

As Jackie looked up, the vaulted ceiling reached all the way to the rafters. A massive chandelier hung gold and glass. Each glass panel was etched with an intricate design.

Jackie noticed that Marna was staring open mouthed at the ceiling. "You'll get used to it," Jackie whispered as she took the girl by the arm.

"There you are!" Katrice said warmly as she bustled into the foyer with an apron over her Sunday dress. She gave both Jackie and Marna a hug and a kiss on the cheek. "Welcome to our humble home. Please come in!" She led Jackie and Marna into the living room.

The living room was more informal. A huge leather couch ran around the exterior of the room, providing ample space for lounging. The walls were a cheery knotty pine, and a thick, plush carpet was underfoot. A large television was mounted into a recess in the wall. Each seat was in easy reach of a coffee or end table, providing space for drinks or snacks. There were a few magazines stacked haphazardly, and there were several TV remotes on the tables. In one corner of the room, a huge pile of Legos spilled out of a box with several half-built toys strewn in the mix. The other corner held a dollhouse with little clothes and Barbies scattered about. Jackie was happy to see the bookcase that held a conglomerate of children's stories. Jackie knew that Chucky's favorites were the third-grade science books.

"Can I get you something to drink?" Katrice asked as Jackie and Marna sat and were enveloped by the cushions.

"I would like a glass of water, please," Jackie said, petting Cassie who had jumped up beside her.

"May I help you in the kitchen?" Marna replied.

"No dear," Katrice answered. "I bought dinner pre-cooked. I'm just heating it up. We should be ready to eat in a few minutes." Jackie thought she saw a look of kindness pass between Katrice and Marna. It was as if some inaudible communication had passed between the two. Jackie wondered why Marna would bond with Katrice.

"Can I please help you anyway?" Marna asked. "I can set the table or something."

"Well…" Katrice thought for a moment. "If you insist. I suppose I could find something for you to do."

As the two walked toward the kitchen, Jackie saw Marna pause in the foyer and stare at the musical instruments.

"I'm part of a classical combo," Katrice explained. "We do a gig once a month or so. We like to practice in the foyer, because the acoustics here are so wonderful."

"I used to play the cello when I was a girl," Marna said longingly.

"Well then, after lunch we'll just have to play a duet." Katrice's face was beaming. She took Marna's arm like they were childhood friends and led her off toward the kitchen.

Jackie's attention was grabbed by Milly who was tapping on her knee with a book in hand. "Grandma, can you read a book to me and Cassie?"

The memory drift hit Jackie so hard that she had to catch her breath.

She was in a war zone. Beirut? Lebanon? Somewhere in Africa? Bullets whizzed overhead, and the screams of men hit in battle drowned out the thunder of guns. Beirut… Yes, that's where she was. There were bombed out buildings all around—they were fighting in the city. The whole street was covered in the dust from exploded concrete and littered with the bodies of the fallen.

Jackie's camera swept the scene. Her long lens captured the faces of the men screaming in anger as they leaned into their rifle sights. In the middle of the street, her camera found the body of a boy—he couldn't have been more than 14. Half the kid's face had been blown off, but his AK-47 was still strapped to his chest.

Jackie felt a tug at her waist and looked down to see a new bullet hole in her camera bag. She ignored the satchel and kept photographing. She was wearing a bulletproof vest, but she knew that bullets didn't always have the decency to strike a person in the torso.

Suddenly, in the melee of death that was transpiring all around her, Jackie saw the little girl. She had emerged from a building right across the street from where Jackie had been hiding. The girl was strapped in a vest. Jackie knew that vest well. It wasn't a bulletproof vest like Jackie's; it was a suicide vest. Jackie knew that it was filled with explosives. The girl was probably five. Under the vest was a threadbare, gray dress. Jackie assumed that it had been white at one point in its life.

The girl was holding a stained blanket to her chest, and was nervously chewing on the ear of a dirty stuffed bunny rabbit. The girl stood for a moment seemingly oblivious to the bullets flying above her and the screams of wounded men. Spits of concrete and brick rained on her head as bullets bounced off the wall behind her.

Jackie knew what was about to happen, but she couldn't do a thing to stop it.

From across the street, Jackie's eyes met the girl's. Every mothering instinct in Jackie made her want to run to the child and whisk her away from the carnage. But it was too late. Already too late. The girl was dead; she just didn't know it yet. If Jackie had tried to run to the child, she would be blown up too. All Jackie could do was take photos, hoping that this story could end or change the war. Her finger was pressing the shutter, causing the camera motor to whine in protest. She could barely see through the viewfinder because of her tear drenched eyes. Her sobs wracked her so violently that she could barely steady the camera.

She let the camera drop to her side for a second and wiped her eyes with the back of her filthy hand. "Take the damned photos!" she shouted to herself over the din. She bit her lip until she tasted blood—the pain helped her to focus. She again pulled the viewfinder to her eye. She became an automaton, pushing her emotions to the side.

Jackie's camera found the head of a young woman peeking from around an open doorway behind the child. She saw the insistent order given to the girl. Jackie had to assume that it was the girl's mother. The roar of the battle drowned out the words, but Jackie knew what the child was being told.

The little girl looked once at her mother's face, then looked up into the building where Jackie was hiding. Through the viewfinder, Jackie saw the girl's eyes lock on her. The moment stretched into eternity.

The girl seemed to come to a resolve, then she began sprinting toward the soldiers at the other end of the street. Her dress flopped wildly as she ran. The blanket and rabbit were clutched to her chest.

The girl ran, and Jackie could hear the soldiers scream, "Bomb Bomb Bomb!"

One of the soldiers shot at the child, spraying bullets all around, trying to stop the coming disaster. But the girl ran on. Jackie's camera whirred and clicked; it was the only thing she could do. Behind the camera, Jackie lost control again, weeping and wailing as the camera whirred. Her heart ached for the life of the child, knowing that death was only seconds away.

The soldiers had come to the battle knowing their lives were on the line. But the child… The little girl was being sent to her death. She had obeyed unquestioningly. Her precious life was but a pawn.

In the midst of the automatic gunfire, Jackie heard the crack of a single rifle shot. She saw the round hit the child in the back. The girl's now lifeless body was hurled forward just as the bullet detonated the dynamite.

From a military perspective, the strike had been perfect. The girl had run right into the nest of enemy shooters. One girl had given her life for ten enemy soldiers.

Jackie's camera swung back to the door from where the child had run. The girl's mother was still visible. She was holding the smoking rifle that had sent her very own child to oblivion. The look on the mother's face was horrid. Rivers of tears were etched in the dust that covered the woman's face. She couldn't have been more than twenty.

Jackie fell behind the cement wall and howled with grief. The scene that she had just witnessed boggled her mind. How could a mother do this to her own child? "I'm here to make the world a better place!" she wailed to no one that was listening. "Oh God! Nooo!"

She had nothing to console her so hugged her camera to her chest and sobbed for the child until she had no strength left in her body.

Jackie was snapped back to the present by a tapping on her knee. "Grandma?" a little girl asked. "Are you okay? Why are you crying?"

Jackie lifted her glasses and wiped her eyes. "She was just your age, Milly," Jackie said. She lifted the girl into her lap. Cassie scooted over to make room.

"Who was my age, Grandma?"

"The girl. You didn't see her?" Then Jackie realized that it was a memory. "Oh, I'm sorry. I was just drifting for a moment." She hugged the child and sobbed into her hair for a minute before she could pull herself together.

Both Milly and Cassie could sense that Jackie was having a bad moment. They hugged and snuggled to help.

"Oh, there you are, Mom." It was Charles' voice.

Jackie wiped her face again, then looked up at her son.

"What's wrong, Mom?" Charles asked, concern in his voice.

"Oh, I was just having a bad memory. I was back in the war zone, reliving an experience of my past." She hiccupped, then took a deep breath to calm herself.

"You know, that little girl's sacrifice ended the war. The story and those photos ran on the front page of newspapers around the world." She was crying again. She hugged Milly tight.

Charles sat on the couch and hugged his mother. "Tell me, Mom. Tell me about it."

Jackie took a shaky breath. "It was a little girl, Milly's age. Her mother sent the child to her death, strapped in dynamite. She shot her own child and blew her up in a nest of enemy soldiers. I caught the whole thing on camera. Then just now when I saw Milly, it happened all over again." She was shaking. She felt like she needed to repeat herself. "The story made a difference. It ended the war."

Charles was silent; he could only hug his mother. His calm strength was soothing.

"Grandma, will you read to me?" Milly asked again, holding up her book.

"Sure, sweetie. I'd love to." Jackie took the book into her trembling hands. She wiped her face again and took another deep breath—forcing calm air into her lungs.

Noticing her hands, she held out her palm and placed Milly's on top of her own. "Your hands are big, Grandma," Milly said.

Charles patted his mother's shoulder. "I've got more reading to do, Ma. I'm going to go back to my study. Let me know when dinner's ready." He turned toward the foyer and headed upstairs. Jackie knew that her son had to constantly stay abreast of his field; long hours of study were required. His family paid the price.

Jackie turned back to the book. "You brought me a story about a monster?" Jackie asked, grateful for something to lighten the mood.

"It's not a monster," Milly said, stabbing the cover with her pudgy five-year-old finger. "It's a story about wild things."

"Where the Wild Things Are," Jackie said, reading the title. "But doesn't that big monster scare you?"

"No, silly," Milly giggled. "He's nice." The little girl bit her fingers in a way that made Jackie's heart melt.

"Dinner's ready!" Katrice called from the dining room, her voice carrying through the house.

"Yum!" Milly squealed and leapt from Grandma's lap. Cassie yapped excitedly and ran after the little girl.

Jackie got up and followed, still shaking from her memory. "Oh, there you are Aaeesha," she said as she entered the dining room.

The girl was putting the finishing touches on the table—aligning the silverware to perfection. "Marna," she corrected. "Are you feeling bad again Jackie?" she asked. "You're calling me Aaeesha."

Katrice came into the room carrying a big pot of roast beef. The scent was intoxicating.

"Oh Katrice, this looks wonderful," Jackie said. Her head hurt, and she was grateful to have remembered the woman's name.

The lady of the house sat Jackie at her place. Cassie scrambled into her lap, sniffing Jackie's hand for a morsel of food.

Marna sat on Jackie's right, and Milly begged to sit on her left. Jackie was pretty sure it was because the little girl wanted to be next to the puppy. But it made her happy anyway, just having the child at her elbow.

They all held hands and Charles graced the table, thanking the Lord for family and for bounty.

As the food was passed, Jackie was still having trouble from the memory of Beirut. Her brain was so fogged that she couldn't think straight. She kept getting confused and passing the plates in the wrong direction.

When the roast beef came, she had trouble serving herself. Finally, Marna helped her.

Jackie sat looking at her plate. She had mashed potatoes and gravy, roast beef, boiled carrots, and green beans. For some reason, she was unsure of how to begin. She looked up nervously to see what other people were doing. She saw that Milly had the stick with the round end—what was that called again? Fork? Um, no… spoon. Jackie picked up her spoon.

She needed her roast beef to be smaller… um… Bite sized. Her brain was totally scrambled. She took her spoon and gently poked at the chunk of meat. That didn't work—it was too big and her prodding didn't make it smaller. She pushed down harder. Nothing happened. She took the spoon in her fist and smashed it down on the stubborn chunk. Potatoes splashed off the plate and onto the tablecloth and silverware clattered noisily.

Everybody stopped eating and stared. Jackie was almost in tears.

"It won't… you know… um… the thing. It won't be small." Her quiet voice carried all the way into the foyer.

Marna patted her arm. "Let me help you, Jackie."

She gently scooped up the mashed potatoes back onto Jackie's plate. Then taking her knife, she cut Jackie's roast beef into pieces.

"Thank you, Aaeesha," Jackie said, embarrassed. "I'm, um, having a bad day since I had that memory."

After Marna had cut her meat, Jackie picked up her spoon. Marna surreptitiously removed the spoon and handed Jackie the fork. Jackie nodded her thanks and began eating.

Jackie was surprised how hungry she was. She cleaned most of her plate, leaving a small bite of beef for last.

She nudged Milly with her elbow to get the five-year-old's attention. With a mischievous grin, she snuck the chunk of beef into her lap for the dog. Cassie, of course, gobbled it with joy. Milly giggled and snitched a piece of carrot off her own plate and fed it to Cassie. The two snickered silently, sharing their conspiracy.

The laughter made Jackie feel better. She felt the brain fog lifting a bit as she played with her granddaughter and the dog. She looked up to catch Charles grinning. Apparently, he'd seen the whole transaction.

After the main course was served, Marna helped Katrice bring in the pie. "We have a choice of apple pie, peach pie, or lemon meringue," Katrice said.

"Yes!" Jackie said loudly.

"Yes what?" Katrice asked, puzzled.

"Yes, I would like one of each, please." Jackie held out her plate, smiling.

Marna shrugged. "She needs extra calories anyway. I guess it wouldn't hurt."

"Me too!" Milly shouted holding her plate in the air next to Jackie's. "I want one of each too, please." She was so excited she was bouncing in her chair.

Katrice sighed and rolled her eyes. "Your Grandmother is to blame for this," she grumbled. But Jackie could tell that she wasn't really upset—a grin was playing at the corner of her frown.

Jackie held her head up triumphantly.

After pie, Marna and Chucky helped clear the table while Charles went back upstairs to his study to read.

"Grandma, can I show you my Legos?" Chucky asked politely.

"I would love to see your Lego set. What have you built this week?" Jackie asked, allowing the boy to take her hand. Cassie and Milly bounced behind them, as they walked toward the living room.

As Jackie sat cross legged on the floor in front of the Lego pile, she wondered if three pieces of pie had been such a good idea after all—her tummy hurt a little. Both Milly and Cassie piled onto her lap.

"What's this one?" Jackie asked, holding up a half-constructed toy.

"Oh, that one is a truck that I tried to build. It didn't turn out right." Chucky was concentrating hard on the piece in his hand.

"So, what are you working on now?" she asked.

"This one is a motor. I have it built so that it spins. See?" He demonstrated. "Then I can stick it onto this airplane."

"Did you say you were eight, or eighteen?" Jackie asked, marveling at the boy's design. "This is amazing." She was astounded at his creation.

"And then I can put these little people right into the cockpit here." He placed a little plastic person into the contraption. "He's the driver."

"Grandma?" the little girl in her lap interrupted. "You never read me my story."

"I didn't?" Jackie asked. "Oh. I think you're right. Do you still have that book? The one with the scary monster."

"He's not scary," she giggled, jumping off Jackie's lap and running for the bookshelf.

"You really are amazing," she said to Chucky. "I am really impressed."

"I'm going to be an engineer," he said proudly.

"You will be an incredible engineer," she answered, fluffing his hair.

His smile was his best answer.

"Do you mind if I read your sister a story? Do you want to come and listen?"

He shrugged. "Nah, I've heard that one before. Besides," he said, "it's for little kids."

Jackie nodded and went to the couch where Milly was bouncing in anticipation. Jackie took the book into her hand and sat as the girl snuggled in. "You're sure you want me to read this?" Her eye twinkled. "I don't want you to have nightmares."

Milly laughed. "I'm big enough."

Cassie and Milly thoroughly enjoyed the story. But before they hit the riveting ending of the book, Jackie heard the piano and cello. Jackie finished the story and made her way to the foyer.

Marna was sitting on a chair with the cello between her legs. Katrice was at the piano. It was obvious that Marna was struggling to remember how to play the instrument. Katrice played like a professional pianist.

They were trying to play a simple piece. As Jackie watched, her young friend's confidence began to grow. Soon, music was flowing. Jackie went into the dining room and got a chair. She brought it into the foyer to sit and listen.

Jackie observed a connection between Katrice and Marna. She looked up to see Charles coming down the stairs, drawn by the music. Jackie motioned him over, and he came and stood behind her, listening patiently.

"You see it too?" she asked her son in a whisper.

Behind her, he nodded.

"You're jealous," she said. "I guess, I'm a little jealous too. I never thought they'd connect like this. They act like they've been friends since high school."

Charles laughed and squeezed his mother's shoulder.

Jackie reached her hand up to her shoulder and placed it on top of her son's. She closed her eyes and let the music wash over her soul.

For a moment, the world was perfect. She started drifting again.

Her hand was on Richard's arm. They were walking up the steps of the Kennedy Center. The night air was hot and humid. It must have been one of D.C.'s infamous summer evenings. Jackie felt the straps of her stiletto heels bite into her feet. The shoes hurt, but she looked fabulous. The evening gown had set her back a month's salary, and the diamonds dangling from her ears could only have been bought with Daddy's money. The broach on her neck was the value of a modest house. She didn't dress decadently very often, but tonight it just felt right.

She leaned into her husband, feeling protected and invulnerable. The huge entrance doors were open. Her face felt the chill of the air conditioning as it escaped from the foyer.

The couple stepped into the red carpeted entryway. Richard fished the tickets out of his inside tuxedo pocket and presented them to the usher. They were taken to a balcony overlooking the right side of the stage.

As the couple settled into their seats, the orchestra was tuning. Life was good. Jackie laid her head on Richard's shoulder. In that moment, she was convinced that nothing in life would ever go bad.

Jackie was pulled back to the present as Milly crawled into her lap. Jackie realized that she was crying again—she seemed to be doing that a lot lately. But this time they were happy tears. She stroked her granddaughter's head. She was glad that she could have good memories too.

CHAPTER ELEVEN

Jackie woke to the smell of coffee. Under the covers, Cassie groaned and yawned when Jackie swung her feet over the side of the bed. Jackie looked around her room and was pleased that she knew exactly where she was.

Jackie found a bathrobe while Cassie jumped to the floor and stretched. "Maybe I'll have a good day today, Cassie," Jackie said.

The pair went downstairs to find Marna already at work in the kitchen. "Morning sunshine," the young woman said. "Sleep well?"

"I've always slept well in my older years," Jackie shrugged. She hooked the leash to Cassie's fancy collar and took the dog to the yard.

"So, what are we doing today?" Marna asked as she slid a bowl of Cheerios in front of Jackie.

"Aaeesha's treasure," Jackie said resolutely. "I've got to find it." She shook her head and took a bite. "I'm not getting better, and I need to find it before I've totally lost my wits."

Marna nodded. "Okay."

"And if you want, you can practice that cello that my daughter-in-law sent home with you. The music really helps me."

Marna smiled. "I can help you look through your boxes."

But Jackie was already drifting.

It was a dark restaurant, and the smell of broiled beef was thick. They were at a back booth, and Jackie had given instructions to the hostess that they were to be left alone. The seats around them were empty—the dim bulb that hung from a cord left them in an island of light in a sea of darkness.

Jackie laid out the photos in front of Congressman O'Connell. "I'm going to submit these to my editor in the morning," she said. She opened the manila envelope and pulled out the bank statements, copies of interviews, and the full, typed story.

She sat quietly as the man read. He began to tremble.

"How did you get this info?" he demanded.

She shrugged. "I've got my sources."

A murderous look passed over his face, then it changed to a beg. "You'll destroy me," he whispered.

She nodded but didn't answer.

"What can I do to stop this? I'll pay anything."

She still didn't answer. She let him sweat a little.

"I'll lose my congressional seat, my wife will leave me, and I'll be homeless on the street."

"You should have thought about that before you accepted the bribe."

"Why are you showing me this? You want something—you want a payoff." The negotiator in the man was calculating his cost.

Jackie shook her head again. "I wouldn't accept your money if you were the last employer on the planet. Dirty money disgusts me."

"Then what do you want? Name your price. It's yours."

"This corporation bribed you for your vote. They want to pump oil from the nature reserve in Louisiana. You're going to pay the money back, and then you're going to vote against their bill."

"You a damned tree hugger? Is that why you're doing this?" Spittle flew from his lips.

"Actually, I don't give a damn what the bill is. I'm angry that a sitting congressman would accept a bribe—it's unconscionable." She let her words hang in silence for a moment. "Whatever they're paying you to do, you'll do the opposite."

"And what do I owe you for keeping my name out of the papers?"

She shrugged. "You'll keep your nose clean the rest of your tenure."

"That's it?"

She gathered up the photos and papers and put them back into the envelope. "I'll be keeping these little goodies on file in case you are tempted to stray from the straight and narrow. I'll be watching. My sources will be watching. If you break the law—even if you get a parking ticket—I'll bust you so fast it'll make your head spin."

"For as long as I'm in office?"

She nodded again.

"These people are evil. You don't know who you're dealing with," he told Jackie. The fear was evident on his face. "They'll kill both of us—they'll kill our families."

"This isn't my first rodeo, Congressman," Jackie said confidently. "A copy of these documents will be in a safe place. My lawyer has instructions to release this to the press if either of us should be harmed in any way. A press release would destroy the company, so it's in their best interest to keep us healthy." She paused to let the words sink in. "I've already had a conversation with them—they understand."

He eyed her suspiciously. "You play a dangerous game."

She shrugged. "It's safer than being a war correspondent."

The man sat back in his seat and sighed loudly. He looked to his left into the darkness of the empty bar. "I didn't want to vote for their bill, anyway. It wasn't right." This time when he looked at her, she could see gratitude on his face. He was glad to be out from under their evil thumb. Jackie had provided an escape for him.

He nodded toward the packet that was in her bag. "You do this kind of thing often? Rescuing the congressmen from corruption?"

She stood, leaving the drink check on the table for the errant congressman to pay. She slipped on her jacket and put the strap of her bag over her shoulder. She pulled out her umbrella to prepare for the rain that was soaking the parking lot. She looked up at him as if she'd only now heard the question.

"Only if I feel the congressman is redeemable," she answered, smiling. She turned on her heel to let the man stew in his own guilt in the dark.

"Jackie?" She realized that Marna was shaking her arm. "You okay, Jackie?"

"Um, yeah." Jackie stirred to her feet, plopping Cassie out of her lap and onto the floor. "Let's go downstairs and sort through those boxes."

Marna turned on the basement light and took a couple folding chairs down the steps. She set them up in the only clear spot in the corner. She brought down a pitcher of lemonade and a few cookies to nibble on.

"This looks like a fun box," Marna said, opening the top one.

"I have dementia; I'm not crazy. Sorting through old crap isn't exactly fun," Jackie said. But she could feel a grin trying to escape the corner of her lips. The woman-child had a way of making dreary tasks seem wonderful. Jackie liked having someone else in the house.

"No really. This is interesting." Marna showed Jackie the contents of one of the manila folders. It was a photo of a fat man in an expensive suit. The man sitting across from him was wearing ratty jeans. His head was covered in a red bandana and his eyes were masked behind wraparound sunglasses. The two were polar opposites. They appeared to be seated in the back of a cheesy restaurant.

"That's Senator Reilly," Jackie said pointing to the guy in the suit.

Marna scanned through the accompanying pages. "It says here that Congressman Reilly…"

Jackie interrupted her. "Oh, sorry. Yes… he was a congressman, not a senator."

"He had a drug and prostitution problem. You documented his actions and confronted him. You got him into a drug rehab program." She looked up at Jackie. "So, this seedy looking character is his drug dealer?"

Jackie sat thinking for a moment, trying to remember the incident. She nodded slowly. "Yeah, I think that's right."

Marna opened another one of the packets. "Um... This one is a story about an Army Colonel."

Jackie tapped her knee. "Is Congressman Reilly still in office?"

Marna pulled her phone out of her pocket and began typing on the tiny screen. Jackie marveled at the technology that kids had these days. "Yeah. He's still in office. He is a Republican from Ohio."

Just then the phone rang upstairs. "I'll get it," Marna called, running up the stairs for the cordless handset.

A moment later, Marna's shocked face appeared at the top of the stairs. "Jackie? It's former First Lady Laura Armstrong on the phone."

"Oh good," Jackie said. "I haven't talked to her in a long time. Would you please bring me the cordless phone?"

A moment later Jackie's old friend was speaking into her ear. "Jackie, we haven't spoken in a while."

"Hi, Laura. How are things?"

"Well, you know that George Sr. is slipping and of course..." Her voice choked a bit. "And, of course, Barbara has passed."

They were silent for a moment. Old friends sharing a moment of grief.

"I'm sorry for your loss," Jackie said. "She was my friend of many years."

Again, they let the comradery pass across the electronic ether of the phone connection.

"I'm slipping too, Laura. Yesterday, I tried to cut my roast beef with a spoon." Jackie held her head in her hands. "My mind is going, and it scares me."

"I'm sorry," Laura said with genuine concern. "Anything I can do to help?"

Jackie sighed to her old friend. "I don't think so. I've got a home helper now. She's terrific, except I keep thinking she's my dead daughter."

Laura laughed. "Well, at least you get to relive some good memories."

At first, Jackie was offended that Laura had laughed, but then she realized that it was really funny. "Maybe you can help me after all, Laura. I need some advice, and my mind isn't what it used to be. Abigail and I came across some evidence I have on Congressman Reilly. I used to know what to do with intel like this, but now..." Her voice trailed off. "I've got soup between my ears, Laura."

Laura pondered the problem for a moment. "I think we should call Williams."

"Who?"

"FBI Director Reginald Williams," Laura said.

"Oh him... Yeah, I suppose we should."

"I'll put in a call for you, Jackie," Laura said. "But I need something from you too."

Jackie was stumped as to what the former First Lady could possibly want from her. "Um... Sure. What do you need?"

"Our publicist is working on some sort of who-knows-what and needs some photos from my White House days. They want something that's been previously unpublished. I thought you might be able to find something for me."

Jackie looked at the huge mountain of boxes that filled her basement. "I'd love to, Laura, but my basement's a total wreck—I've got boxes stacked to the rafters with no organization." She sighed. "I know I have what you want, but I have no way of finding it."

"Maybe you could hire someone to come help you organize it," Laura suggested.

"Can't," Jackie said. "I have sensitive stuff in here—like Congressman Reilly's documents."

Laura was silent for a moment. "I've got an idea. Do you remember Congresswoman Banks from Oregon?"

"Sure," Jackie remembered. "She's the one that I caught…"

"Yeah, that's the one," Laura answered. "Her son, Warren, now works for Williams. He's the smartest guy I've ever met—besides you, of course. Even at the age of thirty, he knows all the players in Washington, and he knows what to do with sensitive intel." She laughed. "He reminds me of what you used to be back in the day… Warren is now an FBI agent. I'll tell Director Williams that you'll turn over your intel to the FBI, if Warren will help you sort through your boxes. He'll help you organize your basement and also find the photos that my publicist wants."

"Those photos about his mother are in this mess," Jackie said. "What if he finds them?"

"He's a grown man. He knows he's the product of that little tryst. And thank God for that, because Congresswoman Banks' husband was dumb as a box of nails." They both laughed.

"Okay, you're on," Jackie decided. "He can stay in Charles' old room. We'll trade my photos for his help in cleaning up."

"Good to hear your voice again, Jackie," Laura said. "I'm sorry you're slipping. Maybe digging out some old memories will help."

"Thanks, Laura," Jackie said sadly. "I'm going downhill fast, and there are some things that I need to do before my mind is totally gone. Sorting out this mess is the first step."

"Well then… I'm happy to help," Laura answered. "I miss you, old friend."

A few minutes later the phone rang again. "Jackie? This is Director Williams."

Warmth flowed through Jackie's body at the sound of her friend's voice. "We've been through some tough things together, Reginald," Jackie said.

"Cut the bull, Jackie." Williams shot. "Laura just called me and told me that you've got dirt on Congressman Reilly. I thought you quit that business after that other deal went bad."

Jackie was silent for a moment. Her head hurt, and she wanted to cry. She didn't know what to say, so she handed the phone to Marna. "Help me," she whispered.

"Hello? This is Marna. I'm Jackie's home helper," Marna said. "She has dementia, and sometimes she gets overwhelmed. What can I do for you, sir?"

Jackie heard the man through the earpiece. "Dementia?" The question was more like an accusation. Then the man sighed. "I'm sorry to hear that."

"Yes sir," Marna said. "She has good days and bad days."

The tinny voice through the speaker said, "Laura asked if I could send over Agent Warren Banks to help. She says Jackie will trade her intel in exchange for help in cleaning out the basement." He sighed again. "Banks is one of my best agents, and I hate putting him on a detail like that." He swallowed as if lumping down a bitter pill. His voice reflected his acquiescence "I had no idea that she was back to her old tricks of collecting dirt. If I'd have known that, I would have raided her place years ago…"

"We could put him up in one of our rooms here," Marna offered.

"That will be up to him. He's based out of Texas, close to the former President and First Lady. He can either stay with you or in a hotel."

Jackie didn't hear any more of the conversation. She was drifting again.

The rain ran in rivulets off the umbrella. Jackie's shaking body was tucked under her son's strong arm. Charles had flown in from med school—he was her only remaining anchor in a world that had just exploded beneath her feet.

The scent of wet earth filled her nostrils. In the distance, she heard the honking of horns by rude people who weren't burying their loved ones.

The preacher stood in front of the two coffins, and he was going on about something that Jackie couldn't understand. It wasn't that he was mumbling, or there was a linguistic problem. Rather, Jackie's mind was trying to wrap itself around the fact that her husband and her daughter were laying in those two boxes. Dead.

The coffin on the right held the body of the man whom she'd grown to love. Their marriage hadn't been love at first kiss. In fact, during the first few years, she felt like she'd settled for second best. But as time passed, she'd come to rely on his strength and fortitude. He was a rock in the storm of her chaotic life. Now he was dead—snuffed out by a horrible car crash.

The box next to him held the body of the young woman whom Jackie loved more than life itself. Abigail was too young to die. The girl had had her whole life ahead of her. Jackie's frame shook with emotion.

Every fiber in her being wanted to crawl into either one of those boxes in exchange for the lives that had been extinguished. The depth of her grief reached the core of her soul.

Charles. While she wept, her son's arm was like a steel pole—helping her to stand erect when fortitude was impossible. She knew that he, too, was grieving. And although he was usually the emotional one of the two, today, he was the stoic.

"It's all my fault," Jackie said through her tears.

Laura Armstrong was standing beside her and patted her on the arm. "No, sweetie. It was just an accident."

But Jackie knew better.

CHAPTER TWELVE

A little before nine the next morning, there was a knock on the front door. Cassie raced to the foyer and barked. Marna was upstairs putting the clean sheets on Charles' bed, so Jackie answered. She gathered Cassie into her arms before opening.

"Hello?" she asked sternly. "How may I help you?"

Before her stood an impossibly handsome young man. He had the size and muscles of a lineman from West Virginia University. He was probably 6'5" and must have weighed close to 250 pounds. She guessed him to be in his early thirties, and only a hint of a paunch showed above his belt. His eyes were the color of a bright but overcast sky. His golden hair cascaded across his forehead and threatened to fall into his right eye. He had on a light, tan suit jacket with a white shirt underneath. A big, black Stetson topped his head. Blue jeans and cowboy boots completed the ensemble. But something in the face troubled Jackie.

"Good morning, ma'am," the man said holding a badge in one hand and extending the other for a handshake. "I'm Agent Warren Banks."

Jackie was confused for a moment, and it must have shown on her face. She let his proffered hand hang in the air.

"Laura sent me… former First Lady, Laura Armstrong."

"Who's Laura Armstrong?" she asked. She blocked the doorway with her body. "I don't know who you are, and I don't like you. You're one of those FBI agents spying on me!"

Jackie felt a hand at her back and realized that it was Marna. The young lady gently pushed her aside. "Hi, I'm Marna Hunt, and this is Jackie

Scott. Jackie has dementia, and sometimes she gets confused." She saw Marna extending her hand to the man.

"He's going to help us find Aaeesha's treasure," Marna told Jackie.

"Oh," Jackie said. "Can he be trusted?" For some reason that she couldn't identify, she still didn't like the guy. It was more than just his badge—something felt amiss.

"Laura Armstrong—remember your friend, Laura? She and Director Williams sent him," Marna said. Still holding the man's hand, she pulled him inside the door.

"Laura… Laura…" The memory hit her like a freight train. She felt so embarrassed. "Oh, Laura from the White House. My friend. Yes. I'm sorry." She hung her head. "I get… um… I, uh, Thanks Abigail. Laura is my good friend… I just forgot." She wanted to run and hide in the bathroom.

"She sometimes calls me Abigail or Aaeesha," Marna explained. "Abigail was her daughter, and Aaeesha was her best friend as a child. If she calls me Aaeesha, she's having a really bad day."

Marna took the suitcase out of the man's hand and set it at the bottom of the stairs to the second floor. She waved with her hand, beckoning the man. "Come into the living room and sit for a minute before we get started."

Jackie followed the two. She could tell that Marna was smitten with the man. She didn't know if she didn't like him because she was jealous of Marna's attention, or if there was something untrustworthy about the guy. She determined to stay on her guard.

The man sat on the couch, and his long legs stretched into the center of the room. Jackie sat in her usual stuffed chair. Marna sat on the chair's arm so she could pat Jackie's shoulder. Apparently, she sensed Jackie's discomfort.

"So, you're from Oregon, but you're now living in Texas, close to the Armstrong's?" Marna asked. "And you work for the FBI?"

"That's the short version," the lanky man answered.

Jackie couldn't remember his name. Wendell? Winston? Warren. That was it. The man's name was Warren.

"My official address is in Texas, but I spend more time here in Washington D.C. I'm sort of a trouble-shooter for the Director. Laura also asks for my time occasionally—she has her fingers in a lot of pies," he said.

"Thanks for helping us out," Marna said. "We've got a big job."

Jackie fought the urge to stick her tongue out at the guy. Instead, she tried to smile, but she was pretty sure that the results of her attempt were a wry grimace.

Marna and Warren chatted for a few minutes while Jackie listened. She knew she was having a bad day. She didn't want to say the wrong thing.

"Well, I'm here to work," Warren said. "Let's go see what we've got."

Jackie led the others to the basement. When the light went on, Warren let out a low whistle from the bottom step. "Looks like we've got a job ahead of us."

"Abigail and I started working on it," Jackie said. "But we didn't get very far."

"Is this intel classified?" he asked picking up a handful of photos.

Jackie shook her head. "I don't know. I... um... I don't think so. But there are secrets. Suddenly she remembered that she had photos of his mother's tryst. "You know that your mother's photos are in here..."

"Yeah, I know," He cut her off. "Laura warned me, but that's old news. No problem." Although he waved his hand dismissively, Jackie could tell that it still affected him. She was impressed.

"Do you think we can get some filing cabinets delivered? I think that's the best way to handle this," he said, taking charge. "Also, if we find some stuff that truly is classified, I'll make sure it gets handled correctly."

"I have Jackie's credit card," Marna said, laying a gentle hand on the man's arm. "I can order the file cabinets and have them delivered this afternoon." Jackie saw the tall man blush as the barely five-foot-tall Marna touched him.

The height difference between the youngsters was shocking. Marna only came up to the man's chest.

"Sounds good," he said, patting her hand.

"Tell me your name again," Jackie said. "You're that congresswoman's son."

"Warren," he said smiling. "But you can call me Bill, or Henry, or anything you want. Since I'm the only guy here now, I'll answer."

Jackie smiled too. She was starting to recover from the funk she felt earlier. "Thanks for helping with my mess."

She stepped back, looking at the pile. She placed her hands on her hips. "You know," she said as a thought occurred to her, "this pile is what my brain looks like right now. It's a total mess, with a lot of really important things buried."

Marna patted Jackie on the shoulder. "That's what we're here to do. We'll help you untangle it."

Jackie wasn't sure if she was talking about the mess in the basement or the tangled spaghetti in her head.

CHAPTER THIRTEEN

By the afternoon, Jackie's house was a beehive of activity. Just a few weeks ago, she had been the only one rattling around her empty home. Now she had two other humans and a canine to keep her company.

Five shiny new filing cabinets sat in the living room, waiting for Warren to clear enough space for them downstairs. Marna was running up and down the stairs, offering Warren a little snack or bringing him water.

Jackie worked with Warren as the two tried to figure out about the photos, reports, and other papers that were strewn through the boxes. She was overcoming her initial misgivings about the man. Having him engage with her life's work seemed to have taken the edge off of her earlier animosity. He seemed truly interested.

The majority of the boxes held photos, old-fashioned negatives, notebooks full of hand-written notes, and articles. The articles that had been published had the date and publication name hand-written in the header. It appeared that almost half of the articles had seen print. In many cases, the newspaper or magazine article had been cut from the original publication and filed in the box.

Most of it was old—the players had long been retired. Since Warren knew all the current movers in Washington, he could sort out the items that were now irrelevant. He also knew what intel pieces needed to be protected.

"You're right," he said. "So far, we haven't found anything that should be classified, but we definitely have some sensitive stuff here."

"My son, Charles, was going to throw it all out," Jackie said, grateful to finally find an ally.

"He just didn't know," Warren said. He stopped his sorting and held a photo up to the light. "Who is this?"

Jackie took the photo, looking closely where Warren was pointing. The picture was of Jimmy Carter. He was in the hallway of a hotel shaking hands with a dignitary—Jackie couldn't remember the dignitary's name. But Warren was pointing to a person down the hall behind the 39th President. There was a man opening the door to a room. It didn't seem like Jackie had intended to catch the man in the frame, but his face was clearly visible.

As Jackie tried to remember the scene, she started drifting. "Stay with me, Jackie," Warren said gently. "Who is that man?"

"That's um…" Her brain spun, then clicked. "That's Horst Sindermann, President of the People's Chamber for East Germany."

Warren nodded. "That's what I thought. This is a meeting that reportedly never happened. But you caught it on film." He set the picture aside. "This is an historic photo, Jackie. It's important."

"So, I caught him by accident?" Jackie asked. She really couldn't remember the incident.

Warren laughed. "Given your reputation, I seriously doubt it. I'll bet you wrote it up…" He rummaged through the box for a moment.

"Ha, here it is." He held up a sheet of paper. "You say here that the Secret Service refused to allow you to publish that photo." He paused as he read the report. "You were quite the reporter, Jackie." He shook his head.

He held up the packet that had prompted the call yesterday. "You wanna tell me about this?"

"Congressman Reilly," she said as she pulled the photos from the envelope. "He had a drug problem and was running wild with a string of prostitutes. He owed a lot of money to the underworld. But after I showed him this packet, he got help. He cleaned up his act—or at least, he was clean the last time I checked." She smiled. "He still sends me Christmas cards."

"You threatened to publish these photos and destroy him if he didn't change his ways?"

"I found that threat of exposure often helped a person back onto the straight and narrow." Her bad funk was definitely lifting. Her head was much clearer.

"So, you blackmailed people into being good?"

She shrugged shyly. "Blackmail is such a harsh word." She was so proud that Warren had discovered her secret. Very few people knew, and Warren had figured it out in a short time. Maybe she was wrong about him.

"But you could have published all this stuff and gotten rich!" he said incredulously.

She shrugged again. "I was already rich—I had Daddy's money. I just did my part to help make the world a better place."

He shook his head. "You're quite something, Mrs. Scott. Even more amazing than your legend tells."

"It went bad one time," she confessed. "Something awful happened. I don't remember what it was."

The doorbell rang. Cassie began barking and ran upstairs. "I'll get it," Marna said. She had been sitting on the bottom step listening to the entire conversation.

A moment later Marna's head popped into the stairwell again—she was holding Cassie. "It's the lady judge who was mad at you in church on Sunday," she said.

"Oh," Jackie said to Marna, "let her in, I'll be right up." She turned to Warren. "Excuse me a moment, would you please?"

"No problem," he said. "But I'm going to be going through this stack a little more carefully from now on. It was just happenstance that I saw Sindermann."

By the time she got upstairs, the Justice was just stepping into the foyer. She had a tin box in her hands. "Jackie," she said warmly, "I was rude to you in church on Sunday. I wanted to bring over some cookies and apologize."

"This is Abigail." Jackie tried to introduce her caretaker.

"Actually, it's Marna Hunt." The girl held out her hand. "Jackie has dementia and she gets confused sometimes."

"Dementia? I'm so sorry to hear that." But her face said that she wasn't sorry. "I'm Charity Keeler." She shook Marna's hand.

"Thank you for the cookies, but it wasn't necessary," Jackie said. She opened up the lid and sniffed. "On second thought, it is perfect." She grinned widely. "These smell delicious."

"Made them myself," the Justice said. "I like puttering around the kitchen."

"Would you like to come in?" Jackie asked, glad that her hostess skills hadn't yet slid into the gutter. "We're having a wonderful time going through all my old memories downstairs."

It was as if the blood in the Justice's face had just been flushed down the toilet. Her face turned white as a sheet of paper. "Really?" She managed to stutter. "That must be so much fun."

"Yes," Jackie said, taking her by the hand and leading her toward the kitchen. "I was talking to Laura Armstrong yesterday and mentioned that I was having trouble finding Aaeesha's treasure. She wanted some old White House photos, so she traded photos in exchange for Warren's help." She felt proud that she was able to remember the man's name.

Jackie sat at the kitchen table and set the tin of treats in the middle. She helped herself to a fat chocolate chip cookie and pushed the tin over to the Justice. Marna reached in and helped herself.

"Really? That's so nice," Charity Keeler said through pinched cheeks. "Warren. That wouldn't happen to be Warren Banks, would it?"

Jackie shrugged. She had enough trouble remembering the man's first name—there was no way that she could remember his surname too. She wiped at some crumbs at the corner of her mouth.

Marna answered for her. "Yeah, it's Warren Banks. Do you know him? He's downstairs; would you like to say hi?"

Jackie noticed that Marna's face went dreamy when she mentioned Warren's name. She also noticed that the Justice's face turned three more shades of white.

"Um... uh, no. um. No thanks. I really gotta get going. Good to see you again, Jackie," she said. "And good to meet you, young lady. Take good care of Jackie, we all need her." She got up and scooted out the door like a man with an axe was chasing her.

"That was weird," Marna said. "Do you have some dirt on her or something?"

"I dunno," Jackie shrugged, "but I like her cookies."

Marna shook her head. "Who knew I'd end up in such an interesting household. All I was trying to do was to get a job, and now I'm in the middle of a political intrigue." She laughed. "Why don't you go downstairs and help Warren some more. I'll see if I can whip up a yummy dinner."

Jackie headed back downstairs to see how the FBI man was coming on her basement project.

"Who was that?" Warren asked, looking up from his work.

"It was that lady... um..." Jackie tried to answer but couldn't remember her name.

"It was Virginia Supreme Court Justice Charity Keeler," Marna said, coming down a few treads of the basement stairs.

"Oh no," Warren said, looking shocked. "You didn't tell her I was here looking through your stash, did you?"

Marna and Jackie looked at each other. "Well, yeah," Jackie said. "Is that bad?"

Warren shrugged. "If she knows, the whole town knows. Might as well take out an ad in the *Washington Post*."

CHAPTER FOURTEEN

That evening after dinner, both Marna and Warren helped Jackie through her sundowning. Warren was keeping a close eye on the things that she sorted to make sure she didn't trash something important by accident. By eight o'clock, Jackie had calmed down enough to go upstairs for tea.

The trio sat around the kitchen table holding hot mugs. Cassie was in Jackie's lap.

"Oh my, it's so nice to have people around again," Jackie said. "I got so lonely in this house by myself. I was so afraid to go out—I'd get confused and lost." She patted Marna's hand.

A thought occurred to her. "This is Tuesday. Marna, aren't you supposed to be going to your AA meeting tonight?"

Marna shrugged. "Missing one week won't hurt. I'll be fine." She smiled largely at Warren.

Jackie noticed that Warren was smiling back. She growled a little inside.

"So, tell me more about yourself," Marna asked Warren. "Where did you grow up, and how did you come to work for Laura Armstrong?"

"I don't officially work for Laura—it just turns out that I do a lot of things with her. She's a busy woman." He shrugged, then went on to answer the question. "I grew up moving between Oregon and Washington, D.C. As you've learned, my mother was a congresswoman."

Marna and Warren were lost in conversation, but Jackie seemed unable to follow. It was as if the words were floating off into a fog.

Jackie knew she was drifting, but couldn't stop. Maybe it was because she was so tired from having sorted all day, or maybe because of the excitement of so many people in the house, but she was falling hard.

It was summer in Washington. Hot, humid, prickly heat clung to everything. Rain had just passed through, and instead of cooling the earth, it had just turned the world into a sauna.

Barbara Armstrong had asked Jackie to photograph their family event at the White House. A few of the ladies had wandered out into the Rose Garden. Jackie followed with her camera bag over her right shoulder. She knew there would be some excellent photo opportunities among the flowers.

"Jackie." She heard a voice behind her and turned to find a woman in her mid-forties carrying two mint juleps. She held one out and Jackie accepted. "Sorry if I offended you earlier. I just get so tired of the press…"

"It's okay. I understand," Jackie said.

They paused their conversation momentarily. The roar of a jet taking off from Washington National Airport rent the sky. Jackie watched Laura's twins, Barbara and Jenna, playing under their nanny's' care.

"I'm just not used to having members of the press at family functions," Laura apologized after the plane's noise had subsided. "I didn't realize that Mom had invited you. She pulled me aside and told me that you were really a family friend."

Jackie led Laura over to a shaded bench. "It's true that I'm a photojournalist, but relationships are far more important than getting a scoop. Barbara knows I would never publish anything about family affairs without her approval."

"But if you got a political scoop?" Laura asked sagely with a raised eyebrow.

"I'm a very curious person." Jackie smiled in a non-answer. Innately, she felt a bond to this woman. She felt as if Laura had sought her out for a reason.

"This whole political scene is difficult for me," Laura confessed. "Washington DC is very different than Texas. I used to just pretend that it didn't exist, but now that we visit Dad so often in the White House, it's impossible to ignore. Sometimes we stay here for a week or two..." She let her voice trail off.

Jackie nodded. "This town can eat you alive. How are your girls adjusting?"

Laura sighed. "Everybody treats them differently." She nodded toward the Secret Service Agent. "And the protection follows us everywhere."

"I understand," Jackie said. "This is a difficult age. Having this kind of attention makes it even more challenging."

Another jet took off above the Potomac River. The thunder of its engines drowned out the conversation for a moment. The women waited until the interruption passed.

"Would you like to bring your girls out to our house for a movie night?" Jackie asked. "Your girls are a year younger than my daughter, Abigail. My son and husband have gone fishing for the weekend, so we could do a girl's night in. We'll make it a pajama party."

"That's perfect!" Laura said, thrilled. "We need some Washington friends."

Jackie was jarred back to the present by Marna's lilting laugh. She looked around her to find that she was still in her kitchen in Vienna.

The big handsome guy was laughing his way through a story about a horse and a very angry steer. Jackie followed enough to hear about his foot getting caught in a rope and winding up with his face in a cow pie.

She wanted to go to bed, but instead got dragged into another memory.

She was walking through a bombed-out street. She was in some African war zone. They all looked the same after a while—ash, dust, bombed-out buildings. The bodies had been removed, but bloodstains inked the pavement. Flies buzzed in the heat.

It was evening, and the shadows stretched long. She walked through the mayhem slowly, her heart aching with every step she took. "I'm trying to make the world a better place, Aaeesha," she said to the empty streets.

She paused to photograph yet another burned out truck. The body collectors must have missed one, because the driver was still strapped into the front seat. Though the truck was burned, somehow, the corpse had escaped the fire. His eyes, still open, stared into infinity, and his mouth gaped in an eternal scream. Flies walked across his eyeballs, and flew into his mouth unmolested.

Jackie's camera clicked. She shot the scene from every angle.

Behind her she heard a whimper. She turned to find a child staring at her. She guessed the boy's age to be two and a-half. He had on a torn, red and blue striped t-shirt. Instead of pants, he had on a diaper—she could smell it even at this distance. His feet were bare, and he was covered from head to toe in ash. Beneath the dirt, she could see that his skin was the color of dark chocolate. His tight, black curls were short and matted. He stood, two fingers of his right hand stuck in his mouth.

The street was silent. There was only the sound of guns and bombs in the far distance, and the flies sucking blood. Everyone in the town had either fled or had been killed—except for this child.

The two stood and looked into each other's eyes for a long moment. Jackie knelt and held out a hand. In Arabic, she said, "Come here. Let me help you." She doubted that the boy spoke Arabic, but her French was very weak.

Instead of coming to Jackie, the boy turned and went into an apartment building. She rushed after him, fearing that he might be hurt in the debris. The child turned to make sure that Jackie was following. He began crawling up a staircase.

By now, Jackie sensed that the boy needed to show her something, so she followed, protectively guarding his every step. When they reached the second floor, the boy went through the doorway.

There on the floor, lay the little boy's family. His mother and his siblings were all dead.

"Mama," the boy said in a confused voice. He said a few more words in a language that she didn't understand. His pudgy hand patted the corpse of the bullet-riddled woman. His eyes questioned Jackie's face.

Jackie's mothering instincts wanted to grab the child and run, but her journalistic instincts caused her to take a moment. She pulled out her camera and began shooting the child sitting among the corpses of his dead family.

She shot a roll, then carefully lifted the boy into her arms. He seemed to sense that Jackie was a source of help, and he clung tightly to her neck.

Jackie prayed over the dead family as a Muslim, as a Hebrew, and as a Presbyterian. She carried the boy to her car and fed him what little water and food she had left. She pulled off her own blouse to clean the boy's bottom.

Suddenly, Jackie was back in Virginia. It was 1972. She was sitting in Monroe Turner's Corvette convertible.

"You've changed," she pronounced. "The Vietnam war broke something inside you."

"War changes everyone," Monroe said slowly. His eyes had a faraway look. "You learn what's important and what's not."

He ran his fingers over the dash of his muscle car. "I may have gotten off that plane two weeks ago, but Vietnam's still in here." He pounded his chest with a closed fist. "I saw things that a man should never see in his life." He sighed deeply.

"Then let it go," Jackie begged. "Help me make the world a better place."

Monroe turned his head and looked out the driver's window into the dark of the Virginia countryside. "No. I can't do that," he shook his head. "We lost that war, because we were screwed up at the top. The generals—the brass—the politicians. Nobody had the balls to do what needed to be done. I'm gonna change that."

"Let it go," Jackie begged again. "Make love, not war." She moved closer, but he didn't notice.

"I've applied to West Point," Monroe said as if she hadn't spoken. "My daddy's got connections and I've been accepted. I'm gonna go to the top, then we'll fix this damned Army, and we'll never have a fuckup like Vietnam again."

"I can't marry a soldier," Jackie said. "Richard Scott wants me. I… I love you Monroe. I always have, and I always will. But I won't marry a soldier. Please hang up your rifle."

"That pussy?" Monroe shook his head with disbelief. "Richard stayed in college the whole time, so he wouldn't get drafted! You deserve a real man."

She didn't answer. The tick of the car's cooling engine was the only sound. The faint scent of the car's oil reached her nose.

"I'm gonna fix this Army, Jackie. You just wait and see. I'm gonna be the top dog; then I'll make it right."

Jackie's memories faded, and she realized that she was laying in her own bed. Under the covers, her faithful dog snoozed happily.

Jackie raised her head off the pillow and looked at the clock. The red readout said 11:21. Downstairs, she heard Marna's voice. Jackie exorcised herself from the blankets and the cuddling dog, and padded her way to the stairs. She made her way down to the living room where she found Marna and Warren laughing. They stopped as she walked into the room.

"Did we wake you?" Marna asked apologetically.

"No." Jackie dismissed the apology with a wave of her hand. "I guess I must have drifted while we were having tea. Did I do or say anything stupid?"

Although she appreciated Warren's understanding of her horde of intel, she still felt uncomfortable with him around.

"You were fine," Marna said. "You just quit talking and became unresponsive, so I put you to bed."

Jackie sank into a large, stuffed chair. "Thank you, Abigail," she said. A huge sigh escaped her lips. "I'm slipping fast. I have to find Aaeesha's treasure before I lose everything. It's important. It's in a box…" She stopped and helplessly rubbed her face with her hands. "That box is the key."

She looked at Warren and Marna with pleading eyes. "Help me find it before I'm totally gone."

She saw Warren glance nervously at Marna. He looked back at Jackie. "If it's downstairs, we'll find it," he said confidently. "I'll go through every box you have."

The three sat in silence for a moment. Finally, Jackie nodded. "Thank you… um…" She looked down, embarrassed. "Oh gosh, if I can't even remember people's names, how am I supposed to remember anything important?" Her voice was almost a whisper.

"Warren," he said gently.

Marna got up and helped Jackie to her feet. "Come on, sweet lady. Let's put you back in bed again. It's time I hit the hay as well. We need to get up early, so we can find that treasure of yours."

CHAPTER FIFTEEN

Jackie was in the kitchen before seven o'clock. She found the eggs and bacon and whipped up the ingredients for a western omelet. She placed the pan in the refrigerator so that it would be ready to cook when her team came to breakfast.

She set the coffee percolating, then went to the back porch with Cassie to watch the sun rise on the W&OD trail and the woods beyond the house. It was a little after eight when she heard stirrings in the house behind her, so she went in and found Marna standing in the kitchen with a gnarled case of bedhead.

"I made omelets," Jackie said. "You proud of me?" She reached into the fridge, and pulled out the pan. She got the stove going, and breakfast was soon cooking.

A few minutes later Warren arrived. "You sleep okay?" Jackie asked. "We haven't had anybody in that bed for a while."

"Yeah, it was fine," he said, rubbing his wild mop of yellow hair. "Man, it smells good in here."

"Sit down and I'll get your coffee and eggs." Jackie served the youngsters. "You two look like you've just been through a hurricane."

Warren and Marna looked at each other's hair and laughed. "If I look anything like you, I'm a total mess," Marna said.

"Trust me, you win." Warren buried his face in his arms and belly laughed.

By nine o'clock, Warren and Jackie were back at work in the basement. They'd made enough room on the basement floor that Warren was able to man-handle one of the filing cabinets down the stairs from the living room.

He sorted the documents and photos according to year and then by name. When a photo had multiple people, it was filed according to the highest-ranking politician or officer.

"Most of the cases you uncovered are on politicians who have already retired," Warren said. "You did a lot of this back in the day, didn't you?"

"I quit because I had one that went bad," Jackie answered. "Then after Abigail died, I left Washington and went back to the field."

"Does the FBI know about all these?" he asked.

She shook her head. "But now I need to turn them over. I can't handle them anymore." There was an empty hole in her chest as she saw her life's work slipping between her fingers.

She began drifting again.

Jackie was livid. "You're telling me that Congressman O'Connell and my husband and daughter are killed in automobile accidents on the same day, and it's only a coincidence?" She was almost yelling at the FBI agent.

They were on the fourth floor of the FBI headquarters at 935 Pennsylvania Avenue, NW. Jackie was in a conference room, and across the table from her was an equally red-faced Agent Reginald Williams.

"If you would have turned this evidence over to us, then we wouldn't be having this conversation!" he shot back. His finger was pounding the packet of evidence that Jackie had shown to O'Connell only a month earlier.

The force of his statement punched Jackie in the chest like an iron fist. She slumped back in her chair and gasped, trying to catch her breath. She blinked back the tears and swallowed. "I know. I haven't slept for two weeks. I know this is my fault. But I was… I was…" She stumbled for words. "I didn't want the man to go to jail if he was redeemable."

Agent Williams' voice was gentle, but he had to ask the direct question. "How many other congressmen and senators have you guided back onto the straight and narrow?"

Jackie shrugged. "People always want the chance to do the right thing, if they are given the opportunity."

"How many?" Williams demanded again.

"I don't know… dozens."

Williams looked at the doorway to make sure it was still closed. "Just between you and me, I understand what you were doing and why." He shook his head. "But it was dangerous and foolish."

Jackie couldn't even look him in the eye. She gasped and grabbed the edge of the table for stability.

"Uh, yeah. I guess I didn't need to say that, did I? I'm sorry."

"The evidence at the scenes?" Jackie asked, bringing the agent back on track.

"Nothing," he said sadly. "Both accidents look completely legitimate. Your husband's car had a mechanical brake failure. O'Connell ran a red light and was crushed by an eighteen-wheeler." He held up his hands in helplessness.

"But we know that these were not accidents," she said, regaining her former rage. It was her turn to pound her finger on the packet of documents between them. "We both know that this oil company is pissed that O'Connell gave back the money and refused to play ball."

"Yeah, I know," he said softly. "But knowing and proving are two different things."

He picked up the photo of the congressman and the unidentified thug passing a case of money. "Are you going to publish like you threatened?"

"No." Jackie shook her head sadly. "No point now. Releasing this information now would crush his family. I wanted to save the congressman, not destroy him." She felt another wave of tears and choked them back. "Now, look what I've done."

The two sat in silence a moment. Finally, Agent Williams spoke. "I want to make a deal with you, Jackie. I will agree to track down these killers to the ends of the earth, if you will agree to let me handle any future cases of political incongruities."

Jackie looked the man in the eye. "If you find my family's killers, then you can have my soul."

"I don't want your soul; I just want your cases."

"Deal," she answered hotly.

Jackie was jerked back to the present with Warren's question. "Huh? What?"

"I said, how did you collect this stuff? You must have a better network than the FBI." He was holding up another photo.

"Laura said that you were a Harvard grad." Jackie told the giant man. "What did you study?"

"I've got PhD's in poli sci, applied physics, and psychology."

She saw that he blushed a little when he gave his answer. Sitting on the bottom step, she heard Marna take in a sharp breath.

"What's poli sci?" Marna asked.

"Political science," Warren answered.

"You look more like a Marine than a guy with three doctorate degrees," Marna laughed.

"I did my four years in the Corps," he said. "Dad's old-fashioned. He made me do my turn in the service before he let me go to college."

"Laura said you were smart…" Jackie said shaking her head.

"How did you build such a wide network of informants, Jackie?" he asked again.

Jackie shrugged. "There are a lot of honest people out there who want to help others go straight." She sighed, thinking of days gone by— never to be recaptured.

"Jackie?" he asked, pushing the photo into her hands. "This is Congressman Reid from Texas."

She realized that she'd started drifting again. "Yes… um… Congressman Reid." She nodded, trying to focus. "He was caught up in a gambling syndicate. When I confronted him, he backed out, cleaned up his act, and shut down the organization."

Warren shook his head. "Congressman Reid is still in office. I had lunch with him several weeks ago. We always knew he was dirty and never had any proof. Why didn't you come to us? Director Williams is your friend."

"I… I… I wanted to save the man without sending him to jail." She couldn't look Warren in the eye. "I always wanted to give people a chance to repent."

He just shook his head and pushed the packet into a briefcase he'd brought with him. "Some people don't take very kindly to being blackmailed. Did you ever get threatened?"

"We have to find Aaeesha's treasure," Jackie said, sidestepping the question. "That's the most important thing. Or… I mean, when we find Aaeesha's treasure we'll find that other thing. You know, the thing. The really vital thing everybody needs to see…" Her head was hurting again.

"You know," Warren said, standing up and looking at the stack of boxes, "I think I'm changing my mind. We're not getting through this fast enough."

"What do you mean?" Jackie asked. She didn't like the way this conversation was headed. Was the man going to walk out and quit? Or did he have something worse in mind?

"I'm wasting my time here. I think we need to take this whole pile back to FBI headquarters and let the analysts go through it."

"You're taking my boxes?" Jackie shouted. "You can't do that; they're mine!"

"There's too much," Warren answered. "Besides that, someone is going to find out that you're going through this stuff, and you might get hurt. I've got to get this mess, and you, to a safe place."

"You can't take it," she pleaded. "It's all I have left."

Warren picked up a fist full of photos. "I know that most of this pile is honest-to-God journalism. But mixed into this stack is evidence of public figures gone astray. How many people did you try to blackmail, Jackie? How many?"

"I don't feel so well," Jackie said, turning toward the stairs. "I think I need to go take a nap." Cassie ran up the steps behind her.

She curled up under the covers with Cassie and cried herself to sleep.

In her dreams, a box full of photos sprouted arms and legs. She chased it around the living room of her childhood home in Basra, but she couldn't catch it. The stupid box kept spilling important pictures, and she'd have to stop and pick them up. But the more she collected, the more got dumped. She eventually gave up and sat on the floor crying, beaten by a box.

CHAPTER SIXTEEN

Jackie woke, feeling a bit better. A glance at her digital clock told her that she'd slept for a couple hours. Beside her, Cassie stretched luxuriously. Jackie scratched the dog's ears. Cassie groaned with pleasure through a big yawn. Jackie wrinkled her nose and slid out from under the covers.

Down in the living room, there was a conference between Warren and Marna.

"I can't get the trucks here until tomorrow," Warren said holding up his cellphone. "And the safe house for Jackie isn't available until tomorrow either."

Marna noticed Jackie walking into the room, followed by the clicking of Cassie's toenails on the wooden floor. "There you are, Jackie. Did the nap help?"

Jackie nodded, wiping a hand across her face. "I'm hungry," she said, her voice sounding childish. It reminded her of Abigail when she was four.

"I made some tortellini for lunch," Marna said. "Let me heat some up for you."

"Thanks, Abigail." Jackie said as Marna went toward the kitchen.

She flopped into her favorite living room chair and looked at Warren. "I don't want to go to a safe house. I want to stay at home."

"Well, we don't really have much of a choice for tonight—we have to stay here." Warren said. "But tomorrow, we'll move you somewhere safe."

Jackie sighed. She couldn't put into words the empty hollow place in her heart—every possession that she considered important was being stripped from her, all because of this stupid disease.

"Jackie, why don't you come out here to eat?" Marna called.

Jackie pushed herself to her feet and made her way to the kitchen. She sat at the place that Marna had prepared. "Pretty fancy for lunch, ain't it?" she said conspiratorially to Marna.

Marna blushed.

"You made this special for tall boy, didn't you?" Jackie grinned. "The way to a man's heart, and all that."

"Behave yourself," Marna said behind her sly grin.

"Sit with me," Jackie said, sliding a chair out from the other side of the table with her toe.

"You're sad," Marna said.

Jackie nodded. Could she make her daughter—no... that wasn't right—could she make her friend understand?

"Tell me," Marna said, swiping a stray hair from her face. Jackie noticed that the girl had let her hair down out of that severe ponytail.

"I feel like he's about to take away everything important to me—except for my family, of course. But... but... I know I can't manage it anymore, and I feel like such a failure. I feel like I'm letting Mother and Aaeesha down." She stirred her food with her fork, unable to put anything into her mouth.

Marna nodded. "I can imagine how difficult this is for you."

Jackie blinked back a tear.

"We'll find Aaeesha's treasure," Marna promised. "You said it's in a box."

It was Jackie's turn to nod. "It's important," she said. "I have to find it before it's too late—before my brain has completely turned to tomato soup."

They sat in silence for a few minutes, enjoying the presence of companionship. "Can I pretend to be your daughter for a moment, Jackie?" Marna said with a twinkle in her eye. "I need to ask my Mom a question."

Jackie grinned. "Sure, Abby. What's up?"

"I wanna ask Warren out to dinner tonight. What do you think?"

"He's pretty handsome," Jackie said. She finally lifted a forkful to her lips and chewed thoughtfully. "But there's something about him that I don't like, and I can't put my finger on it."

They sat in silence for a moment. "Yeah, but Laura and Director Williams sent him. He can't be all bad," Marna said.

"Alright," Jackie sighed. "You can go out with him, but be careful."

"Thanks, Ma!" Marna leapt from her chair and kissed Jackie on the cheek. She ran into the living room and asked Warren if she could speak to him privately outside.

Jackie sighed again. That young lady was really growing on her.

CHAPTER SEVENTEEN

By seven o'clock, the worst of Jackie's sundowning had passed. Marna had Jackie and Cassie fed. Jackie had told the giddy couple that they could borrow the Mercedes and her Master Card. She'd told Marna to call the Seasons 52 over in Tyson's. The maître d' refused to take the reservation until Marna put Jackie on the phone.

Suddenly, Marna stopped and looked at Warren. "What about Jackie? You said that you wanted her to be at a safe house since Judge Keeler knows we're rooting through her stuff. Will she be okay while we're gone?"

"Oh, I'll be fine," Jackie said, waving her hand dismissively. "You two go have a good time."

Marna was standing in the kitchen in her brown silk dress and new shoes, imitating a miniature goddess. She looked like a dime store doll that Jackie had seen when she was a child in Basra. Marna's black hair was down and the tips teased her shoulders. Jackie saw Warren's eyes wander helplessly up and down her form.

"Well um...." he tried to find his words. "Yeah, we'll only be gone a couple hours."

The testosterone-saturated look in his eye reminded Jackie of the senseless spat between Monroe and Reginald when they were all in high school. Sometimes men only thought with their....

"I'm sure she'll be okay," Warren interrupted her thoughts. "It will take a little while for the gossip grapevine to become active. The safe house thing was just an extra precaution."

With that, Warren donned his Stetson and whisked Marna out the door in a cloud of perfume and giggles.

"Well, I guess you'll have to protect me," Jackie said to Cassie. The dog wagged so hard her whole body wiggled. Jackie laughed and scooped the eight-pound fur ball into her arms.

Jackie settled down in the living room with the latest issue of *Better Homes and Gardens*. Cassie snored softly in her lap. But Jackie's mind was drifting all over the place, so finally she gave up and set down the magazine.

Outside, the sun had set and the dim streetlights were casting large shadows. Somewhere, a dog barked.

Jackie stood and stretched. She clipped the leash to Cassie's harness and took a plastic bag from the cupboard. "You wanna go for a walk?" she asked her furry friend.

Instead of replying in English or Arabic, the little dog bounced nearly a foot into the air. As soon as they stepped out the front door, Cassie did her business in the yard. Jackie picked it up in the bag and dropped it into the trashcan by the curb.

She turned left and headed toward Maple Avenue with Cassie prancing proudly in front of her. Cassie would strain on the leash, then stop to sniff at a post or trashcan.

At Maple, Jackie turned right—in the direction where the sun had just set. Streetlights caused the bustling people to glow under neon halos. Jackie stopped in a shop to buy a cup of tea, leaving Cassie tied to the handrail for a moment.

When she stepped out of the coffee shop, she became disoriented. She bent down to untie Cassie's leash from the handrail. "Where is home, Cassie?" The dog licked her face.

"Oh, you're no help." She bit her lip.

She stood and looked around her, panic beginning to grow. She looked to her right, and nothing seemed familiar. She looked to her left, and it might have been a street on Mars.

As terror began to rise in her chest, she turned right again. She walked a block, hoping something would become familiar. It was hopeless.

Tears began to well. She relived the panic that she felt the night she'd gotten lost driving. She turned around and walked the other way, past the coffee shop and to the end of the block. By now, she was crying uncontrollably.

She sat down on the sidewalk with her back against a brick wall and hugged Cassie to her chest. She didn't know what to do, and she was wailing loudly. Her paper cup of tea spilled out onto the sidewalk, but she was too upset to notice.

A horn honked on the street in front of her, driving the dizziness to infinite heights. The headlights of the cars swirled in front of her, adding to the chaos. Down on the corner, she saw the orange do not cross hand flashing at her. A car whizzed by with its turn signal blinking. Her head was spinning, and she felt like she was about to vomit.

"Jackie?"

Her head swiveled around. Through her tears, she saw a tall, thin teen with curly hair.

"Jackie? Is that you? What's wrong? Why are you crying?"

Too many questions. Which one should she answer? But it didn't matter because she was sobbing too hard to say a word.

"It's me—Billy McGee. I live just a few doors down from you. You live over on Center Street."

"Lost," was all that Jackie could blurt out. "Dementia." She gasped, trying to catch her breath.

She lifted her glasses and wiped her face with the back of her hand so that she could see. She saw the compassion on the boy's face. "Help me," she said.

"Come on," the teen said, gathering Cassie into his arms. Jackie couldn't remember the kid's name even though she knew he had told her only a moment before. "I'll take you home," he said kindly. He helped her to her feet, then steadied her when she stumbled.

"Your home is this way." He took her arm and guided her gently. Cassie wiggled out of Billy's arms and into Jackie's.

"Thank you," she managed around her choking. "Abigail is out on a date tonight. And I wanted to take a walk. Then I…" She had to stop talking for fear of crying again.

"It's okay. I'll take you home and make sure you're alright." He patted her hand that was on his arm. "This is a small community, and I know most people around here."

Jackie felt a flood of relief when she saw the front of her house. "This is it!" She cried excitedly. "This is where I live!"

She led the kind teen up her front steps. "Would you like some tea?" she asked.

"No, I'm fine. I need to get home—my mom is waiting for me."

"Please at least sit for a minute," she said. "PLEASE." She realized that she was still shaking from having been lost. She needed some company while she regained her wits.

He must have seen the panic in her face, because he smiled. "Sure. But only for a minute."

After stepping inside, Jackie bent down to take off Cassie's leash. When she stood up and turned around, she noticed that the brass candleholder that usually sat on the table by the front door was missing. There was also an unusual bulge in the teen's front pocket—and it wasn't 'cause he was happy to see her.

But Jackie was so upset about being lost, and so grateful for the teen's company that she didn't say anything about the candleholder. She was too frightened to worry about the silly little brass trinket.

"Come sit on the couch," she said, leading the way into the living room. "I won't keep you long; I just need to calm down."

Jackie sat him on the couch in the living room and took her favorite chair. Cassie jumped into her lap and began licking her hand.

"Tell me your name again," she said, just as the front window exploded and a bottle with a burning wick bounced on the carpet at Jackie's feet.

All those years as a journalist in war torn countries told Jackie exactly what she was looking at. It was a Molotov cocktail.

CHAPTER EIGHTEEN

Without thinking, she pounced on the bottle with both hands. Ignoring the searing heat and the flames that licked at the sleeves of her blouse, she grabbed the cocktail and threw it back into the front yard. As it left her hand, she was aware that gasoline had covered both her hands and was now burning hotly.

Automatic gunfire began raking through the now-broken window. The bottle bounced off the grass and the bomb exploded. A wall of flame rolled back into the house from the front yard.

"I'm on fire!" Jackie screamed, rolling on the floor. Cassie had dived under her chair.

Within seconds, Billy had fallen onto his belly beneath the hail of gunfire. He doffed his jacket and smothered the flames on Jackie's hands.

"Into the basement!" Jackie shrieked. She and Billy crawled under the flying bullets and fell through the door into the darkness below. Billy reached up and pushed the door shut to keep the smoke from billowing through.

He was already on the phone, screaming at the 911 operator. *"They are shooting at us! Oh my God! I need police, and fire trucks! Hurry! The house is on fire and we're trapped in the basement! It's going to burn us alive!" He gulped. "It was a bomb! I don't know the house number, but it's on Center Street North! Hurry!"*

He listened for a moment until his hyperventilation slowed. He looked at Jackie. "Anyone hurt? Jackie, are you hurt?"

Jackie's answer was a whimpered cry.

"Yes! Send an ambulance!" He looked at Jackie in the dim light of his phone, *"Just look for the house with all the bullet holes!"*

They were at the bottom of the stairs before his 911 call was completed. He leaned Jackie against the boxes, freeing up his hands.

"The light switch is at the top of the stairs." Jackie groaned.

Above them, the sound of gunfire ceased, and she heard the sound of tires squealing as the car sped away. Billy turned on the flashlight function of his phone and found the light switch. The bulbs flickered on, then off. They buzzed slightly with an electric sizzle before coming on to stay. She saw his lower lip quivering.

"What the hell?" He turned and screamed at her. "Are you a drug dealer or something?"

"No... It's um..." Jackie wouldn't have been able to tackle a thought if it had been hogtied and laid at her feet. Thoughts were zooming through her brain like lightning bolts.

"What did you do? Who are you? Are you a terrorist?" The teen screamed again.

Which question did he want her to answer? Jackie could only stare. In the distance, she could already hear the sirens. Jackie was shaking. Old memories of war were sucking at her brain, and they were trying to drag her down.

"The little boy," she cried, "they wouldn't let me keep him."

"What little boy?" Billy asked, alarmed. "Was someone in the front yard who got bombed? I didn't see anyone else!"

"The one in that village. The one whose mother was dead! I was going to bring him home and adopt him. But they wouldn't let me!" She was crying hysterically.

The kid shook his head and muttered something about a loose screw.

Upstairs, she could hear the sound of burning wood. The scent of smoke wafted through the crack under the basement door at the top of the stairs.

"We're going to die! How can we get out of here?" he screamed, looking frantically around the cement basement for an exit.

"Can't," Jackie managed through her haze. "No other way out."

"You're one crazy bitch!" He began kicking her boxes in frustration.

She drifted. She did the whole village scene again. This time it wasn't a little African boy; it was two-year-old-Charles. And the woman lying dead on the floor was her.

A pain shot through Jackie's hand, ripping her back to the present.

A woman was kneeling in front of her, putting salve on her burns. "You'll be okay, but we need to get you to the hospital. You've lost a lot of fluid, so you'll need an IV. We need to get this bandaged up, and I want them to do it in the ER."

"Call Abigail!" Jackie said to Billy.

"Who's Abigail?" The paramedic asked Billy.

He shrugged. "The bitch is loony-toons. She said she has dementia. I have no idea what she's talking about."

"Call Charles—or wait, Abigail has Charles' number," Jackie said.

"We're going to take care of you," the paramedic cooed in a patronizing voice.

"What about the fire?" Jackie asked. "Is my house burning?"

"No, they put the fire out," the paramedic said. At least that's what Jackie thought she said—her head was spinning. She realized that she must have been drifting for a while.

"Okay, let's go," the woman said. She and Billy gently lifted Jackie to her feet by her arms, being careful not to touch her hands.

They stepped out of the stairwell into the living room. The whole room was blackened and dripping with water. The smell of smoke caused Jackie to cough.

From beneath her burnt chair, Cassie barked when Jackie stepped into the room. Without thinking, she got down on her knee and opened her arms for the dog. Cassie shot out from her hiding spot and leapt into Jackie's arms.

Jackie howled in pain as her injured hands touched the little dog's fur. Billy instantly scooped Cassie into his arms and helped Jackie to her feet by her elbow.

"We'll take her to a kennel until you get back from the ER," the EMT said. She waved over a uniformed cop and relayed instructions.

A cop with sergeant bars stepped up to ask for a statement.

"Make it short," the paramedic demanded. "This woman needs to get to the hospital."

"Good God, the bitch is crazy," Billy said. "I don't know if she's a drug dealer or a terrorist."

"Start at the beginning," the cop demanded. Jackie was pretty sure it was the same officer who had saved them from Rodney, but she was so bad with names and faces these days.

"Okay. I was over on Maple when I found Mrs. Scott crying. She told me that she was lost and that she had dementia. I live down the street and know who she is, so I brought her home." Billy stopped to catch his breath.

"She invited me in, but when I said I needed to get home, she seemed to panic at the thought of being alone. So, I came in with the intention of just staying for a minute. We sat down in the living room." Billy pointed to the smoldering couch where he had sat. "That's when the bottle full of burning gasoline came through the window and bounced on the carpet. Jackie picked it up and threw it out into the yard where it exploded."

His face turned white. "She may be crazy, but I guess she saved my life. If she hadn't thrown it back through the window, we would both be dead."

The cop nodded. "If the glass bottle had burst when it hit the floor, then it would have exploded on impact. Maybe the thick carpet was what kept it intact."

The cop scratched some more in his pad. "Did he get the story right, ma'am?"

Jackie was drifting and didn't realize the question was directed at her. The cop looked up from his notebook and looked at her. "Huh?" she asked.

"Did Mr. McGee tell the story correctly?" he repeated.

"Um…" she shrugged.

"Look officer. She's in shock. I need to get her to the hospital now," the paramedic demanded.

"Oh, sorry. Sure. Get her out of here. I'll ask Mr. McGee a few more questions."

She felt a gentle pressure on her elbow and realized that the paramedic was guiding her toward the waiting ambulance.

As she stepped through the back doors of the waiting vehicle, Jackie took one last look at her house. In the garish hue of the streetlights, she could see that the entire front of her house had been blackened by smoke.

The yard was full of cops who were scratching through the scorched grass like chickens pecking for bugs. The yaw of the exploded front window made the house look like a skeleton with an open mouth. She shivered and allowed the paramedic to seat her on the bench. She was grateful when the woman placed a blanket around her shoulders and closed the door—shutting out the horror of her former home.

CHAPTER NINETEEN

The Presidential limousine rocked to the left as it exited the beltway onto Allentown Road. The armored machine blasted through the afternoon traffic toward Andrews Air Force Base. Ahead, Air Force One was waiting. Outside the limo windows, the sirens of the police escort blared.

George W. Armstrong leaned back in the seat and pinched the bridge of his nose. "I'm running out of time," he said in a weary voice.

He shook off the fatigue and sat up, focusing on her, "I need you on the ground over there, Jackie. I need a direct link to the mood of the people. I need an unofficial backchannel to Saddam. This war is going to blow wide open, and I need all the assets I can get. You speak the language—these are your people."

Jackie looked out the window, the world whizzing by in a blur. Her true home was Iraq—it was where she was raised. But the Butcher of Baghdad had become a terrorist to his own people.

She shook her head reluctantly. "George... I've spent my whole life straightening out messes. This guy makes my skin crawl. And you're asking me to talk to him and pretend I respect him?" She shuddered.

When they were in the presence of others, she addressed him formally. But here in the privacy of the car, they were just friends. On the other hand, would a friend ask her to...

Her musings were cut short by the President. "I don't know if I'll need you to give him a message or not. I want you on the ground, just in case." He paused, looking her in the eye. He knew her weak spot. "You might save a lot of lives."

"Maybe I'll just pull out my .45 and shoot him between the eyes."

They rode in silence for a few minutes. "Look, I know you're still grieving your daughter and your husband, but your country needs you," he said.

"Don't give me that 'yee-haw do it for your country' bullshit. It might work on a jarhead, but it doesn't work on me. You and I both know that this war is going to happen. I'll go to Iraq and cover the story, because the world needs to see the horrors—the terrors—that you are about to unleash." She paused and lowered her voice. "If you need me to go meet with the bastard, I'll think about it—that's all I can promise."

George W. nodded. "Thanks," he said. He gritted his teeth. "I'm about to send American soldiers to their deaths—I can't sleep at night." The limo shot through the gates of the Air Force Base. Through the tinted limo windows, Jackie could see the guards standing at attention. "I just need every available tool at my disposal."

"So now I'm just a tool?" Jackie's eyes shot fire.

She saw the hurt on his face and instantly regretted her words. They both knew she meant more to him than that. "Sorry," she said softly.

He looked like he'd aged ten years since she'd seen him last. There were droopy bags under his eyes. His exhaustion was palpable.

"Are you getting any sleep at all?" she asked.

He shook his head. "No. Not really. I'm getting ready to send men to their deaths. Now I'm asking my friend to walk right into the lion's den."

They sat in silence a moment as the limo flashed past the base housing. She knew he was conflicted. But she also knew he'd do anything to save lives. Frankly, so would she.

He got a sly grin on his face. "General Turner will be over there, you know."

Jackie didn't even blink an eye. "Three things, Mr. President. Number one: Your intel is old. That affair ended six months ago. Two: General Turner will be with the troops in Saudi Arabia—unless you're in the habit of sending one-stars behind enemy lines. I, on the other hand, will be in Baghdad, right where the General's bombs will be landing. I don't think we'll be able to rendezvous across that distance. And Three: Do you really want to be comparing who's got dirt on whom?"

George W. Armstrong turned a deep shade of red. The limo turned onto the tarmac. Jackie was always amazed by the size of Air Force One.

Finally, the President regained his composure. "I've got a dozen intelligence agencies under my command. Yet, you seem to know the inner workings of this city better than I do."

"That's because I know how to handle the dirt, sir," she answered proudly. "Instead of just throwing creeps into jail, I gently bring them back to the straight and narrow—if they're salvageable."

POTUS shook his head, not finding a retort. The limo pulled to a stop at the foot of the plane's stairs. A Marine stood to attention, then opened the door for George.

The President stepped out of the back of the automobile. He turned and leaned back in the door. "Thanks for doing this for us, Jackie."

"I didn't promise you a thing," she shot back.

"Yes, you did." The man smiled broadly.

She hated it when people knew what she was going to do before she even knew herself.

CHAPTER TWENTY

Jackie found herself lying on a tall bed in a white curtained room. She was aware that her feet wouldn't reach the floor if she sat up. An IV ran into her arm from the stainless-steel tree beside her.

Just as she tried to sit up, a short, dark skinned Indian man pushed aside the curtain and stepped into the room. There was a young, female aide in his wake.

Through the parting of the curtains, she could see that she was in a hospital—most likely the emergency room. She'd seen enough of those in her time. She could see doctors and nurses tending to other patients. Like hers, some of the curtained partitions were closed for privacy. Until this moment, she hadn't been aware of the hubbub of voices in the air.

"Hi, I'm Dr. Patel," the little man said holding out his hand. He blushed and dropped his arm when he saw her bandages.

Jackie smiled. His accent reminded her of that happy summer spent traveling through the lush mountains of India…

"Are you Mrs. Scott?" he asked, interrupting her drifting thoughts.

She grunted as her brain whirled in sludge. "Yeah. I'm Jackie," she finally managed.

"Do you know Dr. Charles Scott who's a surgeon here at Fairfax Hospital?"

"Yes." She suddenly felt so tired—she just wanted to sleep. She laid back down on the bed, but was jerked awake when her hand touched the sheet. She groaned loudly. Remembering Dr. Patel's question, she finished her sentence. "Um… He's my son."

Jackie heard the short doctor whispering to the aide. "Get Dr. Scott down here right away."

The girl scampered off.

Jackie closed her eyes—sleep beckoned.

"Oh, no you don't." She felt Dr. Patel gently shaking her shoulder—it was like an earthquake was rattling her rafters. "I need you to sit up, so that I can tend to your wounds."

Mindful of the trailing IV, he gently lifted her up to a seated position. Jackie could sense that the doctor was a kind man.

He took her elbows in his rubber gloves and inspected each extremity carefully. "Hmm… We have second degree burns over most of your palms." He adjusted his glasses for a closer look. "I don't think we have any third degree." He pointed with a pinky finger as he gazed carefully through his spectacles. He looked up at her. "I've seen a lot worse. You'll be bandaged up for about three weeks or so. I'll give you a prescription for the pain, which will be significant the first week."

Just then the curtain temple was ripped apart by a frantic hand. Charles stepped into the little cotton room. "Ma!" he was nearly ballistic, "what happened?"

Through the parted curtains Jackie saw Warren and Marna rushing through the chaotic emergency room in her direction. "Is she okay?" Marna shrieked from behind the big Harvard grad.

"We came back from the date to find your house had been firebombed!" Warren blurted out. "We rushed right over!"

"Firebombed!" Charles was about to climb the cotton walls. "Mom! What's going on?"

"A Molotov cocktail," Jackie managed. "Automatic gunfire."

"Ma! Gunfire?" Charles was choking on his words. His face was red and spittle was flying from his lips.

"Everybody calm down!" The little Indian doctor took command of the situation.

Silence ruled the little room. A person groaned on the other side of the cotton barrier.

Marna stepped forward to put her arm around Jackie.

The smell coming off Marna was unmistakable. "Abigail! You've been drinking!" Jackie screeched and then turned to Warren. "She's a recovering alcoholic! How could you buy her wine?"

Before either of them could answer, she smelled sex on Marna. The odor was wafting off the woman-child's body like a whole bottle of cheap perfume.

"It was just a little wine," Marna said, holding up her thumb and forefinger to indicate a small amount.

"Don't lie to me, girl!" Jackie was raging. "How could you do this? By your own admission, one little drink could crash your life!"

"Why is it that you can't remember my name, but you can remember details about my love life and my alcohol problem?"

"I can't help what I remember and what I forget!" Jackie felt a hot tear burning its way down her cheek. She wasn't sure if the anger was at her own leaky brain, or if it was at Marna for her self-sabotage.

"Come on," Warren jumped into the fray. "She's in danger. We can't stay here. We've got to get her out of here and hidden somewhere that the terrorists can't find her."

"Mom! Tell me the truth. What's this all about?"

"Stop it!" Dr. Patel yelled. "All of you, get out!" He pointed a finger at the exit.

"Exactly!" Charles commanded. "All of you get out now!"

"You too, Dr. Scott!" Dr. Patel stomped his foot. "Out!"

Charles looked like he was about to go toe-to-toe with the little Indian man, but a withering glare from Jackie melted him. He turned, defeated, and followed Warren and Marna. As soon as Dr. Patel whipped the curtains closed, Jackie heard Charles start in on Warren and Marna with scathing questions.

Dr. Patel sighed. "Now young lady," he said, peering at her over the top of his glasses like a schoolmarm, "behave yourself, and I'll get you all bandaged up so that you can go have fun with your playmates." He jerked a thumb in the direction of the exit. She could still hear Charles' voice carrying through the cloth partition.

First, he sprayed her hands with a topical anesthetic, then he applied a thick salve. He gently bound her hands with gauze.

"You wanna tell me how this happened?" he asked as he worked.

"I have dementia," Jackie said mischievously, "but this time when I say that I forgot, it will be a lie."

He raised his eyebrows at her.

"It's a police matter," she answered. "I was burned with gasoline."

"So that big guy was serious about the firebombing and the terrorists?"

Jackie lowered her voice. "He's FBI."

Dr. Patel's face reflected his concern but didn't reply. He nodded and applied the last bit of tape. Her hands looked like a pair of white clubs.

"You weren't kidding!" she said in despair. "I won't be able to do anything for myself. How will I go the bathroom?"

"You'll need some help with that," Dr. Patel answered honestly. "It may be uncomfortable for a few weeks, but it will soon pass."

She looked at him dourly. "You doctors have your own vocabulary. When you say, 'this may be a bit uncomfortable,' you really mean it will be freakin' embarrassing."

He gave her a wan smile and a slight shrug of concession.

She held up her clubbed hands, almost on the verge of tears again. "I've lost my brains, the big FBI man is taking my boxes, and now I've lost my hands."

"You'll get your hands back," the good doctor said. "I can't help you with the other stuff."

He carefully took the IV needle out of her arm and stepped on a lever. The bed lowered itself until Jackie's feet reached the floor. He took her by the elbow and helped her to her feet. Jackie was unsteady at first, then gained strength as she began walking.

He led her to the reception area, where Jackie found Charles, Warren, and Marna whispering at each other in angry voices. They stopped and stared at her when Dr. Patel walked her into the room.

He handed her off to Charles with instructions for her medical care. "I'd like to keep her a little while, but it sounds like you need to get her someplace safe," he said in acquiescence. He wished Jackie well and headed back into the E.R. to address the next emergency patient.

Charles took charge and led the group into a consult room off the side of the main E.R. He closed the door and Jackie tried to sit but found herself almost falling. Marna grabbed her elbow and eased her into the chair.

"Tomorrow I expect you to take the Mercedes out and have it detailed," Jackie said in a clipped tone. "Please have them concentrate on cleaning the back seat."

Marna turned six shades of red. "I... um...." She was cut short by a curt shake of the head from Warren. Marna's response told Jackie that she was absolutely right—they'd had sex in the back of her car.

"Ma! What is this about being firebombed?"

Clearly, Charles hadn't lost any of his ire, nor had he caught the sexual tension in the room.

"Calm down," Warren tried to take charge over Charles' hysterics. "Never mind that. Let's just figure out what we're going to do now."

"Were you a spy, Mom? Is that what it is? Oh, God! Don't tell me that you were a spy for Iraq!" Jackie pondered the irony that her doctor son looked like he needed a doctor himself.

"No!" Marna said. "She's not a spy." Then she turned her head and looked at Jackie. "You weren't, were you?"

Jackie shook her head. "Not very often. I did a little work occasionally. But for the good guys. I never killed…" She stopped herself as she remembered something. "Well, not very often anyway."

"Oh God, Ma! You were a spy? *You killed people?*"

"Calm down!" Warren repeated, hovering his bulk over Charles in an attempt to intimidate him.

But Charles was wound up so tight that he would have started a fist fight with Godzilla. He tried to unbutton his collar to loosen his tie, but the button popped off and shot across the room, hitting Marna in the face.

"Hey!" she shouted.

"Calm down!" This time it was Jackie. "Son, I've protected you all these years. I've done a lot of stuff that I probably need to tell you about. But now's not the time," she sighed. "This man… what's your name?"

"Warren," the big man said.

"Yes, Warren is a very smart FBI agent. Right now, we need to listen to what he has to say. We are all in trouble." She was proud that she'd been able to string that paragraph together. She took a breath and let it out slowly.

"I want to take Mom to my house," Charles said. "We can straighten out the mess in the morning."

"No," Warren answered. Jackie could tell that he was trying to figure out how to tell Charles what needed to be done without going into too much detail. "Your family and your home are at risk, too. We've got to get your family to safety."

"Why?" Charles asked. "Who's after Mom?"

"Just do it, Charles!" Jackie snapped. She hadn't used that tone on him since he was sixteen. Her voice had the intended effect. Her son was instantly humbled.

"Get on the phone. Tell your wife to put the kids in the car and drive here. Don't take the time to pack; we'll buy clothes and toothbrushes."

Charles got out his phone and obediently dialed.

While Charles was talking to Katrice, Marna leaned over to speak with Warren.

"Where will we go? You said the safe house wasn't available until tomorrow."

"Do you still have my credit card?" Jackie asked Marna.

"Of course."

"Money's no object—my Daddy was richer than a Saudi prince. Get on the phone with the Hilton. Reserve a three-room suite. We should be safe for tonight." She looked at the Fed. "Will that work?"

He nodded. "That will work for now. If these people are connected, they'll eventually track us through your credit card. But for now, it will work." He interrupted Charles who was on the phone arguing with his wife. "Tell her to meet us at the Tyson's Corner Hilton, over by 495 and the Dulles Toll Road."

Charles nodded and spoke into the phone. "This is serious, Katrice. Hurry. They firebombed Mom's house and shot it up—our place may be next. Get out of there now!"

Getting the four into Jackie's Mercedes was like corralling four pit bulls into a dog fighting ring. They decided to leave Charles' car at the hospital in his reserved spot.

"I'll sit in the back with Abigail so you two don't have to smell her dragon breath," Jackie said. She was feeling pretty sharp at the moment, but her anger was not making it a pleasant experience. "I can't believe I have to sit my ass on the seat where you two…"

"Ma! Shut up!" Charles groused. "You're not helping. I wanna know all about this spy thing."

"I never told you because I knew you'd go off like a Roman candle," Jackie shot back.

"Do you two mind?" Warren snapped, holding a hand over his phone. "I'm trying to coordinate with HQ." He turned back to his phone. "Never mind where we'll be staying the night. It's safe, that's all you have to worry about. And I want a friggin' army of agents guarding that house during the night. The terrorists obviously want it destroyed, and I don't want to give them a chance! She's got important documents in that basement." He listened a moment. "I don't care if we have to pay overtime! Get it done!" He slammed the phone with his thumb, cutting off the call.

The second Warren hung up with his call to HQ, his phone rang again. "Yes?" he answered impatiently. Then, "Oh, Director Williams? Good evening, sir."

From the back seat, Jackie couldn't hear the words her old friend Reginald Williams was saying to Warren, but she could tell it wasn't good. Even in the dim light, she could see Warren's ears glowing red.

"N- No sir. I was just gone for a few hours. I didn't figure on them tracking her down that fast…" he was apparently cut off by more yelling.

"Yes sir. It was an… um…" He swallowed hard. "It was a date, sir."

More yelling in the earpiece.

"But sir…" he pulled the phone away from his ear and looked at it. "Shit. He hung up on me."

"Is everything okay?" Marna asked.

Warren didn't answer. He looked out the passenger window as the guard rail flew past. Anger sizzled out from under his ten-gallon hat.

They rode in silence for a few minutes. Charles got onto 495 headed north. The tension in the car was thick as Jell-O. Jackie found it difficult to breathe.

"If you must know," Warren said through clenched teeth. "I've been demoted. Director Williams holds me personally responsible for the attack on your house. He said I shouldn't have gone on a date in the middle of an operation like this…" He wiped at his face. "One more screw up and I'm done."

"Well, if you were supposed to be protecting Mom, then you deserved an ass-reaming," Charles snapped. "I knew I shouldn't have hired that woman. It's all her fault." He glanced into his rearview at Marna.

Warren pointed at a sign. "Here's the exit for 123," he said to Charles.

"I know where I'm going." Charles growled, actually showing his fangs.

"Well, isn't this fun?" Marna said, her sarcasm adding to the tension. Jackie almost choked on the cloud of the girl's alcohol breath.

"Honestly, how much did you drink, Abigail?" Jackie fumed.

Charles pulled the car into the parking lot. Marna and Warren were helping Jackie out of the car by her elbows, when Katrice pulled in. She jumped out of the car and ran crying into Charles' arms. The children attacked Jackie.

"Grandma!" they both cried out with excitement.

"We're on an adventure!" Chucky pronounced proudly.

She bent to hug them, being careful of her bandages. The drugs that the doctor had given her were wearing off and the pain was setting in. She felt her awareness slipping as the ache in her appendages increased.

Jackie stood and stumbled, gasping. The sudden onslaught of pain and dizziness swept over her. She began falling. Instinctively, she put out her hands to stop the fall. She hit the pavement—hard.

The pain shooting through her arms felt as if she had been shot. She screamed loudly.

"Children! *You pushed Grandma!*" Katrice shouted.

"No," Jackie gasped through the red curtain of consciousness. "They didn't do it. I got dizzy. I fell." She rolled onto her back and began panting like they had taught her in Lamaze class.

Warren reached down to help her. "No!" she wheezed. "Just a minute." She closed her eyes, shutting out the world. She felt the cold of the pavement seeping into her back. Pebbles bit into her back through her thin blouse. The sharp pain slowly receded, replaced by a throb that threatened to destroy the foundations of the earth.

She opened her eyes again to see a circle of concerned faces staring down at her. She knew her face was drawn and taut. Laying on her back, she felt the tears streaking from her eyes into her ears.

"Okay," she croaked. "I think I can do it." She extended her elbows and was lifted aloft.

They started to walk again, but Jackie stumbled—Marna held her vertical. Without a spoken word, Charles gently pulled Marna away. He took one elbow and Warren took the other. The rest of the group walked solemnly and silently toward the hotel lobby.

CHAPTER TWENTY-ONE

She could tell it was going to be a bad day before she even opened her eyes. She heard Marna vomiting in the toilet. Served the girl right—maybe a hangover would cure her of drinking forever. Although, Jackie was sure that she'd probably experienced many a "morning after."

Jackie realized that she'd fallen asleep in her clothes. Apparently, Marna had thrown a blanket over her and pulled off her shoes. But she still had on her slacks and blouse.

The pills that Charles had given her the night before had allowed her to sleep. But now that dawn was creeping into the hotel room, her hands were pulsing with pain. She was having a hard time maintaining her grip on reality. She didn't know if it was the pain, the drugs, or just a bad day. She figured that it was probably all three.

She drifted hard—sucked into the jungles of Columbia. It registered that this was her last field assignment. At first, she couldn't remember why. Then the painful memory flooded in.

The jungle air hung hot and humid around her. The stifling mist was thick and difficult to breathe. Her ears were ringing with the loud cacophony of night insects. The smell of damp earth and rot filled her nose.

She lay on her belly beside Lt. Col. Grizzly Beckett. He had a first name, but only Army Human Resources Command knew what it was.

Jackie couldn't believe the moral depths to which she had sunk. Ever since Abigail and Richard had been killed, she'd lost her moral compass. Would she ever find her way again? She'd come to the place where she'd do anything for a story. She revolted herself.

She'd wanted this story. The military brass wasn't excited about having a reporter along.

Surprisingly, it had been Turner who had tipped the scales in her direction. Just when she thought her participation was going to get axed, Turner had cut through the red tape and made the trip happen.

"Don't get yourself shot," he laughed as she had exited his Pentagon office. She'd seen something in his eye that she hadn't understood. It was almost as if he was wishing her ill. She shook her head. No. That was a crazy thought. He'd done this as a favor. It was one friend looking out for another. Over the years, she'd done Turner favors. And now he'd repaid. It was as simple as that.

But Grizzly had been another story. Although Turner had approved the mission, it was only under the condition that Grizzly was onboard with the idea. So, she'd seduced the colonel and had ridden him like a stallion. Now the man was putty in her hands. Apparently, he had been starved for female approbation. From the frantic sessions in that seedy motel, she guessed Grizzly hadn't been getting any at home. She hoped he wouldn't come to his senses too soon. She wanted to get a few more stories out of him before one of them discarded the other.

Even through the heat of the humid tropical air, she could feel the desire radiating off the man. She hoped Grizzly could concentrate on the coming fight—she didn't want to be responsible for someone else's death.

Like the other men in the unit, Jackie was wearing night-vision goggles and a ghillie suit. The suit was covered with a mat of green strings into which local flora could be woven. Properly deployed, a soldier would be mistaken for a bush. It was standard issue for spec-ops troops and snipers.

Her face was covered in mud. Even in daylight she would have been invisible in the underbrush. Grizzly had obtained a special camera for her from the recon armory—it was painted camo green, and was completely silent, taking high-resolution digital images instead of Jackie's familiar 35mm film. It was fully IR capable, so could take excellent photos using only the dim moonlight that filtered through the trees above. Although the technology was cool, Jackie would have preferred her old familiar tools in her hands.

The dark jungle canopy was thick with a dense fog. Insects of all types crawled through the cracks of her soaked clothing and feasted on her flesh. Every bite made her want to flinch but to do so would be to give away their position. So, she gritted her teeth instead.

They were here on a mission to try to make a dent in the drug trade. In front of them was a large clearing—maybe a half mile in diameter. In the middle of that clearing was the mansion of a ruthless drug lord, Ricky Sanchez. It was rumored that when his brother had crossed him, he'd bound his brother's wife and children, leaving their mouths free. He then pushed them into a deep hole that had been dug with backhoes. The brother, who was also bound, was forced to listen to the screams and pleas of his wife and children while the backhoes buried them alive. The brother was then taken into the jungle and tied to a tree. From there, the rumors were conflicted as to whether the man starved to death or a wild animal killed him.

The Sanchez operation produced nearly one-tenth of Columbia's cocaine export. The mission for tonight was to kill Sanchez and destroy his operation.

The first obstacle was a machine gunner 20 yards in front of them. Over the rot of the jungle floor vegetation, Jackie could smell the man's body odor. Richard had always said that she had the nose of a bloodhound.

The thought of Richard caused regret to bloom in her chest. She looked over at Grizzly; her dalliance brought a lump to her throat. For a moment, the shame paralyzed her. She blinked back a tear and forced the emotion aside.

Beside her, she heard Grizzly stir as he inched forward through the insects. Was he regretting the affair? Was he having second thoughts?

Jackie realized that she too was starved for attention. There was a hole in her heart that couldn't be filled with adventure. Sex was meaningless.

It was like biting into a piece of chocolate cake, only to discover that it tasted like sawdust. Worse yet, it made her sick to her stomach.

Everything was empty. No meaning could be found. So, she'd looked for the most dangerous assignments and hoped a lucky bullet would end her suffering.

She blinked again to drive away the thoughts. She focused on what was in front of her. Death, rot, and blood made for a good story.

She pressed the shutter of the camera as a bush-looking wraith silently rose up behind the gunner. The glint of steel flashed in the moonlight. The gunner slowly toppled over backwards into the waiting arms of the soldier.

"He pushed the knife directly through the man's lung and into his heart," Grizzly explained to her in a whisper. "That way he couldn't draw a breath to shout a warning."

Jackie knew all this, but the colonel apparently felt the need to flaunt his intelligence. Jackie had to assume this was the man's mating dance. In that one sentence, she knew he was still under her control. She thought guiltily of the woman back home who called herself Mrs. Grizzly.

The thought of the other woman was like a dagger. She had set out life to make the world a better place. Now she was a homewrecker. She wanted to cry.

The group of six Spec Ops slithered their way through the bugs and the mud to the next outpost. Again, the knife was deployed and another drug-land gunner was sent to his maker.

The group paused as a roving patrolman walked past. A muffled, PFSST, sounded as a bullet found the man's skull. The loudest sound was the guard's body hitting the ground.

"Hector?" a voice called through the dark.

"Shit," Grizzly whispered beside her.

Suddenly, Jackie was very confused. She didn't know where she was or what she was doing. Looking back, it was her first encounter with this deadly disease called, dementia. A surge of fear pounded through her body. She couldn't remember where she was or what she was doing. She didn't remember what continent she was on, or who the man beside her was. All she knew was that she was frightened out of her mind.

Involuntarily, a loud squeak of fear escaped her lips.

"Hey!" the voice that had called out to his fallen comrade shouted a warning. Then he opened up with automatic fire at the Seal Team.

Within seconds, the entire field was alight with muzzle flashes, and bullets rained on the U.S. soldiers. Supersonic sizzlers buzzed over Jackie's head.

By the end of the night, Sanchez was killed and his operation was destroyed, but two of Grizzly's men died in the fight.

When it was over and the last bad guy lay in a pool of his own blood, Grizzly stormed over to Jackie. "It's your fault!" he screamed. He pointed at the mutilated body of Coolhand Jones, "you killed him because you opened your damned mouth! What's wrong with you? Are you crazy?"

Grizzly raised the smoking barrel of his rifle at her. "I have to explain this all to my superiors. I brought a God-damned reporter with me, and she blew our cover. I have to explain that to Coolhand's wife." He paused. "And to my wife!"

For a moment, she thought he was going to empty his clip into her head. She didn't care—she knew she deserved to die. If not for Coolhand's death, she deserved to die for… She couldn't remember the man's name—the guy she paid to have eliminated.

"I'm sorry," she said, shaking her own head. "Do it. Pull the trigger."

Grizzly shook his head and turned away. The man never spoke to her again, and Jackie never went to the field again. That day marked the beginning of her mental slide.

CHAPTER TWENTY-TWO

Jackie felt someone shaking her shoulder. She groaned as the pain from her burns hit her with full force. She was… um… in the hotel. Yeah, that's where she was. The early September light streamed through the pane into the lap of opulence.

"Help me up," she said to Katrice who was standing over her. Her daughter-in-law slid her arm under Jackie's back and helped her to a sitting position, then to her feet.

"Where's Abigail?" Jackie asked.

"We sent Marna out to buy some clothes and some toys for the children," Katrice answered. "Charles ordered breakfast for all of us, and it's on its way up."

Jackie was embarrassed at the next question she had to ask. "I… um… have to go to the bathroom. She held up the white clubs that used to be her hands. "Can you… um… help me?"

"Sure," Katrice answered, smiling compassionately. She led Jackie into the bathroom and undid her slacks and pulled down her underwear. She then lowered Jackie onto the toilet. When she was done, she cleaned Jackie up and redressed her.

Jackie felt a tear trickle down her cheek from embarrassment. "I'm sorry," she croaked. She was ashamed that Katrice had to wipe her.

Her daughter-in-law took her in her arms as Jackie sobbed. "I'm so sorry," she repeated, as she cried into Katrice's blonde hair.

"It's okay," Katrice said. "I've always loved you more than you know." Jackie felt her head being stroked.

Jackie nodded. She knew that the tension between them had always been Jackie's fault. Now, the woman was heaping coals of kindness onto her head.

She thought of every disparaging comment that she'd ever made behind Katrice's back. She thought of the fights she'd had with Charles, calling the woman a money-hungry gold digger.

Suddenly, Jackie was aware of her own selfishness. She had spent her whole life fighting evil, and in the midst of the battle, she'd maligned those who truly cared for her. The hostility had started out as a crusade against evil and changed into a war against the whole world. In the process, she'd trampled those who loved her. At first, her shame had been because of her physical nakedness. But now it was because of her blackened heart.

Jackie wanted to ask forgiveness. But her words were drowned out by body wracking sobs. Clutching Katrice tightly, Jackie wept until her well of tears ran dry.

It was a full two minutes before Jackie could pull away. Through her tear-blurred eyes, she looked into Katrice's face. She knew instantly that Katrice had seen through her façade—she could see that the younger woman had known for years. But instead of fighting back, her daughter-in-law had chosen kindness.

Jackie looked away. The shame of her soot-stained soul was more than she could bear. "I'm sorry," she whispered. "I'm sorry for all of it…"

"Come on. Let's go get some breakfast." Katrice put a finger under Jackie's trembling chin, forcing them to lock eyes. Their gaze conveyed more than words could encompass. Jackie could see that the display of raw emotions had embarrassed Katrice too.

Katrice wiped Jackie's face with a tissue, then smiled. "You look at least a little bit presentable."

"But I've been such an ass…" Jackie said.

Katrice laid a finger on Jackie's lips. "Shhh," she hushed. "It's okay. I know."

She hugged Jackie again, then ushered her out the bathroom door.

Jackie stepped out into the main room of the suite. "Grandma!" Milly shrieked. She came running with her arms wide open, expecting to be caught in a hug.

"Be careful!" Katrice warned and stepped in to block the flying missile. She caught her daughter in her arms and showed her Jackie's bandages. "Grandma has been hurt very badly. She can't use her hands. We have to be careful not to touch them."

"What happened?" Milly asked Jackie.

"I touched something that was burning," Jackie said.

"You shouldn't do that," Milly said sagely.

"Good idea. I'll try to remember that next time." She kissed the top of the girl's head. Seeing her granddaughter helped to shake away the raw emotions of the past few moments.

Looking around, Jackie realized that she hadn't paid any attention to the room last night. She had been so engulfed with pain that the world had been a blur.

The room was beautifully furnished. There were expensive sofas set around a mahogany coffee table. In the corner, there was a desk set up with outlets for a computer. The 55" TV was playing the local news but was muted. The curtains were drawn open, and, from their height, Jackie could see much of Northern Virginia and Washington DC stretched out into the distance. The canopy of treetops was green with a hint of fall colors beginning to show.

"Where's Cassie?" Milly asked.

"She's on an adventure, just like us. She's staying at a kennel—it's like a hotel for dogs."

"They're showing your house!" Charles said and grabbed the remote to unmute the TV.

The news anchor was just launching into the story. Behind him was a photo of Jackie's torched porch. "Sources are now saying that last night's explosion in a quiet Vienna suburb was not a gas line as was earlier reported. The latest information is that this was some sort of bomb. We don't have any knowledge of what prompted the attack. We have also learned that the house was hosed with automatic gunfire."

"I wish we could have kept this out of the news," Warren complained over the newsman's voice. "But bombs and bullets tend to draw the media."

The camera switched from the talking head to a live shot at the scene. The video was either taken from a drone or from a circling helicopter. Jackie could see that the street was blocked off at both ends. She saw Virginia State Police, Fairfax County Police, and FBI agents. The FBI agents were clad in black riot gear and holding automatic weapons.

"We are just learning that this is the house of Pulitzer Prize winning photojournalist Jacqueline Scott," The voiceover said. "Jackie's work has been featured on this station many times over the years."

"Grandma. That looks like your house," Chucky said, pointing.

"That is Grandma's house," Charles told his son. "Some bad people did that."

Jackie could see the fear on her grandson's face. Milly began to cry. Katrice bent to her knee and the children ran into her arms. "Everybody's safe," her mother said as Charles muted the TV—the anchor had moved on to the next story.

There was a knock at the door. Warren drew his sidearm and held it behind his back. He opened the door to let in the caterer and his cart laden with breakfast. Marna stepped into the room right behind the white-clad chef. She was carrying an arm-load of bags.

"Breakfast is served," the man said in a fake British accent.

"I got clothes and toys," Marna said, laying the bags on the coffee table.

"Yay! Toys!" the kids hollered, jumping with glee.

"You've been drinking again, Abigail!" Jackie glowered at the young girl. She could smell the scent and recognized the look in her eye.

Marna didn't reply. She just went into the bedroom and closed the door behind her.

"She's crashing," Jackie announced to Charles. "And it's all his fault." She pointed her white-clubbed hand at Warren.

"Come on, Ma. Let's not start again," Charles said. He tipped the waiter and sent him away.

Marna came out of the room again wearing a new t-shirt. A tag still hung from the sleeve. While the others dug into their breakfast, Marna made a plate for Jackie. She had to feed her with a fork. Jackie was mortified.

"Don't cry," Marna whispered to Jackie, wiping a tear from her cheek. Jackie didn't know if she was crying from embarrassment, from the pain, or because she knew Marna was crashing. She thought that mostly she was crying because her life had become such a mess.

Jackie had been so independent all of her life. She had always been the strong one. Now she was losing her mind. She couldn't go to the bathroom without having somebody wipe her bottom, and she couldn't even feed herself.

She was cognizant enough to realize that the young woman feeding her was on a rocket ship headed for her own destruction. She hiccupped and shook her head at Marna's proffered spoon.

Jackie started drifting again.

Agent Williams and Jackie walked along the W&OD trail. Above them, the sky threatened snow. The air around them seemed to absorb the sound of their voices, but even so, when a jogger or biker approached, they stopped their conversation until the intruder passed.

"How are Amy and the kids?" Jackie asked, trying to break the ice.

He didn't answer for a moment. He stopped and picked up a rock to throw into Piney Branch Creek. She could tell there was hostility behind the action. "She left me," he replied around a lump in his throat. "Took the kids and moved back to her mother's house."

"Oh. Sorry." Jackie truly felt sad for the man. Separations were hard. Nobody deserved that.

"She said I worked too much. Said I was cold and uncaring," he sighed. "I think she's having an affair with another woman. I could find out, but I really don't want to know."

"Sorry," she said again. She meant it. "That sucks."

"I should have had you—back in high school. It should have been you and me." There was bitterness in his voice.

"Is it true that Monroe kicked your ass over me?"

He grimaced and didn't answer. She could still see the green in his eyes after all these years. She felt there was an undercurrent to the relationship between those two men that she didn't understand. It was a love-hate thing. She was surprised that one of them hadn't put a bullet into the other's head in Vietnam.

"I'm not here to talk about high school," he finally said. He shrugged in helplessness. They both knew he was here to talk about the murders of her family.

"Nothing yet?" Jackie was frustrated. "It's been six months. We know it's somebody in that oil company." She didn't tell the agent that she'd pulled the strings of every contact her father had known in the oil business. She hadn't been able to uncover anything either.

Reginald looked around to make sure they were out of earshot. "A lower-level VP gave the order. We know it, but it's not something we could prove in court. The upper management is livid. In fact, the man has been fired."

Jackie nodded. "I'm leaving the White House and going back to the field," she said, picking up a stick and tossing it off the trail—saving a future bicycler from disaster. "Charles is in med school in Massachusetts and is so consumed that I never see him anyway. I get tired of living in my little house with the ghosts of my dead family. I want to get back out into the world where I can make a difference again."

"You lose your family, and the asshole loses his job," Williams said bitterly.

Jackie pulled a manila envelope out from under her jacket and passed it to Williams. "I gave you my word that I wouldn't handle these cases on my own," she said, her eyes indicating the folder. "A light colonel has sticky fingers. Seems he's selling Vietnam-era weapons off the backs of trucks to the Michigan Militia and padding his personal nest egg."

Williams took the envelope and stuffed it into his jacket. "A few more of these, and I'll get a promotion," he smiled.

They walked in silence for a few minutes. Here and there, a snowflake began to fall. Her mind was still on the man who gave the kill order for her husband and daughter. She didn't want to know, but she felt like she didn't have a choice—animal revenge drove her sleepless nights. "Give me a name," she growled.

"Antonio Jackson Randall, III, of Dallas, Texas."

"And if some unfortunate accident were to happen to Mr. Randall?" Jackie asked.

"Accidents happen all the time. They're a part of life," Agent Reginald Williams said with gravel in his voice.

The two turned around and started walking back toward Jackie's house. "Just make sure that it looks like an accident," he warned her. Jackie knew this moment and this decision was the beginning of her moral slide—she was about to become one of them.

Jackie was brought back to the present by Marna's gentle prodding. "Come on, Jackie. You need to eat more."

"I can't. I'm so tired. So much pain," Jackie said.

Apparently, Charles overheard the comment. "I can give you some more pain meds, Ma," he said. "Take these and go lay down for a little while. Warren needs to finish making plans, but I'm pretty sure we have a big day ahead of us. You'll need the rest."

He fished the pills out of the bottle. "I don't want to give you more than you need. They'll make you feel loopy."

"You mean even more than my dementia?" she asked.

He nodded solemnly and put two pills into her mouth. Marna tipped a glass to her lips and Jackie swallowed obediently. Marna led her to the bedroom, helped her lay down, and covered her with the blanket. Jackie was asleep in minutes.

CHAPTER TWENTY-THREE

The street looked worse at ground level than it did from the TV's camera. Her grass was burned down to the roots. The once-white-paint on the porch was either burned away or blackened and blistering. Her front, bay window was smashed—the broken glass looked like the teeth of a ravenous animal.

The rental truck had arrived at about ten o'clock and the loading had commenced. She stood in the bombed-out living room watching the progress. Every box that was hauled up from the basement was like a piece of Jackie's heart being ripped away.

She looked at Katrice's cello, which was badly burned. Strings had popped and slinked down across the metal stand.

Charles came and stood beside his mother as the boxes streamed by. "You didn't always have this stuff in your basement, Mom. Where did you keep it before?"

She leaned against him in an attempt to keep the world from swimming. Charles had been correct about the pain meds making her loopy. She shrugged in an answer to his question.

"I don't remember," she said. "All I know is that for years I kept this stuff somewhere safe—maybe it was a storage locker or a secure room at the newspaper…" She shrugged again. "When I knew I was slipping, I didn't want to lose it. So, I guess I must have moved it home." Her voice trailed off. "All I know is that one morning I woke up and it was in the basement. I've spent the last year looking for the box that holds Aaeesha's treasure."

Charles pondered the boxes as they passed. "I was always aware that you were a journalist, but I never knew you were doing things that could get your house firebombed."

"I'm sorry," she whispered. But in her heart, she knew that Charles would have never been able to handle the thought of his mother doing dangerous work. He was too protective. He'd only tolerated her war reporting because he knew there was nothing he could do to stop her.

"Well, we'll figure it out," he said. "Warren told me that once the intel becomes property of the FBI, you'll no longer be a threat to the bad guys—whoever it is that you pissed off."

"I've done some evil things, Charles," Jackie confessed. "Things I'm not proud of."

"You were a good mother."

They stood in silence for a few moments as men continued hauling out her stuff. "Where's Abigail?" Jackie asked.

"Marna's upstairs packing clothes for you."

"You think we can save her?" Jackie asked.

It was Charles' turn to shrug. "It depends on whether she wants saving."

"Promise me that you'll do everything you can to help her." Jackie was feeling the exhaustion rolling over her again.

"I promise, Ma."

Outside, and through the shattered window, Jackie could hear Warren barking orders at the truck loaders. Apparently, they weren't being careful enough.

"I don't ever want to come back to this house, Charles," Jackie said. "I want the carpet from my bedroom, the vanity that Richard bought me, and the photos on the walls." She shivered. "This house has too many ghosts in it."

He nodded. Through the foggy haze of her brain, she could tell that her son was sad at her words. This was the house he had grown up in. It was the end of an era for him as well as for her. She knew that feeling—her mind went back to the time she'd said goodbye to Aaeesha in her childhood home in Basra.

"It's hard, isn't it?" she asked. "I wish I could be young again," she sighed. "Back when I was smart."

"We all wish that, Ma." She didn't know if that was a tear in his eye or just allergies.

Marna came downstairs. "Our clothes smelled so smoky; I don't think we can wear them. I'll take them to the cleaners to see if they can fix them."

"We can buy new clothes," Jackie said.

She was drifting again.

Everybody thought that these things had to happen in a dark sinister back alley, but Jackie met the guy in a sports bar over in Merrifield—just on the other side of 66.

The raucous crowd made normal conversation impossible, and the two had to lean close to be heard. The beer flowed while young single girls flirted with the opposite sex. There were dozens of TV screens circling the walls, and each table had its own audio box so that the patrons could listen and watch their preferred sports channel.

She didn't know his real name. She figured that he probably had a dozen identities. He was balding and in his fifties. When she'd known him in her former life, he was doing wetwork for the CIA. At the time, she had loathed him. But now, she had the need for his specialized skills.

Tonight, he wore blue jeans and a Redskins jacket. His scruffy, graying beard made him look like just another football fan. The man had the ability to blend in anywhere.

They had each ordered a burger. Jackie had taken one bite and eaten three fries. Nothing else would go down.

She took a slip of paper from her pocket and pushed it across the table to the man. She'd done her own research on Antonio Jackson Randall, III, of Dallas, Texas. She didn't want some innocent man to get hurt. The man's name and address were on that piece of paper.

She held her finger on the note for a long moment, not wanting to release it. It seemed to sizzle with heat. She knew that she was crossing a line from which she would never return. In this moment, she was becoming the slime that she'd fought against her whole life.

Coming to a decision, she released the paper. She reached into her other pocket and took out an envelope containing a large stack of currency. She slid it across the table to the murderer as well. He nodded and slid the packet of bills into his pocket.

Watching the envelope disappear, she felt as if she had just accepted thirty pieces of silver instead of paying out cash.

"Make sure it looks like an accident," she yelled over the crowd noise, even though his head was only a foot away.

He nodded.

"How much would you charge to do me?" she asked. She honestly didn't care if she lived or died.

He smiled and patted her face. Without a word, he got up and wound his way through the tumultuous crowd toward the door, leaving her alone with her guilt and the half-eaten burgers.

CHAPTER TWENTY-FOUR

Jackie was grateful that she'd slept on the ride down to FBI headquarters. Charles had given her another dose of the pain meds before they'd left Vienna. Now she was coasting at the perfect balance between pain and dopiness.

Someone had found her an easy chair, and she sat in the middle of the gymnasium in the Hoover building. Chaos was king and the sounds of every voice echoed and reverberated through the room.

Jackie counted twenty analysts who were working through the pile of boxes in the center of the floor.

She could tell that, at one time, it had been a full-sized basketball court. Now there was only one hoop. The other end of the room was filled with treadmills, weight benches, and rowing machines. Even as the analysts dug through the boxes, there was a woman who was working out on the heavy bag that hung from a steel girder. The Fed appeared to be in her early thirties, and was grunting and cursing at the bag.

The ceiling was vaulted as one would expect in a gym. There was a set of roll away bleachers that had been collapsed against one wall.

Katrice had taken the kids to the zoo. They had also been assigned a female agent to follow them around. Nobody expected them to run into trouble, but the director had been adamant about the security.

In front of her, a team of analysts was carefully sorting her boxes into file cabinets. She was impressed with the intelligence of the group. Most of the cabinets were being filled with normal journalistic entries—photos, negatives, reports, and notes. There were a few boxes with family memorabilia. Intermingled were historical documents, like the picture of the Sindermann-Carter meet. And of course, there were the packets of political dirt that she'd collected over the years. This final group was sorted according to the active or retired status of the subject. Warren told her that the director himself would handle the active cases involving sitting politicians.

Every once in a while, people would ask her questions about events and make notes as they filed. Jackie told them everything that she could remember, but most of the questions were answered by a puzzled look and a shrug. She was tiring quickly.

Another team of people were wading through the filed documents. Everything that wasn't personal was being scanned into the FBI's database.

A desk had been pulled into the middle of the room, and a pair of analysts was linking the new data with things they already had on file.

Director Williams strode into the room and the chaos ceased. "Carry on," he said in his authoritative voice. "I'd like to speak to Jackie in private if I could." He looked at his watch. "Somebody wrangle us up some lunch."

Marna helped Jackie to her feet, and the retired journalist followed the director into a tiny conference room off the gymnasium. Through the window, she could still watch the team working.

"How are you doing?" he asked with concern on his face as he closed the door. He helped her sit.

"I'm tired and confused," she replied honestly. "Dementia is hell. I highly recommend that you avoid it at all costs."

This won her a wry smile as the director sat across from her. He closed his eyes and rubbed the back of his neck as if to drive away a headache.

"You've set this town on its head, Jackie. I thought we agreed that you'd stop playing the cop and turn all your stuff over to me."

She looked at him with a blank expression. She didn't remember what she'd done or failed to do.

"I put a hit out on Abby and Richard's killer," she said looking at her bandaged hands.

"I'm the top cop in the nation," he said angrily. "Don't tell me things like that!" He shuffled uneasily in his seat. He lowered his voice so that she had to lean toward him in order to hear. "You did the right thing, Jackie," he said. "If you hadn't stopped him, then he would have continued polluting our political system, and he would have killed others."

"That was the beginning of my own moral decay," Jackie said.

"You came to the wrong place for absolution," he sighed. "Anything you've done, I've done worse."

"Don't I have a file on you somewhere?" she asked, a grin playing at the corner of her mouth. He didn't answer, and she was reminded that the man certainly had one on her.

"I'm an old senile woman," she told Reginald. "I've got a mind like a steel sieve. Everything just flows right through it," she sighed. "Somewhere there's a box that has Aaeesha's treasure. That is my most important box. I've got to find it before my mind is completely shot."

"If it's here, we'll find it," he said with certainty in his voice. "I never was able to find where you kept your intel. If I'd have known you moved it to your basement, I'd have come and gotten it a long time ago."

Her mind started drifting back to her bombed-out house in Vienna. "After your people loaded up the boxes, the only thing left in the basement was my old camera bag," she said nostalgically. "It's still got the bullet holes." She smiled wanly. "My bag got shot the day I took the photos of the mother who blew up her own daughter." She paused reliving the horror. "That photo series won me the Pulitzer prize and it stopped a war." She sighed, picturing the little girl's face that was permanently etched in her memory. "But the price was still too high."

"The cases that you turned over to me back in those days helped me to rise to my current position," he said as if ignoring her reminiscing. "But I'm still pissed that you were holding out on me."

"Why am I on your watch list?" she demanded, coming back to the present.

"There's actually about six answers to that question. First of all, you're on that list because I personally want to see that you're protected."

"And the other five reasons?" she asked, already guessing at some of the answers.

"You've pissed off a lot of very powerful people. Several important people identified you as a *person of interest*. I think it was their way of harassing you without being overt."

"You think one of those people bombed me?"

He shrugged. "Possible, but not likely. They wouldn't be stupid enough to put their name on an official document if they wanted you killed."

"So, you don't know who's trying to kill me?"

"Probably somebody in one of those files." He nodded through the window toward the gymnasium. "We'll be looking very closely at those individuals."

"Warren says that the danger is past now that you have the documents. He says that I'm no longer a threat to the bad guys."

"I hope so. But we're going to keep you safe for a week or so, just to make sure." The director rose and extended a hand. Out of reflex, Jackie raised her bandaged hand toward the shake. "Oh, sorry," he said, withdrawing his proffered paw. "I've got to get back up to my office, but you take care of yourself. I'm sorry about the dementia."

"Thanks." She struggled to her feet without assistance, stumbling once, but catching her balance with her elbows on the tabletop. "Good to see you again, Reginald."

The chaos had ceased by the time Jackie made it back to her easy chair in the gym. A stack of pizza boxes was being ransacked by the hungry crew. Marna sat glumly on a folding chair beside Jackie. She could see that Marna had already eaten. So, when Jackie came out of her meeting with the director, Marna set to feeding the older lady.

"I'm sorry," she whispered in her alcohol-stink breath as she held a slice for Jackie to eat.

Jackie didn't answer. She was too tired, and she knew the girl's mind was made up.

After she'd eaten her fill she said, "Take me to the bathroom, Marna."

"You got my name right," Marna smiled. Then the smile disappeared like a snowball on a hot stove.

Jackie did her business, and Marna helped her clean up. On the way back, Jackie stopped her in the hallway. "Don't do this, Marna. I love you."

Marna bit her lip and looked at the floor. "I'm garbage," she said. "I'll never be able to fit in with people like you, Charles, and Katrice." She scuffed her tennis shoe on the floor. "I'm not good like you. I'm street trash."

"Stop it!" Jackie demanded. She put her clubbed hand under the girl's chin to look her in the eye. She gasped at the pain of the touch and dropped her arm. "Look at me. Don't do this. I love you."

Marna hesitated, then reached into her pocket. She pulled out the keys to Jackie's Mercedes and the credit card. She pushed them into Jackie's pocket. A tear spilled down her cheek and splattered loudly on the white, tiled floor. "I've gotta go," she hiccupped, then turned and ran.

Jackie sighed, watching the form disappearing around the corner. "I loved you like a daughter." She said to the air.

Jackie pushed her way through the gym doors and found Charles. He was talking to one of the analysts. Amazement showed on his face as the young woman told him of his mother's exploits in a world that he didn't even know existed.

"Your mom is a legend," the young woman was saying to Charles in a hero-worship voice. The girl looked to be about Marna's age. When Jackie walked up, the woman-child looked at her with doe eyes the size of grapefruits.

Jackie flopped down in the easy chair. She knew she was interrupting, but she didn't feel like a hero at the moment. "Call the Home Care agency," she said to Charles. "Marna just quit. We need a new nurse."

"What happened?" Charles asked, standing up as if to run after her.

Jackie sighed again. "Sit down. She made her choice. She's run off to her old boyfriend."

Jackie knew that Marna's problem wasn't the bombing or the FBI involvement. It was the alcohol.

"It's Warren's fault!" Charles said, balling his fists. "He gave her the wine that knocked her off the wagon!"

"Sit down!" Jackie commanded again. "The guy is twice your size. What are you going to do—punch him in the kneecaps?" She shook her head. "You can't fly off the handle every time you think there's an injustice."

"But you made me promise to do everything I could to keep her…."

"Let it go—she doesn't want to be here. Get me somebody new."

The analyst went back to her work, and Charles stomped off to the corner to make his call. Jackie leaned back and closed her eyes. It took all her strength not to cry again. Her mind went back over every conversation and interaction that she'd had with the girl. What had she done wrong?

She remembered the CIA analyst that had the drinking problem—what was her name? Julie Something? Jackie was drifting again.

She rarely visited her desk at the newspaper while she was working the White House. Most of her time was spent meeting with informants and doing interviews. Because of her reputation, the paper gave her anything she wanted—including a plush corner office. Right now, she was sitting at her desk looking out across the city.

She had gone back to the office to check the reliability of a source. Although the desk was strewn with papers, the tiny envelope stood out.

Jackie called out to her secretary. "Sandy, where did this come from?" she asked, holding up the little envelope.

"Some lady dropped it by this afternoon. It looked personal, so I left it on your desk."

Curious about the note, Jackie settled back in her chair. She picked up her letter opener.

It wasn't just an ordinary letter opener. It was a knife that had been given to her by an African terrorist. She held the ornate blade in her hand remembering the story. She'd somehow found herself in an impossible situation, brokering a deal between two warring factions. Her goal had been to save lives and stop the conflict. But the creative deal she had negotiated was beneficial to both parties. The toothless hoodlum had been so grateful that he'd given her the gift of the knife. The handle was ornately carved ivory. She guessed it was illegal ivory, but she had no way of knowing.

She set aside the knife and turned her attention to the note. "I'm a CIA analyst. I think that my coworker, Julie Styles, is in trouble. Can you help her?"

Jackie dropped the note into the trash. The world was full of people who needed rescuing. She was tired. This was somebody else's problem.

But her conscience bothered her. She stared at the piece of paper at the bottom of the trash can. She thought of Abigail, who was now in the tenth grade. If Abby was in trouble, she'd appreciate a stranger's help.

She sighed. "I'll pay it forward," she said to the note. She reached into the can and pulled it out again.

The message gave details and a photograph of the woman in need. It was late in the day, so Jackie grabbed her camera and headed for the door.

She waited in her car outside the woman's apartment for a couple hours before the young woman came home. She was inside for about thirty minutes, then came back out, wearing a slinky, revealing dress. Jackie watched as the girl traipsed away on her high heels; she was continuously pulling down on the dress to keep it from creeping up to reveal her hoo-ha. From Jackie's vantage, it was a losing battle.

Jackie slid out of her car and crossed the street. She pressed a random button on the entry pad, and a tinny voice came through the speaker. "Is that you, Amanda?" She had gotten lucky—apparently someone was expecting a visitor.

Jackie grinned at her own ingenuity. "Yeah, it's me," she lied.

The door buzzed and she slid through. She went up the stairs and found Julie's apartment door. In the movies, people could pick locks in seconds. But in reality, it took Jackie five minutes to get in.

The apartment was small, overlooking a dingy portion of Q Street. But since it was in Georgetown, it probably cost a fortune. Jackie began looking through Julie's desk, careful not to leave a mess.

For a CIA analyst, the woman wasn't very clever at hiding evidence. There were a stack of notes from a person calling himself, Alfonzo. From the context of the notes, it was clear that the man had sex with Julie. He referenced her alcohol problem and was obviously trying to blackmail Julie into giving him state secrets.

Jackie put the stack of notes into her pocket. She picked up Julie's phone and called home, telling Richard that she'd be out late. Wandering to the kitchen, she opened the fridge and made herself a roast beef sandwich and washed it down with a glass of milk.

She grabbed a J.A. Jance novel off Julie's shelf, admiring her taste in literature. She sat by the window and began to read. As she read, she continued to scan the street below, keeping watch for the returning girl.

A little after eleven, she saw the woman staggering up the street with a man on her arm. They were laughing loudly, and Julie was no longer bothering to keep the skimpy dress in place. They passed under a streetlight, and Jackie saw that the man looked Cuban.

She turned off the lights and tucked herself into a corner. She pulled out her .45 and pointed it at the door. She didn't intend to shoot anybody; she just wanted to put the fear of God into the kids. They needed a dose of reality.

A minute later, she heard the key trying to find the doorknob. There was loud laughter on the other side of the entryway, then a male voice said, "Here, let me try."

There was the sound of keys falling to the floor and a girl's giggle. Finally, the key slid home and the door opened. The tipsy couple staggered into the hallway and fumbled for the light switch. They were sucking face and the woman's dress was half off before Jackie spoke.

"Good evening," she said calmly.

Julie let out a little scream, then clamped her hand over her mouth when she saw the gun. The man just stared. Apparently, the sight of the gun was as potent as an entire pot of coffee, because the couple appeared to be suddenly sober.

"Come on in." Jackie invited the pair into the living room with a wave of her hand.

She could see that Julie was trembling slightly. The girl was a thin slip of a thing topped by bleach-blonde hair. Jackie guessed she was originally a dark brown.

The young man was calm on the outside. But his eyes gave away his fear. He had a sparse mustache that made him look fifteen.

Jackie held up the notes. She set the gun on top of the novel that she had been reading. "Julie Styles," she said looking into the girl's eyes. She looked at the guy. "And what's your real name, young man?"

"Perez," he said with a quaking voice. "Alfonzo Perez."

"Where are you from Alfonzo?"

"Cuba." His voice had pubescent quality.

"And you're trying to blackmail Miss Styles?" She clicked her tongue and shook her head. "Ain't gonna happen." She thought for a moment. "How old are you, Perez?"

"Twenty-four, ma'am," he said respectfully.

"How'd you get in this business?"

He hesitated before answering. Then his eyes said that he came to a decision to tell Jackie the truth. "My sister's still back in Cuba. This guy met me on the street and told me that they'd kill my sister unless I seduced Julie and forced her to give up secrets." He had a wild look in his eye. "I don't wanna do this, but I gotta."

Julie tried to say something, but Jackie cut her off with the palm of her hand. "I'll get to you in a moment, missy."

"You like living here, Perez? In the US?"

"Yes, ma'am. I don't want to go back to Cuba."

She nodded thoughtfully. "Tonight is your lucky night. I am your fairy godmother, and I'm about to make all your dreams come true." She paused. "As long as you play ball with me."

The look on his face said that he'd believe in Santa Claus, the Tooth Fairy, and the Easter Bunny if it got him out of trouble.

Jackie shifted on the couch. "You work for me now, Perez. I'm going to be feeding you the data to give to your contact."

She turned her attention to Julie, who was no longer shaking, but was looking very sheepish. "How old are you, Julie?"

"I'm twenty-four also, ma'am."

"And you have a drinking problem?"

"Yes, ma'am." A tear trickled down her face.

"So, you're a drunk and you've been passing State secrets. If your boss at the CIA finds out what you've been doing, then you'll be canned and perhaps prosecuted?"

"Yes, ma'am."

"You work for me now too. Understand?"

She nodded. "Who are you?"

"I'm your best friend." Jackie picked up the phone and dialed a number by heart.

Agent Reginald Williams picked up on the second ring. "Go," he said.

"It's me. Jackie. I've just turned a Soviet spy and a CIA mole. They're ready to play ball and feed misinformation upstream. But they're my agents, and you have to promise me to treat them right. If you don't give me your word, then I'll set 'em free to do their thing for the Ruskies."

There was a pause on the other end of the line. "What are your terms?"

"The spy is a kid from Cuba. They are threatening his sister's life who is still back home. You'll give him full immunity and citizenship if he wants it. After he serves you five years, you'll rescue his sister and bring her stateside."

There was another silence. "Okay done. What about the mole?"

"First thing is that you'll square it with her supervisors and tell them she's been working for you all along. Next, she has an alcohol problem— you'll get her into a program. I'll let her know that if she falls off the wagon, we'll throw her under the bus. That ought to be incentive to keep her on the straight and narrow."

"I can do that," Williams said. "Where and when can I meet them?"

"Right now." Jackie gave him the address and apartment number.

The kids were sitting on the couch holding hands. Both of them had tears running down their faces.

"Why are you doing this for us?" Julie asked.

"I'm paying it forward," Jackie answered. "Someday, my daughter is going to need someone to help her."

She'd started life with the goal of making the world a better place. She still wanted to do that. But now she was also driven by love. She would do anything for her family. And for Aaeesha who was still in Iraq.

Jackie was brought back to the present by the pain throbbing through her singed hands. She thought of the kindness that she'd tried to bring to the world and how it had all turned sideways in the blink of an eye. Now, there was no kindness that anyone could do for Abigail. Jackie had become bitter and disillusioned by Abby's murder. She had been hoping to redeem Abby through Marna. And now, even that opportunity was gone.

"She just walked away from it all," Jackie said to Charles. "Just walked out that door."

He nodded sympathetically. "We'll get you another nurse, Ma. She's on her way right now."

She shook her head. She didn't know why she had thought that Charles might understand. She sighed loudly and realized she was shaking from the pain.

"As much as I hate to do this, I need more pain meds."

Charles reached for the pill bottle in his pocket as Jackie finished her thought.

"Ask Warren if the safe house is ready. I think I need to go to sleep."

CHAPTER TWENTY-FIVE

Instead of going to the safe house, Warren had arranged for Jackie to take a nap in one of the assistant director's offices. The woman was in Louisiana for the week, and she had a cot in the back of her room.

Jackie looked around the lush office that was almost the size of her entire house. There was a huge gilded, walnut desk in the middle of the room, topped by an ornate brass lamp. The owner of the office was obviously meticulous, because there wasn't a book or paper clip out of place.

Jackie didn't care about the office. The pills that Charles had given her were slamming her hard, and she had to lay down. Warren led her to the cot and helped her into it.

"I'm sorry about Marna," he said sadly. "I wasn't going to let her drink, but she begged me." He sighed. "I'm a tough guy on the outside, but I'm a sucker for a pretty woman."

Jackie was sick of thinking about Marna, the woman that she had previously thought of as her daughter. "If they find anything about Aaeesha, set it aside. That box is important."

She fell into a fitful sleep. In her dreams, secret agents kept popping up out of a whack-a-mole game. They would point a little gun at her and shoot tiny darts. The little arrows stuck in her hands and caused pain to run through her arms. Every time she'd whack one, three more would pop up and shoot her.

She woke with a throbbing headache, which of course, matched her throbbing hands. She sat up on the tiny cot, having no idea where she was. It looked like she was in somebody's office. There was a fancy clock on the wall and its little hand was on the three, the big hand on the one.

She tried to push herself off the cot and was instantly reminded that her hands were injured. The pain shot through her, and she sucked in her breath and rocked on the cot until it subsided.

Just then the door opened and Warren rushed in, followed by Charles. "Oh good, you're up," Warren said excitedly. "We found a box with Aaeesha's things." He rushed over and helped Jackie to her feet.

"Who are you?" She asked Warren.

"I'm Agent Warren Banks. I'm helping you sort through your boxes."

Jackie pulled away from him. "Are you one of those FBI agents who's stalking me?" Panic was rising in her voice.

"No, Mom," Charles said in a placating voice. "He's been helping us, remember?"

"Who are you?" she asked, terrified of these strange men. She tried to hug herself, but the bandages made it impossible. She knew the face was familiar, but she was really frightened.

"I'm Charles, your son," he said sadly.

"Richard is dead!" Jackie said. "You can't be him."

"No, not your husband Richard. I'm your son, Charles."

"Oh," Jackie said. She had to take the man's word; he seemed so sincere. "Of course. I know who you are."

"Mom, I'm worried about you."

"Well, that makes two of us. I'm worried about me too. What happened to my hands?"

By the time they made it back downstairs to the gymnasium, Jackie's mind had caught up with the present. She remembered who Charles and Warren were, and she remembered getting burned. Seeing her boxes in the middle of the gym floor with more than a dozen people rooting through them was quite a shock, but she recovered quickly.

"Is this what you're looking for?" Warren asked, opening a box that he'd set on a table.

Jackie tried to reach for one of the pages, but her club hands wouldn't work right. Warren held up the page for her to read.

"No," Jackie said sadly. "These are letters that Aaeesha wrote to me after I moved to America." Her friend always had such beautiful handwriting. "Aaeesha didn't know English," Jackie said as way of explaining the Arabic scrawl. "We wrote every week. I saved all her letters."

"Hey, what's this?" Warren asked. He rooted to the bottom of the box and pulled out a cloth bag. It jingled slightly as he withdrew it.

"Oh, that's some of the gold that Aaeesha gave me," Jackie said.

Warren tipped the bag up and spilled the contents onto the table. Five gold coins spun themselves into a loose pile. He let out a low whistle. "I'm no coin expert, but these things are worth thousands each," he said.

Jackie nodded. "Aaeesha's husband was a mid-level official in Saddam's government," she said. "He was high enough that he had a little disposable income but not so high that he was one of Saddam's direct reports. They didn't have a mansion or anything like that. Um… they lived in an apartment like normal people."

She realized she was rambling a little. She tried to pull herself back onto the subject. "Aaeesha and her husband developed a hobby of collecting coins—they actually made a little money at the craft."

Jackie closed her eyes to shut out the pain. "When Richard and Abigail were killed, she sent me this bag of gold coins." Her head hurt. She was so tired. "Aaeesha told me that she had purchased them with the express purpose of giving them to Abby when she graduated from college."

She felt a tear rolling down her cheek. "But since Abby wasn't going to graduate…" She couldn't finish her sentence. She opened her tear-streaked eyes to see everybody looking at her.

She looked at Charles. "Remember the coins she gave you when you graduated from med school?"

He nodded. "They helped pay down some of my college debt."

"Aaeesha was like that," Jackie said wistfully. "She was a good friend."

"So, is this Aaeesha's treasure that you've been looking for?" Charles asked expectantly.

"Oh no," Jackie answered confidently. "Those coins are only worth several thousand dollars. No. It's true that Aaeesha's treasure, the real treasure, has monetary value. But it's more than just money. It's worth… um… Oh, I hope I didn't throw it out. It's very important."

"But this box is important?" Warren asked hopefully. He patted the box on the table.

"It's very important to me," Jackie said brightly. "Aaeesha was my best friend, and this is all I have to remember her. But no, it's not the treasure that I was looking for. There's something else."

A sudden burst of remembrance shot through her head. "The box has a backpack… and… um… and some papers. And of course, some coins…. It's real important!" She could suddenly picture the backpack in her mind.

"That's awesome Mom! Can you remember anything else?"

"The papers…. They, um, tell about somebody." She stopped short and looked up helplessly.

"That's it?" Warren asked. "Do you remember anything else? Are the papers about a congressman, or maybe the President?"

"It has a backpack," Jackie said defeated. Tears were beginning to well again. "Bullet holes. Dried Blood."

She could see that Warren and Charles were both very frustrated, but there was nothing more that she remembered. She was so upset with herself. She crossed her arms angrily and flopped back into the easy chair.

At six o'clock, Warren called a halt to the operation. "Alright folks, let's knock off for the day. We'll pick up tomorrow at eight. Looks like we've made it about halfway through. Good work."

A googly-eyed analyst brought a 12x14 shot of Laura Armstrong. "Ms. Scott? May I make a copy of this photo? I'd like to hang it in my office. I'd ask you to sign it, but…" She pointed at Jackie's bandaged hands.

"Sure, you can have a copy," Jackie said, smiling. "If you bring it to me after my hands have healed, I'd be happy to sign it for you."

CHAPTER TWENTY-SIX

The FBI van inched its way through DC in the late rush hour traffic towards Virginia. Jackie was alert enough to recognize that they were on Rt. 66. Once they had passed the exit for Rt. 243, the one that would normally take them to Vienna, the sludge of vehicles began to move a little faster.

Warren was driving, and Charles held down the shotgun seat. The middle bench of the van held the new certified nursing assistant (CNA) and Katrice. Jackie was sandwiched between the kids in their booster seats on the very last bench. Chucky and Milly were chatting endlessly about the animals they'd seen at the zoo.

Jackie couldn't remember the name of the new nurse. Jackie guessed her age to be a little north of 40. She was dressed all in white. Her feet were clad with white, rubber-soled Merediths.

The moment Jackie had met the woman, she had an instant dislike for her—she was the polar opposite of Marna. Where Marna was dark, short, and thin, this lady was paper white with ultra-blonde hair. She was large boned and large breasted. She had an air of intimidation that said she was used to being in charge. Marna had been warm and caring, but this nurse was taking her idea of professionalism to an extreme— she had a soul made of ice cubes. Marna had let Jackie take the lead— asking her what she wanted to do next. The new woman only barked orders.

When they were getting ready to leave the FBI gymnasium, she had commanded that Jackie visit the restroom even though Jackie didn't have to go. While Katrice and Marna's help in the restroom had been compassionate, this lady's attitude made Jackie feel like an insignificant infant.

Trying to ignore the new nurse, Jackie had her arms around the children. She forced them to take turns telling her stories about the zoo—trying to teach them to respect the other's right to speak and how to listen patiently. Milly's favorite was the monkey house. Chucky was enthralled with the lions. They'd been lucky enough to be there when the lions were fed.

In spite of her earlier episodes, Jackie was feeling rather alert. It felt wonderful to feel her brain firing on all cylinders. If it weren't for her bandaged hands, she would have fired Attila the Hun. Instead, she just glowered at the back of the woman's severe bun.

As the children chatted, Jackie looked into the cars as they passed. Warren was driving gently, so vehicles were passing on the left.

The first vehicle was a young couple in a hot sports car. The rocket-on-wheels was a sleek, red thing that advertised the verve of the engine and the insignificance of the man's penis. Given the body language of the two, Jackie wondered if it were an affair. She hoped the woman wasn't about to be disappointed when they undressed.

Next, a minivan passed. The driver appeared to be a soccer mom. She had coiffed hair and armor-thick makeup. Jackie wondered how the woman blinked. The passenger, a teen girl, about fourteen seemed to be talking non-stop. Her light-brown curls were bouncing as she spoke. She was gesturing with her hands—fully animated.

In her right ear, Chucky was telling how the lion had viciously attacked the meat. His story held the tale of a wild carnivore, ruthlessly attacking his prey. Her eyes scanned to his sweet face, then back outside to the parade of traffic.

It was a black Chevy Suburban. She could tell that there were four men in the vehicle, but the back windows were tinted black so that she couldn't see the faces—just the outlines. The driver had wrap-around sunglasses—the kind that she'd seen on American soldiers all around the world. It was the rider in the front passenger seat that caught her attention.

Their eyes locked. He looked different without his beard, and he had aged several years. The man's hair was dyed black: he had obviously tried to mask his identity, but the eyes of her former lover hadn't changed. He had on body armor—she could see it under his expensive, black jacket. Everything about him said death.

Without looking away from the man, Jackie said to the children, "Take off your seatbelts and get under the seat, kids." In spite of her quaking, her voice carried an edge of steel.

"What's going on?" Charles said as he turned to see his children crawling onto the floor of the van.

"Warren, we have a problem," Jackie said loudly enough for Warren to hear.

"What's wrong?" Warren asked in a placating voice.

"Grizzly," Jackie answered. "He's in the car next to us. He's a Spec Ops soldier that I followed into Columbia on a drug raid."

"Shit," Warren swore, and Charles strained to look. "You think it's a coincidence?" Warren shook his head at his own stupid statement. "Right. Dumb question."

"It's the black Suburban," Jackie said, pointing.

In the other vehicle, Jackie could see an animated conversation, as Grizzly realized that he'd been made. She saw him looking at her again and speaking into a handheld radio.

"We've got another one on our tail," Warren said, glancing in the mirror.

"Pass me a gun," Jackie demanded.

Jackie began ripping at her bandages with her teeth. The sharp bolts of pain tearing through her hands brought tears to her eyes, but she had to protect her family. She got enough ripped away to free the palm and fingers of her right hand and her index finger on her left.

Charles noticed what she was doing with her teeth. *"What are you doing to your bandages?"* he shrieked.

Unhooking her seatbelt, Jackie reached all the way from the back seat to retrieve the Glock that Warren passed over his shoulder.

"You sit back down!" The nurse demanded, shaking a finger at Jackie. "What's this about?" she asked of Warren.

"Mom! You don't even know how to shoot!" Charles crowed.

Jackie answered him with a withering stare. "I may be senile, but there are certain things that you don't forget." She was glad that she was having a lucid moment. Right now, she felt like her old self—in control and on top of the situation. She knew what she had to do.

The pain that shot through her wounded hand as she gripped the gun took her breath away. She knew that if she fired the weapon, it would probably pull the skin from her burned palm. She saw Charles' look of concern. As a doctor, he could tell that she was hurting. But the pain in her hands helped her to focus past the dementia and the painkillers that were swirling through her brain.

Katrice had taken off her seatbelt and crawled on the floor with the children—covering them with her body.

The nurse, who had seemed unflappable earlier, had turned into a quivering bowl of jelly when she saw the gun. She was crying and holding her head between her knees. Jackie was pretty sure that she was praying the rosary. But right now, she didn't have time to placate Attila. If she peed on the seat, it would be somebody else's problem.

Apparently, Charles could see from her handling of the weapon that she knew what she was doing. "You have to be careful with the Glock," she told him. "The safety is built into the trigger itself, so all you have to do is point and squeeze. The danger is that there's no external safety."

"I don't even want to know." Charles turned around and buried his face in his hands. He seemed more nervous about his mom holding a gun than the bad guys that were pursuing them.

"They won't shoot at us while we're in traffic," Warren said, hopefully. "They'll wait until we're on an unpopulated country road."

"You have a leak inside the FBI," Jackie said. "They shouldn't know where we are."

Warren didn't say anything. He was apparently concentrating on the present danger. He pulled out his cellphone, dialed a preset number, and handed it to Charles.

"Tell them where we are. Stay on the line and tell them every turn we make. Tell them we've got bad guys on our ass. Tell them to send the state police, county cops, and even call out the National Guard if they can."

Charles nodded and began speaking in a frantic voice.

"Everybody hold on!" Warren said.

He had just pulled past the exit by about twenty yards. Without signaling, he stomped the gas and yanked the wheel to the right. The van shot through the grass back toward the exit ramp that they had just missed. The van's side grazed the end of the guardrail. The boxy beast bounced heavily as the steel rail ripped through the sheet metal of the driver's door. The grating sound caused shivers to run up Jackie's spine.

The vehicle bounced wildly, then popped up onto the Rt. 50 ramp—tires squealing. For a moment, Jackie thought the high-centered van was going to roll. Then Warren had it under control, the engine and tires screaming with protest.

For a second, Jackie's mind started drifting. In that moment, she stared at the gun in her hand, terrified that she'd kill one of her loved ones. But she was able to angrily swat the thought away, and her mind was once again on track and in the moment.

Bouncing around like popcorn kernels under the seat, the children began to wail, but Jackie had other things on her mind. Katrice was down there and would have to control the situation.

"Grizzly's vehicle is stuck in traffic, but the other Suburban made the exit behind us!" she shouted. She was now up on the bench seat on her knees watching out the back of the van, pointing her pistol at the car behind them and knowing the futility of firing a handgun at a moving vehicle. She wasn't going to fire, but she had to track the bad guys.

She glanced over her shoulder at the windshield. She saw an opportunity. "Left!" she shouted.

Warren whipped the wheel to the left, and the van screamed toward the Fair Oaks Mall. Behind them, a yellow Prius swerved to avoid Warren's van and crashed into a box truck. The Prius was launched into a 360-degree spin, and bounced off of a black minivan. Jackie watched a hubcap roll crazily through the intersection.

The pursuit vehicle full of bad guys had to slow and swerve to avoid getting collected by the evolving accident. Warren roared around the back side of the mall. He skidded to a stop in a handicapped parking spot, shutting down the engine. *"Go Go Go!"* he shouted. "Hide your gun and get into the mall! Now!"

Jackie jammed the pistol into her sweater pocket. She saw Warren pull his backup .38 out of his ankle holster and wrap it in his coat. Jackie grabbed Milly in her arms while Katrice picked up Chucky.

The nurse still had her head between her knees and was babbling incoherently. Charles was pulling on her arm to get her on her feet.

"Leave her!" Warren demanded. "They're not after her—she's in no danger!"

Jackie finally got Charles, Katrice, Chucky, and Milly out of the van. In the distance, she saw a black Suburban rounding the corner. Charles wrenched Milly out of his mother's wounded hands.

"Run!" Jackie shouted.

The ragtag group ran for the Mall entrance. Warren held the door as everyone else ran through. Jackie was the last through the door. Behind her, she saw the Suburban stop and three hardmen piled out.

Warren was on her heels. "Run into the Target store!" Jackie hollered at the group. Ahead of her, she saw Charles pulling his family toward the big box store.

The glass doors of the main mall entrance were tinted, allowing Jackie to see out, but the pursuers couldn't see in.

The store was big, with waxed floor tiles so reflective that they looked like glass. The store's red theme was displayed everywhere. The aisles were wide and clean. The air was filled with Muzak, intended to soothe the customers' souls and make them happy so that they would overspend. Jackie was anything but soothed.

They met in the toy department, panting. Jackie kept an eye out on the main hallway of the mall. She saw the bad guys running past the Target entrance, heading toward Macy's. She slumped back against the steel shelving in relief.

"What's the plan?" she asked Warren.

"Help's on the way," he said. "State police will be here in a few minutes. We'll swarm the place with cops—they won't be stupid enough to attack numbers like that." She saw that he had taken the phone from Charles and was now in direct contact with the Hoover Building himself.

Jackie nodded, then let a curse word slip. In the mall's hallway, she saw Grizzly. He was headed straight for them. His jacket bulged with concealed weapons.

CHAPTER TWENTY-SEVEN

Surprised at how well her brain was working, Jackie took charge. She instructed Charles, Katrice, Milly, and Chucky out of the area. She then told Warren her idea.

Her plan was to act as the decoy, drawing Grizzly to her, and allowing Warren to approach the man from behind.

"Go!" she whispered hoarsely.

Warren ran. She saw that Katrice and Charles were having a heated argument in muted voices. In a commanding posture, Charles was pointing off into the distance. Then a red-faced Katrice scurried off with the children. Somebody was going to get killed if they didn't get out of here—fast. She couldn't figure out what he was thinking.

"Get out of here!" she whispered hoarsely.

He just ignored her and casually sauntered out into the main aisle in front of the approaching soldier. She wanted to slap him. There was no time—it was too late to grab her idiot son and shout in his face. She just had to move and let the scene unfold.

Seemingly without a care in the world, she walked into the main aisle, being careful to not look in Grizzly's direction. She gazed up at a display of plastic turtles. Her bandaged left hand reached out as if to touch one of the toys. Her right hand was painfully gripped around the Glock in her sweater pocket.

Out of the corner of her eye, she saw Grizzly's pace quicken. The bait was set. She stepped back into the side aisle, hiding her body from the killer. She was hoping the disappearance of his target would increase

Grizzly's urgency. The more her attacker was focused on her, the less he would be watching for Warren to step out from between the toys.

Her ploy worked. She waited until she heard the rubber soles of the killer's combat boots squeaking on the polished, white-tiled floor. She stepped out into the aisle to face him.

The world seemed to go into slow motion. She looked straight into her former lover's eyes. She saw the shock of surprise register on his face. His hand started coming out of his jacket with a shiny chrome handgun. It was a fancy 1911 with wooden handgrips—she couldn't tell the manufacturer. The hammer was already cocked. At the same time, Jackie was raising the Glock in her pocket—she didn't even bother to pull it free.

Just as Grizzly's gun cleared the fabric of his jacket, Warren stepped out to the killer's left. Sensing the threat, Grizzly turned to assess.

Jackie was about to fire, when a movement caught her eye. Somehow, in her concentration on Grizzly, she had lost track of Charles. A cloud of anger crossed her face—her son was now in her line of fire, right behind her target. Her finger eased off the trigger of the Glock. Grizzly was continuing to turn toward Warren. Warren's hand was bringing his own pistol up toward the killer's head.

There was a blur of movement behind Grizzly. Jackie caught the rage on Charles face as something in his hands swung toward the soldier's head.

Booooonnggg! A metallic echo rang loudly through the store.

Grizzly's eyes rolled back in his head. He stood for a moment, then his knees buckled. He collapsed, face-first, onto the white tile.

Jackie's eyes locked onto Charles. The fury on his face was like nothing she had ever seen. *"Leave my mother alone!"* he shrieked in a bloodcurdling scream. It registered that her son was holding an aluminum baseball bat—it was dented on one side where it had collided with Grizzly's skull.

He raised the bat again to pummel his mother's attacker. Another scream escaped his lips—spittle flying. His eyes held the wild sheen of a man out of control.

Before he could pounce again, Warren had tackled him. The bat clattered across the floor. Even though Charles was half his weight, Warren was barely containing the man.

"He's down!" Warren screamed at the struggling doctor.

Jackie bent down to listen for Grizzly's breathing. "He's still alive," she said, standing.

The words seemed to drive the rage from her son. He ceased his struggle beneath the gargantuan FBI agent. The two untangled and looked at the man lying unconscious on the floor.

There was a commotion and shouting in the main hallway of the mall. Jackie looked up to see a dozen state cops running into the store with weapons drawn.

"Freeze! Police!"

Warren held up his badge. "FBI!" he yelled back. "Call an ambulance!"

They were swarmed. Jackie found herself face down on the floor with a uniformed cop on her back. She wailed in pain as her wounded hands were wrenched behind her back.

With her cheek pressed against the floor, she looked over to see Warren and Charles squished against the cold tile as well.

"FBI!" Warren yelled from under the pile. "Set up a security perimeter! There are more gunmen loose in the mall!"

One of the cops picked up Warren's badge off the floor. "Let 'em up," he said in a gravelly voice. He handed the badge-wallet back to the big Fed. "Sorry 'bout that sir. We just needed to get the situation under control."

"Let me up!" Charles squeaked. "I'm a doctor, and that man needs medical attention."

Jackie was helped to her feet as she watched in amazement at the transformation of her son. One moment he had been a raging, bat-wielding protector; the next he became a compassionate doctor. She was impressed and proud.

"Grandma!" a little voice cried in terror. Jackie turned to see that Chucky had escaped from his mom and was running toward his father and his grandmother. In Katrice's arms, Milly had a look of panic on her face.

"Don't look, Chucky," Jackie said. She turned and deflected Katrice and her little ones into a toy aisle.

"What happened to that man?" Chucky asked.

"Your daddy conked him with a baseball bat," Jackie said. "He was trying to hurt me, so your daddy stopped him."

Jackie saw a look of surprise and wonder on Katrice's face. "Charles did that?"

"Is he going to be okay?" Chucky asked.

"I don't know," Jackie said, honestly. "Your daddy's trying to save his life right now."

Ignoring the commotion in the aisle behind them, Jackie told the children. "I'll buy you each three toys. You get to choose."

After the excitement of the attack, Jackie could feel the fog of dementia creeping back into her mind. She turned to Katrice. "I'll take care of the children for a moment. Go ask one of the cops to check on that nurse out in the van."

Katrice nodded and put Milly on the floor. Chucky wanted to find a science kit, and Milly wanted to check out the book section. Jackie followed them dutifully.

Katrice was back in a moment. "No need," she told Jackie. "The agency called Charles' phone. The woman quit and took a taxi back into the city. She said she didn't want to work for a lunatic." She grimaced and shook her head.

"Can't say I blame her," Jackie answered. She wanted to ask a question but didn't want to impose.

"Don't worry." Katrice gave her a side hug, apparently reading Jackie's mind. "I'll take care of your bathroom needs until we find somebody else."

"Thank you," Jackie breathed, blinking back a tear of emotion. Suddenly, the adrenaline that had been coursing through her veins ceased. She wanted to collapse on the floor.

Her wobbly knees carried her as she followed the children up and down the toy aisles. Scores of cops continued pouring into the store. She caught sight of a stretcher being wheeled toward Charles' vanquishment. She watched as Warren and Charles cleaned up the mess on aisle six.

The kids picked out their prizes, totally excited about their new loot. Chucky wanted to open the science set right there on the floor, but his mother made him wait. Finally, Warren and Charles were done; they came over to join the family.

Jackie realized that the store had been totally vacated of customers. "I want to buy these for the kids," she told Warren. "There's nobody at the checkout."

Warren shrugged. "I'll find the manager."

"Wait!" she said, pulling the pistol from her pocket. "Take this. I'm starting to sundown. I'm afraid I'll shoot somebody." Her hands were already shaking as she held the gun out butt-first.

Warren nodded and stuck it into his holster. He flagged down a cop, who in turn started talking on his radio. A few minutes later, a short, balding man in a white shirt and Target-red tie turned up. Apparently, the police had herded all the employees into a safe area during the scuffle.

"I need to buy these toys," she told him. "And also, I need to buy more dressing for my hands." She held up her arms; shreds of bandaging material hung down like fringes from a cowboy's coat.

"Bandage material would be this way," he said in a nasal-tinted voice. "I'll give you want you want on the house. But please, get these cops out of here—they've driven away all my customers!"

The short, copper-skinned man led the group to the pharmacy department. Charles found some ointment and an armload of gauze. He handed the stuff to Katrice while taking a wallet out of his pocket. "Here," he said, handing over a pair of $100 bills, "this ought to cover our purchases." He nodded back in the direction of the downed terrorist. "Sorry about the mess."

"Is it ok to go to the safe house?" Katrice asked Warren.

He shook his head. "Jackie's right. The FBI's got a leak. Somehow, the bad guys knew where we were heading. We've got to go off-script for the night."

"You think the danger's over now that Grizzly's out of action?" Katrice asked.

Warren shook his head. "I hope so, but we can't be sure. We need to go somewhere safe—somewhere unexpected."

"Back to the Hilton?" Charles asked.

"No, that's the first place they'd look."

"There are lots of hotels out toward Dulles," Katrice suggested.

"The Westin," Jackie said. "It's a 4-star place. They'll have a suite for us."

Warren nodded. "And they have an underground garage. Maybe they have a place where we can hide our van."

Katrice walked around the store with Jackie for a little bit, trying to take the edge off of Jackie's sundowning energy. But it felt like a hopeless cause without the use of her hands and Marna's kind help. Finally, Jackie gave up and just gritted her teeth.

On the way to the hotel, Jackie started drifting again. It was Baghdad, before the bombs fell. It was 2003—fifteen years ago. Aaeesha was still alive. If she'd have known what was going to happen, she'd have kidnapped her childhood friend out of the country.

The street around her was teaming with children and pedestrians. She was wearing a chador, in spite of the heat that was undulating off the pavement. Today, the breeze was still, causing her to gasp for each breath.

She stood across the street from the Presidential Palace. Saddam was always on the move, and you never knew where he could be found, but she needed to get a message to him.

Earlier, she had considered using Aaeesha's husband, Aakav, who was a member of Saddam's government. But using him as a conduit for communication would have put his life at risk—Saddam might think he wasn't loyal, and that would be a death sentence for Aakav and for Aaeesha.

A car whizzed by in front of her, blowing its dusty horn loudly. Its rusted fender flapped in a nasty state of disrepair. She waited until it passed, then stepped into the hot street.

She'd watched the guards for a few days. She found that there was an older veteran who made the rounds, checking on the vigilance of his soldiers. The colonel had a purple scar that cut diagonally across his face—most likely a souvenir of the Iran-Iraq war. She guessed that the man had pull in the Palace, and he may be able to pass her message on.

The man rounded the corner of the Palace wall right on time, on his way to inspect the guards standing at this side gate. She pulled the note from beneath the folds of her abaya. She stepped in front of the man, blocking his path.

"Out of my way, woman!" he snarled, raising his hand in preparation to backhand her.

She proffered the note. "For His Excellency," she said bowing and handing over the paper. "I carry a message from the President of the Great White Satan." She knew Saddam preferred to think of the U.S. in those terms. She kept her head low in deference. "If His Excellency would permit me an audience, I would be honored." Knowing the place women took in society, she averted her eyes to the ground.

The man growled and snatched the paper. "I will deliver it," he spat. "Now get out of my way."

"Many lives may be saved," she added softly as she stepped aside, permitting him passage.

She watched him walk toward the pair of guards and hoped that her message would reach Saddam before the bullets started flying.

CHAPTER TWENTY-EIGHT

Jackie was back in her easy chair in the gymnasium of the Hoover building. Sunlight streamed through windows high in the room. In front of her, the buzz of the hive of analysts danced.

The previous evening had gone off without further event. Since hearing of her husband's heroism, Katrice had been fawning over Charles like a star-struck teen. She was batting her eyes and lightly touching him with her fingertips.

Katrice had doted on Jackie—feeding her and dressing her. Charles had applied salve and re-bandaged Jackie's hands. They'd eaten from the room service menu, and everyone had gotten a good night's sleep. True to her word, Katrice had helped Jackie with her bathroom needs.

Now Jackie was watching her life's work being analyzed and sorted. Milly was in her lap, and Jackie was reading the girl's new book to her while analysts occasionally interrupted her with questions.

She caught movement out of the corner of her eye. It was a woman in her mid-thirties, stepping into the gymnasium. The woman looked around the room, then caught Jackie's gaze. Her face lit up. She rushed over.

"Hi, you may not remember me. I'm Julie Perez—I mean I was Julie Styles when we met. I heard you were in the building." She stretched out a hand but then saw Jackie's bandages. "Oh, sorry. I didn't know you'd been injured."

Chucky was at Jackie's feet, playing with his Legos. Katrice hovered, watching over her chickadees. Charles was out of earshot, talking with his office on the phone.

Jackie was having a fairly good day, but she couldn't remember Julie. "You saved us—me and my husband, Alfonzo. I'm so grateful." She bit her lip. "We were both in so much trouble—we didn't even know how bad it was." She blinked. "Then you swooped in and fixed everything."

"You had a drinking problem. The Russians had Alfonzo's sister in Cuba," Jackie remembered, the cogs starting to turn. "You were so young."

"I've been sober ever since that night. Alfonzo and I eventually got married. I now head the FBI's physical evidence labs."

"Good for you," Jackie said proudly.

"I couldn't have done it without you." Her lower lip was quivering. "I never got a chance to thank you properly."

"You did it all yourself," Jackie said. "You just needed to be pointed in the right direction."

"If you ever need a favor..." the woman said, holding out a card.

Jackie reached for it, but her bandaged hand got in the way. Katrice, seeing her plight, took the card from Julie's hand.

Jackie's eyes shot a "thank you" to Katrice, who pushed the card into her pocket.

"I'm serious. Anything you ever need. Anytime of day or night. I wrote my personal cellphone number on the card." She bent down and pecked Jackie on the cheek before heading back to her office.

Katrice watched the woman walking away. "You really did a lot of good in your life, didn't you Jackie."

"I also did some horrible things," she said sadly. "I couldn't save Abigail or Aaeesha. And I let that skinny girl slip away."

"Marna?" Katrice asked.

"Yeah, her. I couldn't save her either."

"You're not Jesus Christ," Katrice said softly. "He's the only one who's ever been perfect. You did good. Stop beating yourself up."

Jackie shook her head. Any secrets not in that dwindling pile of boxes were going to go to the grave with her. Many had already been lost in her gray fog of dementia. She knew that her life after Abigail's death had been a train wreck of sin.

"Grandma, what's this word say?" Milly asked in her five-year-old voice. She was trying to sound it out.

"That word is 'love,'" Jackie said. "As in 'I love you.'" She squeezed her granddaughter and kissed the top of her head.

"I love you too, Grandma. I like it when you read me books." A shadow of thought crossed the little girl's face. "The bad guy that tried to hurt you last night—was he your friend?" she asked.

"Yes," Jackie answered. "A long time ago, he was my friend."

"Then why did he try to hurt you?" Her tiny face was puzzled.

"I don't know," Jackie said. "It doesn't make sense to me either."

CHAPTER TWENTY-NINE

The crew had taken a lunch break. There were only six more boxes in the middle of the floor—everything else had been filed into the row of cabinets. Several nice photos had been set aside for Laura Armstrong and were being prepared to be sent to Texas.

Just as Katrice was pushing the last bite of the Subway sandwich into Jackie's mouth, FBI Director Reginald Williams and Senator Monroe Turner walked into the gym. After all these years, she could still sense the camaraderie and the tension between the men.

"Hi Monroe," Jackie said shyly to the first man she'd ever loved. "Why are you here?"

She saw Williams turn green because of the connection between her and Monroe.

"You didn't know?" Monroe asked, picking up a bag of chips off of the lunch table. "I'm on the Senate Intelligence Oversight Committee." He gestured with his hand. "You've done some fine work here, Jackie. We're going to have chats with five sitting congressmen and Justice Charity Keeler."

"Remember that most people just want someone to help them go straight," Jackie said with her last swallow of lunch.

Williams shook his head. "You've put this town on its ear. It will be months before this calms down."

"Do you think I'm still in danger?" Jackie asked.

"I don't see how," Monroe answered. "You took out Grizzly. So now that the leader is out of action, you should be safe."

"But why would Grizzly attack me?" Jackie asked. "I mean, I know we had a bad history, but I don't think I had any dirt on him… Not that I remember anyway."

"Maybe he just wanted revenge," the Senator answered. "I read the report—he blames you for the deaths of several of his squad members."

"But why wait until I start hauling out my boxes?" Jackie asked, waving her white-clubbed hand at what was left of her life's work. "It doesn't make sense."

Williams shrugged. "As an agent, I've seen crazy minds do insane things. Maybe he saw your name on the news, and it triggered his rage."

"If we can assume that he's the one that bombed my house, then we have to look at some other trigger than seeing my house on TV. I wasn't on TV before I got bombed," Jackie said. "What triggered him? Was it rumors that Warren was looking through my boxes? But that doesn't make sense either, because I didn't have dirt on Grizzly—at least none that I remember."

"Maybe he thought you did," Williams said.

Senator Turner turned to the FBI chief. "I want you to keep a guard on her for at least a month," he said. "Just to make sure that there's no one else out there that wants to do her harm."

Williams nodded. "I'll do that, but we'll keep digging. I need to find the connection."

"Is Grizzly talking?" Jackie asked.

"No." Williams shook his head. "He's awake, but he's not saying a word. And frankly, with his training, I don't expect him to."

In a moment of clarity, Jackie blurted out what nobody in the room had been able to articulate. "Grizzly didn't do this on his own. He was hired. Somebody wants me dead because of something I know."

Every head turned toward her. It seemed as if even the echo in the gymnasium had been arrested. The silence was thick as everybody pondered her statement.

"It's the only thing that makes sense. There's something in the box that holds Aaeesha's treasure. That's what the bad guys are after," she said to the quiet room. "We've got to find that box."

The analysts in the room went back to their work, but the three old friends stayed silent thinking through the problem.

"You look good, Jackie. Nice to see you again," Senator Turner said, placing a hand on her shoulder. Even after all these years, his touch made her skin quiver with excitement.

She sighed. "I'm having a good day, Senator. At one point yesterday, I couldn't remember my son's name. My mind comes and goes." She hugged Milly, who was sitting patiently in her lap. "I'm just trying to hang onto the important things in life while I can."

"Thanks again for what you've done for your country."

CHAPTER THIRTY

By three o'clock, all the boxes had been sorted. Charles made arrangements with a storage company to have all her file cabinets full of articles, notes, and photos transported and stored safely. The FBI had all the incriminating evidence and had kept the originals, just to keep Jackie safe. According to Warren and Director Williams, the bad guys no longer had a reason to attack her.

"You have a leak in your house," Jackie told Director Williams as he stood beside her easy chair in the gymnasium. "Let's use that to our advantage. Put out the word that I no longer have any dirt in my possession."

"Yeah, I know." The Director sighed and ran his fingers through his hair. "Tracking down a leak like that is difficult. The best way to find a leak is to put out false information, then watch how the enemy responds. But in this case, I don't think that's such a good idea—I don't want to put you in danger."

Jackie looked sadly at the empty gym floor. "We never found Aaeesha's treasure." She had started to fade again. Memories were sucking at her like the drain in a bathtub. She gripped the arms of the chair to keep her head from spinning.

"And you can't remember what it is?" her friend asked.

"Huh? Remember what?" Jackie said, blinking.

"Aaeesha's treasure. You can't remember what it is?" he asked again.

"Oh that... um... No, but I would have recognized it. It was more important than all those boxes combined. I hope I didn't throw it out."

In front of her, Milly was spinning on the gym floor with her hands spread wide. "Look at me, Grandma, I'm getting dizzy."

Jackie allowed a wry smile. "I see sweetie. I get dizzy a lot."

"Come do it with me!" Milly shouted with glee.

"No pumpkin. I get dizzy enough just sitting here," she said sadly.

Milly wobbled drunkenly across the floor before plopping on her butt. She leaned her head back and laughed until everybody in the gymnasium was laughing with her. One of the young female analysts went over and spun with the child, laughing wildly.

"You have a wonderful family," Director Williams patted her on the arm. "I really enjoyed having you around here for a few days."

"Will I ever see you again?" Jackie asked.

"We'll stay in touch," the director promised.

"I might not recognize you the next time we see each other—this disease is a cruel master."

"But I'll know you," he said assuredly. "That's all that matters."

As the analysts cleaned up their computers, tables, and scanners, Jackie was drifting again. The memory was of her dark days—she was running from Abigail's death, angrily trying to make sense of the world, not caring if, maybe even hoping, she caught a bullet. Or was she lashing out?

She was doing the only thing she knew how to do—run down stories that nobody else was willing to write. Somewhere inside her, she still had a spark of decency. Buried under the landslide of despair and raw anger, the flicker of kindness burned dimly.

At the moment, she was once again sitting across the table from the bald hitman. "What ever happened to Antonio Jackson Randall, III?" she asked.

"You don't want to know," the man said, avoiding her eyes. "I sent you an email that the problem had been solved."

She had gotten so used to the rage, that it had become part of her. "I need to hear it from you. What happened?"

He shrugged. "He was a pilot. He owned a single engine Cessna. It seems that he had engine failure over the Rocky Mountains somewhere in Montana."

"Good." She was amazed at the vehemence that still boiled through her blood at the man who had killed her family.

"I need your services again. His name is Robert J. Young of Seattle," she said, sliding a picture across the table. "He's running a sex trafficking ring out of China." Three months ago, she'd gotten a tip from an informant. The operation she'd uncovered was staggering. In the process of digging out the dirt, she'd been shot at three times.

"Take it to the police," the man said, sliding the picture back.

"He's got a man on the force. Every time they try to take him down, he gets warned by his inside man. He makes all the evidence disappear." She slid the picture back across to him. "You're trying very hard to turn away business."

"Call the FBI," he demanded. "I understand that you're friends with Agent Reginald Williams." The picture now lay untouched on the table between them.

"I'm really pissed at Williams right now. I hold the FBI responsible for the death of my daughter and husband."

He sighed and sat back. "Jackie, I've known you since before Jesus was in diapers. You're a good person. Then your family gets killed as the result of one of your operations. You are blame shifting—the FBI isn't responsible for their deaths. Randall was."

Rage once again boiled. She was about to yell at him but caught herself, remembering that she was in a public restaurant.

She pounded the picture with her index finger, her voice an angry whisper. "If this guy is dead, then the cops can roll up the whole operation—everybody from Shanghai to Vancouver to Seattle."

"Jackie, what's happening to you?"

She held her face in her hands. "I… I don't know. I'm all messed up inside."

They sat in silence listening to the clink of forks on plates coming from the rest of the diners. She looked up from her introspection. "So, will you take the job?" She pushed the picture to the killer once more.

He nodded solemnly. "It'll be my last job. Then I'm going to go live on a beach and drink cold margaritas and dance all night with hot señoritas. I'm too old for this shit." His eyes searched her face. "Wanna come along?"

She shook her head.

"Still too angry at the world?"

She answered by pushing a Ziploc bag of gold coins across the table at the man. "Kill Young," she demanded. "It will save a lot of girls from sexual slavery."

He opened the bag and held one of the coins up to the light. "Damn," he muttered half to himself. He looked at Jackie. "This is some serious coinage. If it's what I think it is…this is a 1907 Proof Double Eagle."

"Do the job," Jackie glowered. "It's worth more than you think."

"Where did you get it?" he asked.

"Aaeesha…she was my best friend as a child. She left me her life savings—her treasure. She told me to use it to make the world a better place."

"So, you're using it to fund a murder?" he asked incredulously.

"Just do it!" she shouted. She was seething that the man was trying so hard to avoid what needed to be done.

Startled by her own outburst and anger, she looked around to see if anybody had noticed. Guests and wait staff were looking at her, mouths agape.

She gathered her pocketbook and slung her coat over her arm. She stood and threw a twenty on the table for the waitress.

Through clenched teeth she leaned into the hitman's face and whispered. "Don't give me a morality lesson. Just do the job!"

She turned to leave and a thought hit her.

She wheeled back on the man and grabbed the front of his shirt. "And this time," she snarled in his grill, "you'd better not tell anybody who hired the hit."

Jackie stomped through the crowd of startled restaurant patrons and stormed out into the bleak night.

"Jackie?" She was jerked back to the present by somebody shaking her shoulder. She looked up and found that the gymnasium was empty except for her easy chair, her family, and Warren. "It's time to go." Katrice was the one shaking her shoulder.

"I was drifting again, wasn't I?" she said sadly. "How long was I gone?" She looked up at the pity in Katrice's eyes.

"A little while. Not too long."

"You're not a very good liar, Katrice," Jackie said sadly. She sighed. "Help me up, would you please?"

Katrice hooked her hands under Jackie's arms and lifted her to her feet.

"How many people have I killed?" Jackie asked her daughter-in-law.

"We're about to leave; do you have to go to the bathroom? I'll help you again."

Jackie nodded. "Yeah, I need to go. There's going to be a special place in heaven for you," she said to Katrice, "and a special place in hell for me."

CHAPTER THIRTY-ONE

Jackie snuggled in beside Milly and her new book. They were at the Willard Hotel across the street from the White House. Jackie knew the manager from her days on 16th street. Of course, back then, the manager had just been a clerk.

The manager gave them the suite at half the normal price. But still, one night's stay at the Willard cost more than the average person made in two weeks.

The suite was beyond decadent. Gilded molding and gold leaf adorned the ceilings. Chandeliers were suspended on gold chains. The furniture rivaled the settees found in the White House across the street. Even the beds were outfitted in pure silk.

Jackie had gone through her sundowning on the van ride from the Hoover building to the Willard. She'd gritted her teeth the whole time and tapped her toes trying to release the anxiety. By now, she'd calmed down a bit and was mostly through the event.

From the room, they could see that the lights had just come up on the White House lawn. Charles was standing at the window with his hands in his pockets. "Ma, I've gotten to see a whole new side of you this week," he sighed. "On the one hand, this has been the worst week in my life—what with you getting firebombed and terrorists trying to kill us. But on the other hand, I've never felt so alive." He was looking out the window as he talked.

He turned back to his mom. "I always knew that you worked in the White House and were friends with famous people. But I never really knew what you did until I started digging through all your boxes." He shook his head. "You really did a lot of good for a lot of people."

She started to tell him about the people she'd killed and the lives she'd ruined but decided against it. She knew she would sound like a bitter old woman.

"You're a hero to all those analysts at the FBI. And then there was that lady that came downstairs to thank you..." He turned back to the window. "Why does it take a week of violence for me to really get to know my own mother?"

Jackie turned sideways so she could launch herself to her feet without help this time. She went up behind Charles and hugged him. She laid her head against his back. "It's my fault," she whispered. "I pushed you away and held walls of secrets between us. I never let you in."

He turned around and held her in a full hug. "Ma, you keep beating yourself up. You did the best you could. You made a lot of mistakes, but you also did a lot of good."

The phone in Charles' pocket rang. Jackie held her son tight.

"I gotta answer this, Ma."

"Let somebody else fix the world tonight," Jackie said. "I'm tired, and I want my family."

Charles shook himself free and reached into his pocket. "Interesting. I don't recognize that number." He hit the button. "Hello? This is Dr. Charles Scott."

"What? Oh my... Yes... Really? Where? Alright, we'll be right there." He hung up the phone.

Warren, who had been reading a novel written in Japanese, stood. "Who was that, and where do you think you're going?" he demanded. Jackie noted that the man could do a very good imitation of a pitbull.

"That was a nurse from Sibley Memorial Hospital. It seems that they've just admitted a young lady into the ER. She's been beaten badly—she's sustained a kidney rupture. She's in surgery now. She gave them my phone number before they put her under."

"So?" Warren demanded. "They've got doctors, why are they calling you?"

"It's Marna."

CHAPTER THIRTY-TWO

"Who's Marna?" Jackie asked. The exhaustion and mental concentration of the past two days caused the fog to swirl thickly in her brain. Looking around the room, Jackie realized that she didn't know the name of a single person.

The mention of the name Marna had triggered something inside Jackie. It was compassion. She didn't know how, but she knew it was someone she loved.

"Marna is the woman that you sometimes call Abigail," the man by the window told Jackie. She remembered the man was her son, Charles. Names slowly came back to her.

Jackie realized her face was wet. It was so frustrating, knowing that her mind was turning to oatmeal.

"And Abigail is in trouble," she said, thoughts fighting hard to align themselves.

"Rodney beat her. She's in surgery," Charles said. "She needs our help."

"Abigail has a drinking problem," Jackie said as another thought fell into place. She looked at Warren with a murderous glare. "You gave her wine. She got a taste and crashed her life."

The big genius nodded as streaks of embarrassment ran up his neck.

"Who was that friend that you saved from the drinking problem?" Katrice asked, fishing in her pocket for the card and squinting at it. "Um... Julie Perez," she read. "She'll know how to help."

"That's her," Jackie said, her mind beginning to come back to life. "Call her and tell her that we need that favor." She stood. "I need to go help Abigail. She's hurt. She's in the hospital."

She stopped. "On second thought, the hospital won't be the place for the woman who can help... um... Julie. She should come to the house after Abigail comes home."

"I'll stay here with the kids," Katrice said.

"No," Warren answered. "We still don't know if we're safe yet. We have to stay together—I have to protect you. Director's orders."

Katrice pinched the bridge of her nose. "Um... okay. We don't know how long we'll be at the hospital. Maybe the kids can sleep in the waiting room." She looked longingly around the fancy hotel room. "This place was so nice," she sighed.

Jackie was still spinning from her senior moment. "What do we do?" she asked, confused.

"We'll take some blankets and pillows," Katrice said. "The kids didn't have time to get pajamas when we left the house two days ago, so they'll just sleep in their clothes."

"We're all a little grungy," Charles said. "But we'll manage."

Given their lack of luggage, it only took them a few minutes to get ready. They went downstairs. Jackie told her manager friend what was going on and that they'd borrowed a few pillows and blankets for the kids. Within minutes, they were headed for Sibley.

After arriving at the hospital and parking, it took thirty minutes to find the waiting room for the O.R. The tribe trooped into the small, florescent-lit room and settled in. Milly was already asleep in Charles' arms, so he laid her out across a couple chairs for a makeshift bed.

Chucky was trying hard to keep his eyes awake, so he leaned up against Jackie while she read him one of Milly's stories. He had to turn the pages himself because of Jackie's bandaged hands.

Jackie's voice filled the little room, as three Billy goats tried to cross a bridge. Jackie knew the frustration those goats must have faced. In her gut, she feared that perhaps she'd taken a hit out on the troll sometime in past history.

She read until Chucky's head dropped into her lap, and his little hands let the book fall. Milly woke when the book hit the floor. She crawled onto the seat beside Katrice, and, laying her curls in her mother's lap, snuggled under a warm blanket. Within seconds, the girl was asleep again. For a moment, the group sat in silence—Jackie's mind still wondering if she'd killed the troll.

Warren cleared his throat. It sounded like a thunderclap in the tiny, white room. "I um…" He looked like he was choking on a brick. He tried to start again. "I um… I have something I need to say." Red was creeping up his neck. He looked down at the children. He seemed to gain strength from their innocent forms.

"What is it?" Jackie prompted. She really wished she could remember the man's name. But she felt an attachment to him. Although the name was gone, she remembered the person. That was the important thing.

"I've always been the tough guy and the smart guy. But I've been those things to hide the emptiness inside." He looked out the door of the little waiting room, and Jackie saw him blink back the emotion.

"Over the past few days, I've gotten to be a part of this family." He breathed to calm himself. "And I know you have your differences, but what you've got is damned precious."

"I guess you know that my mom cheated on dad, and I'm the product. Dad was Italian and very dark. It was obvious to everyone that I wasn't his biological son. Having a blond little boy running around his house irked him to no end. He wound up taking it out on me with his fists."

He paused, blinking for a full thirty seconds—his eyes were pointed out the waiting room door, but they weren't focused on anything. He gestured toward eight-year-old Chucky. "When I was eight, I would go to school with black and blue eyes. I'd always have to tell the teacher that I ran into a doorknob. Later on, Dad learned how to hit me so that the bruises wouldn't show."

Jackie placed a hand on his knee. Through her bandages, she could feel him quivering. "I told you earlier that I joined the Marines right out of high school, before I went to college. What I didn't tell you is that I haven't been back home since I left, not for Mom's birthdays and not even for Christmas." He sighed. "I swore that I'd never have a family."

He shook his head. "Then I was forced to live in the middle of your family for days." He slowly turned his head, looking into Jackie's, Charles', and Katrice's eyes. "Now I understand why people have families."

Jackie was about to speak, but he cut her off with a glance. "Then I screwed it up for you. I bought that wine for Marna fully knowing the risk." He looked at his big hands. "I think I was subconsciously trying to sabotage myself and a possible relationship. I wound up torpedoing the whole family. Look at you now. You're sitting in a hospital waiting for a woman to recover—a woman you've only known for a week. You care enough about her to waste your night in a waiting room."

He wrung his hands. "And you still treat me like I'm a friend."

"We're not all that great," Jackie countered. "You don't know the things I've done."

Warren laughed. "I know none of you are perfect. Charles is always trying to please his mother, but she never seems to notice. Jackie doesn't trust her son because she doesn't think he's mature enough to handle sensitive information. Katrice first married Charles for the money, but over the years she's grown to love him more than life itself—and both Jackie and Charles are too self-absorbed to notice the change." He chuckled afresh. "I get it; you're a Frankenstein family that has lots of warts and flaws. But you're a family, and you stick together, even to help a friend."

Jackie stared at the floor; she couldn't look into anybody's eyes. She didn't know she was that transparent. She was paralyzed thinking of the other things Warren may have seen.

"And I torpedoed everything." He scratched the back of his neck in embarrassment. "I just wanted to say I'm sorry. I'll do anything to fix it."

Before anyone could respond, a doctor stepped into the room breaking the mood. He seemed to sense tension and looked from face to face. He cleared his throat and meekly asked. "Is someone here for Marna Hunt?"

"Yes," said a chorus of four adult voices.

"I'm doctor Saeed," the dark-skinned man said. "Marna has come through surgery just fine. She'll be in recovery for another ten minutes or so before she starts coming around. I'll allow one person in to visit her."

"My maiden name was Saeed," Jackie said. "I was born in Iraq."

He smiled broadly at her. "We are a big family—perhaps we are kin."

"Mom, you're the one that needs to be there when she wakes up," Charles said. "We'll all wait here."

She nodded and Warren helped her to her feet, catching Chucky's head in his big hand. The child sighed and settled down to sleep again.

"You need to keep track of me, Doc," Jackie said, walking toward the doctor. "I have dementia and get confused. One time I got lost and drove all the way to Harrisonburg."

"I'll personally put you beside her bed," he promised as he took her arm.

When Jackie walked into the recovery room and saw Marna's face, she began to cry. Her left eye was swollen shut, and there was a big cut on her lip. Five butterfly bandages decorated her face. There was an oxygen tube running under her nose, and another tube was going into her mouth. A machine beside the bed beeped with every heartbeat.

"Oh Abby, what have you done?" she sobbed, covering her mouth with a bandaged hand.

"She'll be fine, Mrs. Saeed," the doctor said. "The man gave her a good beating, but she'll recover as long as she doesn't go back to him."

"My married name was Scott," she said, correcting the man. "But my husband has passed."

"I'm so sorry. That must have been difficult."

But Jackie didn't notice the condolence. Her eyes were filled with Marna at the moment. "How bad is it?" she asked.

"We repaired her kidney. She'll be sore for a few weeks. I'll want to keep her overnight. I may let her go tomorrow, if there are no complications."

"Thank you, Doctor," she said softly. Her eyes never left Marna's face.

"Stay with her until she wakes," the doctor said. "Let the nurses know if you need anything."

As the doctor left, she heard him softly talking to one of the nurses. She heard the word, "dementia." The nurse nodded and he left.

Jackie stroked Marna's hair with her bandaged hand. "Oh, dear child," she whispered.

Before Marna's eyes opened, she began groaning. She rocked slightly on the gurney. "I'm here, Abigail," Jackie said softly. "You're safe now."

"Jackie?" she whispered with her eyes shut. She tried to reach her hand, but she didn't have the strength. "Am I fired?"

"Just rest, sweetie."

CHAPTER THIRTY-THREE

Jackie jerked awake as the shaft of sunlight hit her face. Her neck had the kind of kink that could only be removed by a steamroller and a team of construction workers with jackhammers. "Where am I?" she asked, sitting straight up in the chair. Fear laced her heart—she felt lost and disoriented.

Beside her, on a bed, was a young woman whose face was beaten badly. Her left eye was swollen shut. There were butterfly bandages on each cheek.

"Good morning, Jackie," the woman said through swollen lips.

"Who are you?" Jackie asked. "And, where am I?"

"We're in the hospital, and I'm Marna. Sometimes, you call me Abigail."

Jackie looked hard at the young woman. The face was too disfigured to recognize, but the voice sounded familiar.

"Abigail's dead," Jackie said.

"Do you remember last night?" Marna asked.

Jackie shook her head. "Did I do something wrong? Did I hurt you and send you to the hospital?"

"No," Marna whispered. "I'm the one that did something wrong. I ran out on you and went back to Rodney. He's the one that put me in the hospital."

"That snake," Jackie hissed.

"I told them that you were my mother," Marna said. "I hope that's okay."

Jackie sighed. "I guess your lie isn't too bad considering all the things I've done in my life."

"Ah, there you are." A pretty, young lady walked into the room. She had raven hair, just like Marna's. She was dressed in those pajamas that doctors and nurses like. "I see you're awake. Dr. Saeed said that the surgery went well. I'm Dr. Wright." She smiled brightly at Marna.

She came and shined a flashlight in Marna's good eye, felt her pulse, then pulled back the sheet to look at the incision. "Looks good from here. How are you feeling?"

Marna groaned. "I feel like I tried to stop a train with my face—and my chest."

"Good. A little humor. I like that," the little doctor said. "If things progress well, we'll send you home tomorrow. You'll have to walk around a bit later this afternoon—these nurses can be Nazis." She laughed a bit at her own humor. Jackie thought the laugh even sounded childish.

"I have to pee," Jackie said.

The child-looking doctor looked down at Jackie's bandaged hands. "Oh yes. You're Marna's mother. The rest of the family is in the waiting room. I'll show you."

The doctor helped her to her feet. "How old are you?" Jackie asked. "You look like a teenager."

"She has dementia. She sometimes says inappropriate things," Marna managed to say quietly from the side of her mouth that wasn't swollen. "Don't let her get lost."

The tiny doctor patted Jackie's arm. "I'll help you find your family."

"Thanks, Mom," Marna said. Jackie turned to see a tear slide down the side of her face. "Thanks for not giving up on me."

Jackie went back and kissed the top of her head. "You just get better."

The short, black-haired doctor took Jackie to a room where people were sleeping on benches. "Who are these people?" Jackie asked.

The man on the chair sat up straight. "Oh, hi Mom."

"She says she needs to use the restroom," the doctor said.

"I'll help her," the blonde woman said, sitting up straight and rubbing her eyes. She apparently saw the confusion on Jackie's face, because she said, "I'm Katrice, Ma. Your daughter-in-law."

Jackie blushed. "Sorry," she whispered. "I remember now."

Warren left the family long enough to raid a McDonalds for breakfast. He brought back enough food to feed a rugby team. Katrice fed Jackie her Egg McMuffin, and patiently wiped the crumbs from her face.

"Can we go back home today?" Katrice asked Warren. "I think the kiddos need baths and a fresh set of clothes."

"I don't see why not," Warren answered. "I'll go with you to check the place out first. But I would think the threat should have passed. The terrorists know that the FBI has all the data. The director said I'd have to stay with you for the rest of the month."

Jackie remembered that Marna fell off the wagon when Warren had taken her on that date. "You have to see her before you go," Jackie said sternly.

Jackie stepped into the corridor with Warren on her arm. She didn't remember which way to go, but Warren asked at the nurses' station.

When they stepped into Marna's room, Jackie could sense Warren's unease. She felt him shuddering at the sight of the pretty, young woman who had been beaten to a pulp. "Rodney was the man with the fists," Jackie told him. "But her real enemy is the alcohol."

Warren nodded with a pained expression on his face. She could see he felt guilty and ashamed. He timidly approached the bed and sat down on the chair to be eye level with the patient.

"Go away," Marna whispered. "I don't want you to see me like this." She tried to cover her face with her arm, but the IV limited her motion.

"You're beautiful no matter what's been done to your face," Warren said softly. "Your grace comes from within."

Marna rolled her head away from Warren. Jackie could tell she didn't believe a word he said. "Inside I'm a mess too," she said in her hoarse whisper.

"I know," he said honestly. "But you'll get better, I promise. And I'll keep checking on you to make sure you do." He found an unbruised spot on her arm to pat.

Jackie nodded as she watched the interaction—she was glad that the dementia hadn't killed her ability to observe. The tension between the two was palpable. There was embarrassment on both sides, guilt, and compassion. She could sense that Marna wanted to run and hide but was strapped down to her hospital bed by the weight of a simple IV.

For a moment, Jackie thought Warren was going to enfold Marna in his arms to protect her from the world. He stopped himself as he glanced at her injuries. But the guilt written on his face said that he saw himself as the monster that had driven the woman to her own downfall. Jackie knew that the mistake would haunt him. Underneath it all, she could feel that the sexual tension between the youngsters had been almost killed—what was left was the mustard seed of attraction. Jackie smiled to herself. Maybe if properly nurtured, the allure could bloom into a lifelong relationship.

"I'll hold you to that," Jackie said sternly. "She'll need a law officer to check up on her weekly."

He nodded seriously, totally missing Jackie's amusement. That was a good sign. "Yeah," he said. "I think that would be a good idea."

"I don't need anybody to check up on me," Marna protested weakly.

"She needs to get to her meetings once a week," Jackie said. "I might forget."

"I'll make sure she goes," Warren said.

"Leave me alone," Marna said, gaining enough strength to sound offended. "Why are you doing this to me?"

"It's what mothers do, sweetie." Jackie bent and kissed the top of the girl's head. "You're the one that told them I was your mom. Now you gotta live with the consequences." She stood and winked at Warren.

She saw him smile for the first time since he had confessed the night before.

CHAPTER THIRTY-FOUR

"It's over, isn't it?" Jackie asked. She laid her head back on the seat cushion. They had dropped Charles off at the hospital so that he could catch up on his work, which had piled up unmercifully. Katrice was behind them in Jackie's Mercedes with the children. Jackie was alone with Warren in the FBI's van.

Warren nodded his head. "I think it is," he said.

In her lap, Cassie snuggled warmly. The kids had squealed with delight and Cassie had run in circles when they picked her up from the kennel.

Now they were headed for Charles' mansion. A contractor had put plastic over the front of Jackie's bombed-out house, but Jackie didn't want to go back. She wanted to be with Charles and Katrice.

"You were right about the FBI having a leak," Warren repeated. "By now, the bad guys know you're no longer a threat."

Jackie was alert enough to realize that he'd made that statement multiple times. She figured that he was trying to convince himself.

"We never found Aaeesha's treasure," Jackie said sadly as she watched the trees fly by her passenger window. "It was important," she sighed. "I probably threw it out with the trash." She growled at herself. "I hate this disease."

They lapsed into silence, and Jackie started drifting.

Jackie's mind wandered back in time, reliving her visit with Saddam Hussein.

Who was that man she'd seen in the market place in Baghdad on that horrible day? She couldn't remember. She sighed. What did it matter? The past was gone, washed away in a river of fog.

CHAPTER THIRTY-FIVE

"Jackie?" Warren was shaking her arm. In her lap, Cassie stirred. "We're here."

"I was drifting again, wasn't I?" she asked, embarrassed.

"Just a little bit," he said. "At first, I thought you were sleeping, then I saw your eyes were open."

"I had a memory," she told him. "I remembered the time I had to talk to Saddam. It was right before the bombs fell in the second Gulf War."

"Wait here," he ordered.

He got out of the van and drew his Glock. Jackie waited as he walked around the house, looking for intruders.

She sighed. She was disappointed that people didn't believe her when she told them things. They just thought she was a senile, old lady. But then again, that's really what she was. She wanted to pound her head in frustration. *Stupid disease!*

Jackie saw Warren walk to the Mercedes that had followed them and ask Katrice for the keys to the house. He walked up the steps and unlocked the door. He leaned back against the house wall, and pushed the door open with his toe. He popped his head around the sill twice before entering.

Ten minutes later he came to the front door and waved everybody in. "Coast is clear," he called.

Jackie fumbled for the door handle, forgetting her bandages. She stopped, frustrated. "Help me," she called through the window glass to Katrice who was carrying Milly in her arms.

Katrice stopped and opened the door for her mother-in-law, then helped her out of the van. Cassie skittered into the yard, yapping happily. Milly wiggled out of her mother's arms and ran after Chucky and Cassie.

"Welcome home," Katrice said.

Overwhelmed by emotion, Jackie put a bandaged arm around Katrice. She couldn't even speak for a moment. She looked over at the marble statue of herself in the middle of the circle driveway and reflected on the petty argument it had caused. She felt ashamed.

Katrice, sensing her struggle, tugged Jackie toward the house. "You'll stay in the guest room. When Marna comes home from the hospital, she can stay with you. After that?" she shrugged. "We'll figure it out."

The next day, Jackie met a moving company at her bombed-out house in Vienna. She and the foreman walked through the house, finding the things that were worth saving. She hoped the scent of smoke hadn't permanently saturated everything, but after the past few days, she realized that these were just things.

She decided to throw out all her clothes—they weren't worth the effort to get them smoke free. She gathered her jewelry from her upstairs safe and her camera bag from the basement.

She also contacted a rug company. They came out and rolled up the Persian rug from her bedroom with a confident promise of removing the smoke smell.

The mover promised to carefully pack each item that she wanted saved and put it into climate-controlled storage, which was important in Virginia. If the storage wasn't climate-controlled, the heavy humidity would encourage black mold to grow thick, ruining everything.

In the afternoon, Katrice dropped the children and the dog at a friend's place. The two women headed to Tyson's Corner for a round of clothes shopping.

Charles called. Katrice put him on speakerphone so they could both hear.

"I called down to Sibley," he told them. "They want to keep Marna for another night. If all goes well, we can pick her up in the morning."

"She'll be disappointed," Katrice said. "I know she wanted to get out of there. We'll go by this evening to cheer her up."

"I'll have my sundowning this evening," Jackie reminded them. "I'll be a ball of nerves."

Katrice slapped her forehead. "I almost forgot. I was doing some reading about dementia and came across an idea called a *fidgeting quilt*. It should help with your sundowning. I ordered one, and it should be waiting for us at home."

"What's a fidgeting quilt?" Charles asked.

"It's a little blanket that can sit in Jackie's lap. There are lots of different types available, but the one I ordered for her has bows to tie, snaps, buttons and zippers. It gives her fingers something to do."

Jackie shrugged. "I'll give it a try."

CHAPTER THIRTY-SIX

Jackie was awakened to the sound of excited children. Marna stirred in the bed across the room. "Merry Christmas," Jackie said. She rolled to a sitting position, able to move her blankets by herself. She still remembered her bandaged hands. It had taken eight weeks to be free from her clubs, as she called her bandages.

In the twin bed on the other side of the room, she saw the top of Marna's head. Jackie did better at remembering Marna's name these days. Marna turned and opened a bleary eye at her charge. The woman's face was healing nicely. Jackie could still see the faint outlines of the scars, but the doctor had told her those would fade.

Cassie poked her head out from under the blanket and licked Jackie's elbow. "Hey, that tickles," Jackie laughed.

Jackie could tell that Cassie was torn. Half of her wanted to snuggle under the blankets again. The other half wanted to go play with the squealing children. And the third half wanted to go outside to pee.

"Make up your mind, silly dog," Jackie said out loud. "You have too many halves." She picked up the canine and hugged her tight. She was rewarded by some licks on her chin. "Come on. I'll take you outside."

At the magic word, outside, Cassie squirmed out of Jackie's arms and onto the floor. She bounced in circles.

Across the small room, Marna rolled to a sitting position. Her hair looked like it had been caught in a mini-tornado. "You'd better doll yourself up a little, Ab... I mean Marna," Jackie said. "Warren is coming over a little later."

Marna nodded and rubbed her eye with the heel of her hand. "You remembered. Good job," she said, trying to push a smile onto her sleepy face.

Jackie threw on a warm housecoat and opened the bedroom door. Cassie squirted out into the hallway and down the marble steps. Jackie fumbled her way to the front door and stepped into the cold. Cassie ran out, barking wildly at her new environment. "That's called snow Cassie," Jackie called, wishing she had on a warmer coat. "Hurry up before I freeze to death."

Cassie chased a squirrel up a tree before she settled down to do her business. Jackie was very glad to go back inside when the dog was done.

In the living room, Milly was crying because she had to wait to open the gifts. Katrice was trying to console her. Jackie saw Chucky leading Charles by the hand down the steps.

"Come on, Dad! It's Christmas!" He was bouncing so hard that Charles' arm was in danger of being dislocated.

Marna stumbled out of the guest room to descend the stairs right behind Charles. Jackie saw that, although she was still in her pajamas, she had made an attempt at taming her hair.

By the time everybody got to the living room, Milly had stopped crying. She crawled up into Jackie's lap with Cassie, while Charles read the Christmas story from Luke chapter 2.

They took turns opening presents.

Chucky opened a gift. "Star Wars Legos! Thanks Grandma!" He came over to give her a hug and show her his treasure.

"Did I give you this?" Jackie asked. "I don't remember."

"Yeah," he said. "It's cool!"

Jackie had apparently bought gifts for everyone, although she didn't remember. "Somebody must have been helping me," she laughed.

Katrice gave Jackie another fidgeting quilt. This was one she had made by hand. It had a patch of fuzzy cloth, which Jackie held to her cheek. "Mmmm… that feels nice," she said smiling.

Milly helped Cassie unwrap a chew bone. Cassie was in heaven.

Marna placed another box in Jackie's hand. "What's this?" Jackie asked. She carefully peeled the colorful paper away. She looked at the box, puzzled.

"It's a new camera," Marna told her. She came over and helped Jackie get it out of the box. "It's digital, and it's real simple to use. You don't have to remember the f-stops or aperture settings. You just point and click, but you can zoom in and out."

"Really?" Jackie asked, intrigued.

She turned it on and Marna showed her how it worked. She took a picture of Cassie with her chew bone, and was able to see the photo instantly.

"Wow," Jackie was amazed. "It's so simple. I think I just may be able to use it!" She felt a tear trying to escape her eye. "It's been so long since I've been able to take pictures."

"Can you take some pictures of me and Warren when he comes over today?" Marna asked shyly.

"I'd love to," Jackie said. She was already snapping photos of each person in the room.

"I have one more present for you, Mom," Charles said, taking a long tube from under the tree. "Actually, this one will affect Marna as well."

Marna helped Jackie unwrap the gift. "What is it?" Jackie asked, perplexed by the cardboard tube.

"There's something inside," Marna said. She reached in and pulled out a fat roll of paper.

"It's plans for your new cottage," Charles said. "We'll build it out back, so you and Marna will have your own place. But we'll be right here in case you need help."

Marna rolled out the blueprints. "Look, it's got an enclosed passageway," she said. "You can walk between the houses without going out in the weather."

"We thought of just adding onto this house," Katrice said. "But we thought it would be better if you had your own place."

Jackie was deeply moved. "I... I don't know what to say. This is so wonderful."

"Just say yes," Charles said, kissing his mother's cheek.

Jackie went to the kitchen with Katrice and tried to help get breakfast going. But she kept getting confused. "I don't think I'm being much help," she said, embarrassed.

"I'll help," Marna said, coming into the room. She had changed into jeans and a sweater. "You go play with the kids."

Warren arrived at ten. Under his leather cowboy jacket, he had a warm, green sweater. "You look so good that I'd eat you myself if Marna didn't have dibs on you," Jackie said, winking.

Warren blushed.

"Behave yourself, Jackie," Marna said, coming down the steps.

Jackie turned. Marna had changed out of her jeans. She had on a Christmas dress that would have been fit for a princess. It was a red little number that showed a lot of leg and an acre of cleavage. Jackie didn't realize how long her hair had gotten over the past few months, but it was now cascading over her left breast. Her black heels complemented the outfit.

Beside her, Jackie heard Warren swallowing hard.

Jackie jabbed Warren in the ribs with her elbow. "You payin' attention, young man?" she asked conspiratorially.

"Holy cow," Warren whispered in reply.

Marna sashayed down the stairs and pirouetted in front of Warren. "You like?" she asked coyly.

"Me like," Warren agreed. "Me like very mucho."

After lunch, Julie Perez dropped by. "Julie!" Marna called. She ran to the door and gave the woman a hug.

"You staying clean?" Julie asked in her schoolmarm voice.

"Yup," Marna announced proudly. "Three months sober, going on a lifetime."

"Good," Julie said. "Christmas can be a tough time. Call if you're tempted."

Julie came to the house every week to pick up Marna for their AA meeting. She had been beside Marna every step of the way—even through Rodney's trial. Marna complained quietly that Julie was a Nazi, but Jackie could tell that the girl appreciated the attention and the help.

The kids wanted to go sledding, so Katrice and Charles took them to a neighborhood hill that was popular with the little ones.

"Time for the photos," Marna said, bouncing with joy. She cleared out the mess of torn wrapping paper in front of the Christmas tree and plopped Warren down. She then crawled into his lap and kissed his cheek dramatically, while Jackie flashed the shutter on her new DSLR.

Jackie was thrilled to be behind the lens again. Her eye instinctively saw the lighting and captured the mood. Things came back to her that she'd forgotten for years. In front of her, Warren and Marna put on a show.

"Oh no, the battery's dead," Jackie said as the camera clicked off.

"I got you a spare," Marna reached into Jackie's camera bag for the new battery. "We need to get you a new bag too, Jackie," she said. "This one has a hole in it."

"That's a bullet hole," Jackie answered. "I got that hole in Beirut. That was the day I took a photo series that stopped a war."

Marna was reaching for the battery, but her hand came out with something else. "What's this key for?" she asked, holding it up.

Jackie sucked in a breath. Suddenly, everything came back to her. "That..." she said, gently taking the key from Marna's hand. "That is the key to Aaeesha's treasure."

CHAPTER THIRTY-SEVEN

Marna and Warren stared at her in disbelief. "You mean you didn't make that up?" Warren asked.

"It was in your camera bag the whole time?" Marna said.

"I guess it was," Jackie replied.

"But wait," Marna said, confused. "You always said that Aaeesha's treasure was the key. But what you really meant was that this is the key to Aaeesha's treasure." She held up the gold colored key in the light.

"Yes… I mean. No." Jackie held her head in her hand. Her moment of lucidity was trying to slip away. Then her mind cleared. She took the key from Marna's hand. "This is the key to Aaeesha's treasure. But Aaeesha's treasure is the key to the other thing. You know. The big thing."

Warren started to say something, but Jackie held up her hand. "Let me think. It's all here in my head right now, and I don't want it to slip away." She tapped her fingers on her knee for a moment.

"Today is some sort of special day, right? Everything is closed today."

"It's Christmas," Marna said.

"Right. They're closed today. But tomorrow they'll be open."

She puzzled how to handle the problem. "Call my lawyer," she said. "We need to meet him at ten o'clock tomorrow morning. He needs to bring an armed security guard with him."

Marna nodded. She pulled out her phone and made a note. "Where are we meeting?"

"Commonwealth Vault in Ashburn, VA," Jackie answered. "Everything is under lock and key. They have my name on file." She was amazed how seeing the key had unlocked this section of her brain. She felt like her former self. "We need to call the vault company and reserve a conference room for tomorrow morning."

Marna wrote another note.

"Then I need to have Senator Turner and Director Williams meet me at eleven o'clock. Warren, you will be at that part of the meeting."

"There's no way that they'll drop everything on a moment's notice," Warren said. "They're busy men."

"If you tell them that I've found Aaeesha's treasure, both men will be there in a heartbeat," Jackie answered. "They know how important this is. Trust me on that. They've both been waiting for this."

"Do you want me there?" Marna asked.

"Of course, darling," Jackie patted her knee. "You need to be at both of the meetings."

She thought for a moment. "Warren, are you armed?"

"Of course." Warren pulled up his sweater and showed his Glock. "I've also got a .38 strapped to my ankle."

"Good," she said. "We're under threat again. Call Charles and tell him to come back home right away."

"Should we go to a hotel again?" Warren asked.

"Um. Yes. That's a good idea."

"Should I call the director and the senator now?" Marna asked her voice was tinged with fear.

"No. Wait until we are at the hotel. Remember that the FBI has a leak. And we don't want to tell anybody where we are. Nobody."

Marna made more notes in her phone.

"Abigail, where is my .45?"

"We sold it," Marna said. "We didn't want it in the house with the children."

She thought for a moment. "That's okay. I think I have another one in the box."

"What if you're having a bad day tomorrow?" Marna asked with concern in her voice.

"Then I'll likely die," Jackie said gravely.

CHAPTER THIRTY-EIGHT

Jackie sat at the desk in the small conference room. On the way in, the guard had shown Marna and Warren the steel that comprised the facility. "This is six-inch steel that's concrete reinforced," the man said proudly. "It would stop a tank."

Jackie had seen tanks in action and wasn't quite sure. But she didn't say anything.

Katrice and the children were enjoying the morning at the Willard Hotel across the street from the White House. Since their previous visit had been cut short the night that Marna had landed in the hospital, Jackie decided to treat them to a repeat stay.

"How are you doing?" Marna asked, patting her hand and jerking her back to the present. The youngster was seated in the chair on her left. Across from them, another pair of chairs awaited the coming visitors.

"As long as I keep the key in my hand, I'm good," Jackie said.

Outside the room, the facility guard stood. Warren also stood with his back to the door. He had pulled himself to his hulking size, making the Glock on his hip look small.

"It's the physical connection to a memory-inducing item," Marna said.

Jackie remembered that they were talking about the key. She looked around the small, institutional room. It was tiny and cramped, and the florescent lights gave Jackie a headache.

"I don't understand," Marna said to Jackie. "You've been looking for Aaeesha's treasure all this time. Now you've found it. Is her treasure so important that people would kill for it?"

Jackie shook her head. "Aaeesha's treasure is very valuable in two ways—monetarily and sentimentally. It's the only tangible item by which I can remember my friend. It is also going to change your life." Jackie patted Marna's hand, ignoring the puzzled look on the young woman's face. Under the table, Jackie felt the tattered backpack that was sitting in the vault box at her feet.

"But Aaeesha's treasure was the one item that I could remember, so I stored my most important documents here in the same vault. My hope was that I'd be able to remember Aaeesha's treasure, thereby remembering these important documents as well. It's these documents that the killers are after."

"So, Aaeesha's treasure was sort of like a mental bookmark," Marna said.

Jackie nodded. "Yes, but it was a mental cue that I nearly lost." Jackie shook her head again. "I came this far from forgetting everything." She held up her thumb and forefinger to indicate a sliver of light.

"What did you mean that Aaeesha's treasure is going to change my life?" Marna asked.

"The lawyer needs to hurry up before my mind slips away," Jackie complained.

As if on cue, she saw her lawyer through the glass of the door. She waved him in with her hand. Behind him came a rent-a-cop. She saw the gun on the man's hip.

Jackie reached her hand under the table into the security box and pulled out the heavy backpack and placed it in her lap.

The door opened and her lawyer walked in, trailed by his rent-a-cop. "This is Doug." The lawyer motioned toward the rent-a-cop who was warily eyeing Warren. Although Doug was big, he looked tiny next to the Fed. Doug was very dark-skinned. Jackie's mind wanted to drag her back to Africa, but she wrestled the thoughts under control.

"I'm Thurmond Wine." The lawyer held out his hand to Marna. They shook hands. "Good to see you again, Jackie," he said, shaking her hand as well.

"Sit down, please, Thurmond," Jackie said.

The man sat. He was a short man, barely five-and-a-half feet. But he was impeccably dressed, in a tailored suit.

"London?" Jackie asked, gesturing at his suit.

"Rome," he corrected. "I like their silks better."

She smiled.

Doug, the rent-a-cop, stood in the corner where he could keep an eye on the table and also see Warren through the glass door.

"Thanks for coming," Jackie said as she pulled the backpack out of her lap and onto the table. Nobody noticed that she'd pulled the 1911 pistol out of the backpack and allowed it to drop into her lap.

She knew it was loaded with .45 ACP rounds. She knew from experience how devastating it could be to a human head. Her smile remained steady as she fingered the gun. She jiggled the backpack with her left hand to cover the sound of the hammer falling to the cocked position. She left the safety locked in place.

The backpack on the table was obviously old. It had several tears and rips through the army-green canvas. Some of the holes looked suspiciously like bullet holes. It was utilitarian in design and lacked a modern aluminum support frame. It had ancient, dried blood splatters on it.

"This is Aaeesha's treasure," Jackie said. She tipped the bottom of the bag up, and hundreds of gold coins fell out its mouth.

The room was silent as Marna, Thurmond, and Doug, the rent-a-cop, stared in awe. Warren, who was outside the door, caught sight of the gold and stared agape. He then composed himself and retook his stance of vigilance.

The gold coins were tarnished and dusty. It was clear that some were worn and almost unidentifiable.

"Please read this aloud. This is a report I wrote on the day that my best friend, Aaeesha, died," Jackie said, pulling a report from the manila envelope that she had taken from the box.

Thurmond took the paper and began reading:

> March 21, 2003

> The report that was submitted to my editor is a heavily edited account of the events that transpired over the past two days. This report, the real one, can never be published until after my death.

> Two months ago, I was sent by my publisher to Baghdad to cover the impending invasion by U.S. forces. Unknown to my publisher, I was also tasked with a mission from President George W. Armstrong, to be an unofficial backdoor conduit to Saddam Hussein. It was the hope of President Armstrong that this effort could avoid the second Gulf war.

> Since I was in Baghdad, I decided to stay at the home of my childhood friend, Aaeesha Aswad. Her husband, Aakav, was a high-ranking member of Saddam Hussein's government.

> Yesterday, at 5:34 AM local time, I was awakened by the sound of jet engines, anti-aircraft gunfire, and explosions. I ran to the roof of our building and began photographing the huge fireball in the center of the city. Later, I learned that the fire was the result of a U.S. air strike on Saddam Hussein's Presidential Palace.

> The bombing was proof that my attempts at diplomacy had failed.

> As I photographed, I began hearing small arms fire in the streets. Although the shooting was several blocks away, I ran down to Aaeesha's apartment in time to see Aakav rushing out the door. He told Aaeesha that he would be needed to help restore order to the chaos. He instructed

Aaeesha to gather their grandchild and their belongings and flee to her mother's home in Al-Falluja.

Minutes after he left, we heard gunfire right outside the building. We ran to the window and saw that Aakav was lying dead by the door of his car. I learned later that Aakav had been accused of treason by Saddam himself—somehow being blamed for the U.S. bombing raid. My personal feeling is that Aakav had been killed because he had the audacity to keep me in his home. I believe that Saddam was angry with me and had sent the Palace Guard to kill Aakav and his family in retaliation.

Still standing at the window, Aaeesha was paralyzed by the sight of her husband lying in a pool of his own blood. I saw that soldiers were running into the front of the apartment building below us. I surmised that they were heading up to kill us.

I snatched the baby from the crib, grabbed the backpack of Aaeesha's family treasure, my camera equipment, and the handgun that Aakav had kept in the cupboard above the kitchen sink. I pushed Aaeesha out the apartment door, and we ran to the back stairway. By this time, Aaeesha was functioning enough that I was able to hand the baby to her.

In all my years as a photojournalist, I never had the need to kill another with my own hand. But when that soldier rounded the corner of the stairwell, I shot him in the forehead.

Aaeesha and I hurdled the soldier's dead body. We continued to the ground floor, and I shot another commando who burst through the back entrance. We ran out the back and jumped into her car—she was in the passenger seat cradling the baby who was now crying.

I got the car to the street, but the soldiers spotted us and opened fire. The car was riddled with automatic gunfire and all of the windows disintegrated. I continued for five blocks before I realized that Aaeesha and the infant were dead—murdered by the bastard dubbed The Butcher of Baghdad.

The car engine seized and refused to roll another inch. I did the only thing that I knew to do; I took a photo of Aaeesha clutching her dead grandchild to her own bullet-strewn chest. I then reached over and closed her eyelids for the final time.

Looking through the shattered back window of the dead Mercedes, I saw that the soldiers were running my direction. I abandoned my friend's body, taking her backpack with me—hoping to turn over the treasure to Aaeesha's mother. But I have now learned that her mother was also killed in retaliation for Aakav's alleged treason.

Today I worked up the courage to open the bullet-ridden backpack. In it, I found that Aaeesha left me a note. She said, "If I don't make it, use this to make the world a better place."

Thurmond finished reading the report. It was as if the air had been forced out of the room. Even Doug, the rent-a-cop, was wiping his eyes. The silence was almost deafening.

Jackie slid the photo of Aaeesha out of the envelope. It was black and white, making the scene even starker. Blood seeped through the woman's breast and ran down her abaya. In her arms, the infant was forever stilled. Aaeesha's eyes stared into eternity, and there was a look of permanent horror on her face. She was sitting in the passenger seat of the bullet-riddled car. Beyond the shattered window, the empty, dusty streets of Baghdad could be seen.

Jackie realized that her hands were shaking, and beside her, Marna was weeping softly.

"Thurmond, I've done some terrible things in my life," Jackie said, breaking the silence. "But in the past few months, I've made things right with God and with my family. I've accepted that I am a soul undone, but I've also accepted my forgiveness—or at least I've done the best I can to get my soul right." She stirred her hand around in the pile of gold on the table. She sighed. "Aaeesha wanted me to use this to make the world a better place." She shrugged. "I don't know if I made it better or not."

She pulled herself together—memories were trying to pull her under. She fingered the key to the security box, and that brought her mind back to the present. She suddenly couldn't remember the lawyer's name. "Get out your notepad, please. I need you to write down my instructions."

The man composed himself enough to open his briefcase. He wiped his eyes and blew his nose loudly in a white handkerchief. Pushing the soiled linen back into his pocket, he pulled out a notepad and a pen. He nodded that he was ready.

Jackie cleared her throat. "My son, Charles, is going to inherit my estate. He is well cared for."

She tapped the pile of gold. "This gold is to be sold and the proceeds are to be deposited into a custodial account for Abig…" She stopped herself. "I mean, Marna Hunt." Beside her, Marna gasped. Jackie continued talking to the lawyer. "You will be the trustee. She is to use it for her further education. She needs a doctorate degree—from an Ivy League university of her choice. Any remaining funds may be used to purchase a house or for the education of her children."

"Jackie…" Marna's protest was cut off with a wave of Jackie's hand.

"Here." Jackie picked up a coin and firmly placed it into Marna's hand. She slid the photo and the report over to the young woman sitting beside her. "Keep these items. You will remember Aaeesha forever. She gave her life so that you could be educated. Make your life's journey worthy of the honor."

The blood had drained from Marna's face. She tried to speak, but no words left her lips.

"Anything else?" the lawyer asked.

"Oh yeah. One other thing," Jackie said. "If Marna ever drinks again, she is to be cut off from the funds." Inside, Jackie was fighting off the swirling memories. She wanted to get this right if it was the last thing she'd ever do.

Thurmond nodded and wrote down the instructions. "I'll have this typed up and bring a copy for you to sign," he said. "And I assume you want me to take the gold with me?"

Jackie nodded. "Thank you," she said. "I'm sorry. I forgot your name already."

He chuckled quietly. "I'm Thurmond. When you called, I thought you were in trouble again. I'm glad to do something like this for you, my friend."

He stood and held out his hand. Jackie shook it. Then they all helped to scoop the coins into the backpack. The lawyer handed the bag to Doug.

"Wait," Jackie said. "Give me one of the coins. I want to have something to remember my friend, Aaeesha."

Doug scooped out one and handed it over. It was a British Gold Sovereign dated 1853.

"Perfect. Thanks," Jackie smiled. "Make sure this man gets paid well today," Jackie instructed the lawyer. She couldn't remember rent-a-cop's name either.

The two left, leaving Marna and Jackie alone. Marna hugged Jackie and wept. "Thank you," she said. "I never expected anything like that."

"I know," Jackie answered. "Stay sober and make me proud."

"I will." Marna meekly nodded and wiped her eyes.

Jackie pushed Marna away. "You have to pull yourself together. Our next meeting will be dangerous." She showed Marna the Smith and Wesson in her lap. "This is the gun that I used to escape Saddam's men. It was Aaeesha's husband's gun."

"They're here," Marna said, looking up from Jackie's lap.

Jackie wrapped her right hand around the pistol with her thumb on the safety. With her left hand, she motioned the FBI director and the senator into the room.

"Help me stay alert," she whispered to Marna. "This is one of the most important moments of my waning life."

When the door opened, she called into the hallway. "Warren, would you please come in too?"

Warren followed the two men into the room. She caught Warren's eye and tried to give a look of warning. He gave an almost imperceptible nod in acknowledgement. He went and stood in the left corner, his Glock in his hand.

"Gentlemen, have a seat," Jackie said. "Thanks for coming out on such short notice. And especially on the day after the um... holiday... You know...."

"Christmas," Marna prompted.

"Oh yeah. The day after Christmas," Jackie said.

She could feel the tension between the two men. Nothing had changed since high school; they were still friends and still enemies. Monroe thought himself superior, and Reginald wore green eyes. Under the table, she switched the gun to her left hand, and extended her right to accept their greetings. She did not rise as they sat.

"As both of you know, I have dementia. I forget a lot of things. But yesterday I found the key to Aaeesha's treasure."

Director Williams forced a smile. "That's amazing. What was it?"

She waved her hand dismissively. "Aaeesha's treasure wasn't all that important to you. But it was the key to unlocking my memory about the other important things. And that's why you gentlemen are here."

She leaned under the table, reaching into the security box at her feet, and pulled out a stack of manila envelopes. Each packet had the name of a U.S. President. She slid them across the table. "I am going to entrust these packets to the FBI for future keeping. If these documents were to reach the public, entire sections of our history would have to be rewritten."

"You have dirt on every sitting President?" Monroe Turner asked.

She nodded. "Apparently the ones that were sitting while I worked the White House." She pointed at her head. "It's not in this bowl of alphabet soup anymore, but fortunately, I wrote it down." She tapped the stack. "The only thing I remember now is that this stuff is really important."

The men looked at her expectantly, saying nothing. Each man leaned over the table hanging on her every word. For a moment, she thought that maybe they'd forgotten their own animosity.

She sighed. "But that's not the reason that you two gentlemen dropped everything to come see a senile, old lady."

They continued staring, saying nothing. "Seriously gentlemen, this stuff is more important than anything else I have to offer. These documents would change the history books." She pushed them further across the table, but both men refused to touch the packets. "They aren't toxic," she said.

Jackie hadn't prayed much in her life. But now, she breathed a prayer. "Help me. Please help me stay sane until this is done." She squeezed the key until it left jagged imprints in her fingers. The pain helped.

Both men knew what she had in the box under the table—they sat on the edges of their chairs. She caught Warren's eye to warn him. He nodded back and tapped his Glock with his index finger.

Jackie knew she was running on fumes. Any second and her brain would turn into mashed potatoes again. She gripped the key and ground the jagged edges into her finger. She bit her lip—the pain keeping her lucid.

Jackie reached down into the box and retrieved the final two packets. She slid them onto the table. The one on the left had the name, Reginald Williams. The one on the right had the name, Monroe Turner.

Jackie's head was swimming. She blinked back the dementia. "Marna, would you please read these reports?" She was proud that she'd gotten the girl's name right.

Marna selected the envelope with Director William's name. She slid it to herself and opened the packet. She opened it far enough to look inside, then retrieved the report laying on top. She began reading.

September 8, 1997

One month ago, today, I responded to the home of Senator Gregory Tillman. My initial report told me that the Senator had been murdered. I arrived to find that Agent Reginald Williams was in charge of the crime scene. Agent Williams lived only a block away and personally knew the family. From what I gathered, after the murder, Senator Tillman's wife called Williams instead of the police. Williams, in turn, called 911 after arriving and took charge of the scene personally.

The senator's body was found in a state of partial dress—he was wearing only an undershirt and his briefs. He was lying dead in the upstairs hallway, right outside his thirteen-year-old daughter's bedroom door. He had been shot once in the stomach and a second time through the heart. According to the coroner, he died within seconds.

The story that Mrs. Agatha Tillman gave to the police was that there had been an intruder. Her proposed theory was that the gunman entered the home in retaliation for legislature that the Senator had championed. She also claimed that the bruise on her left cheek was delivered by the intruder as she tried to defend her husband. She claimed that the gunshot residue found on her hands was due to the fact that she was wrestling with the intruder as he fired at her husband.

My curiosity was piqued, because the daughter had never been interviewed by the authorities. Even as a minor, she could have possibly had pertinent information on the case.

At one point in the evening, Agent Williams left the scene. I followed him discretely and photographed him throwing an object into the Potomac River.

In most murders in a domestic situation, the spouse is the prime suspect. However, since no weapon was ever found, Agatha Tillman was eliminated from the suspect list.

Two weeks later, Agatha and her daughter flew out-of-state and visited an abortion clinic.

Although my evidence is circumstantial, I believe that Agatha Tillman caught her husband sleeping with their daughter and shot him dead. I believe that Agent Williams illegally disposed of the weapon, thereby eliminating the possibility of a murder charge.

As illegal as Agent Williams' act was, I agree with his actions. I would have probably done the same, given the circumstances.

"Good for you," Marna said through clenched teeth, looking up at Williams. "He deserved to have his dick cut off."

"There's no evidence to say that she shot her husband," Williams said. "Is that all you had on me? I'm not sure why I was worried." He laughed a little.

"Keep reading, Abigail," Jackie said. Her dizziness had subsided a bit for the moment.

Marna pulled out the next sheet and continued reading.

December 3, 1999

On November 6, Congressman Roy Angler was arrested by the FBI on charges of receiving a bribe in the amount of $500,000. In exchange for the money, it was alleged that the congressman was to champion legislature for the purchase of one hundred aircraft from a defense contractor.

The key evidence in the investigation were files found in the office of the congressman. Agent Williams was not in charge of the case but was assisting the lead investigator.

The warrant executed on the Congressman's premises, permitted the removal of all of Angler's file cabinets. The intent was to have the FBI analysts see if they could find further evidence.

However, the key documents were inexplicably lost in transport. There was no evidence as to what happened. As a result, the charges against the congressman were dropped.

Last week, I found that an account had been established in the name of Agent Williams' son. The amount deposited was enough to fund his education at an Ivy League university.

Unfortunately, I don't have enough hard evidence for a case to stand up in court. But it is clear to me that Williams accepted a bribe in exchange for destroying the evidence against Congressman Angler.

"Well that doesn't sound good," Marna said, looking at the FBI chief. "What school did your son go to? Whatever it is, I'll choose a different one."

"These are groundless accusations," Williams said. "Is there anything else in there?"

But Jackie could tell that the story had hit a nerve. There was a bead of cold sweat at his temple.

Marna picked up the next story.

March 9, 2010

Three weeks ago, this reporter received a tip concerning our newly minted FBI Director, Reginald Williams. I did my due diligence with the information I received from my source.

According to my informant, Director Williams' position had been bought. The margin of congressional approval was tight. Two weeks before the confirmation vote, experts predicted that Williams would be three votes short. One congressman wanted to have his own man installed as head of the FBI, another was mad at the sitting President, and the third was getting a kickback from the first.

Then, according to my source, each of the three received a new Corvette and a ski trip to Switzerland. Suddenly, there were enough votes to confirm Reginald Williams into the director's position.

I contacted the Chevrolet dealership where the cars had been purchased. I then traced the money back to an offshore account. The account was a front for a shell corporation owned by a gentleman in North Carolina.

I found the owner of the corporation on a horse ranch outside of Durham. The gentleman in question had been in business with some questionable characters, one of whom has been implicated, but not convicted, of human trafficking.

By buying off the congressmen, and obtaining Director Williams' confirmation, the "businessman" hoped to gain leverage in the event that he was charged with a crime.

As a result of this man's actions, Director Williams, obtained his political position by fraudulent means. I believe Director Williams to be the best man for the job.

I could not find any evidence that Williams was complicit in the bribe. However, if the facts were to surface, Williams would lose his political footing forever.

This leaves me conflicted. Do I reveal the corruption and destroy the career of my friend, or do I allow the malfeasance to perpetuate?

Since it was not Williams' intent to deceive Congress or to subvert the system, I have decided to file the evidence and let sleeping dogs lie.

Marna looked up from the article. "You were approved by a fraud."

Director Williams' cheeks were red. "I didn't know," he said quietly. "I swear, I had no idea." He turned to Jackie. "Give me the name of the man who did this. I'll find a way to bury him."

The man was lying like a cat who had just found the world's warmest sunspot on a shag carpet. The guilt couldn't have been any clearer if it had been written on his forehead in a fat, black sharpie. It was like his face was saying, "I knew about this, and I approved." She didn't know if he had arranged the deed, but it had certainly been in his sphere of knowledge, and he'd done nothing about the bribes. Nor had he taken any action to rectify the transgression.

Jackie shrugged. She had been concentrating on reading the novel that Williams' face was telling, so she almost forgot the question. She was struggling to stay with the group. She paused and replayed the words back through her mind until they made sense. Then she squeezed and cajoled her brain, trying to formulate an answer that could at least sound intelligible. Finally, she gave up and shrugged. "I don't remember the guy's name," she said helplessly. "If it's not in the packet, then I don't know."

She saw Williams' hand start to move toward the envelope. But something told him to wait. He withdrew his hand and stared angrily at Jackie.

"What about his packet?" Marna asked, nodding toward Jackie's former lover. "Should I read Senator Turner's?"

Jackie nodded again. "Do it fast. I'm struggling to stay lucid."

Across the table, she could hear her friend and former lover breathing hard. It was as if he knew he was about to take a brutal shot to his solar plexus, delivered by a world-class heavyweight. He gritted his teeth and steeled himself in preparation. His laser eyes tried to penetrate the packet; he was wondering which of his many sins had been documented by the previously lucid and incredibly thorough, Jacqueline Saeed Scott.

Marna nodded and opened the packet and began reading.

March 3, 2003

A copy of this report is to be kept on file with my lawyer in Vienna, Virginia with instructions that it should be released to the public in the event of my untimely demise.

Two weeks ago, on February 17, I was returning to Aaeesha's house from my meeting with Saddam Hussein. The meeting with the dictator had been at the direction of President Armstrong. I was tasked with creating a backdoor communication conduit between the two presidents in the attempt to avert the second Gulf War.

The meeting did not go well, and I felt lucky to have escaped with my life. After the meeting as I was trying to compose myself, I wound my way through a street market in Baghdad.

By sheer circumstance, I observed Monroe Turner, Brigadier General of the United States Army, walking through the crowd. I personally know the general, because we dated in high school and, later on in life, after my husband died, I had a brief affair with him.

I was shocked to see him. He was supposed to have been hundreds of miles south in Saudi Arabia preparing for the Iraqi invasion. Yet to my amazement, he was walking in the heart of the enemy's capital.

At the time of the sighting, the general was in civilian clothes, but the big Caucasian with the military haircut stood out like a wolf at a sheep shearing.

Wearing a Chador, I was able to follow unobserved. I watched as Turner went into the offices of a man named Abhid Abdigar.

Further investigation revealed that Abdigar was involved in the illegal arms trade, supplying arms to insurgents, terrorists, or anyone else that couldn't obtain arms legally. After some digging, I discovered that Abdigar owned a warehouse on the south end of town. I began a nightly stakeout from the roof of a building half a block away.

I was rewarded on the fifth night—a caravan of trucks rolled into the warehouse. This meeting was only days before the invasion.

I do not know how the trucks entered the country—I can only assume they came in through Jordan. I was able to slip inside the warehouse unobserved. There, hidden beneath a truck in a dark corner of the cavernous building, I photographed General Turner making an exchange of money for the truckloads of arms. Those photographs are attached. It is clear from my pictures that the general was selling surplus US weapons to the dealer.

Further investigation (documentation attached) revealed that the proceeds from these sales have been going to a shell corporation in Switzerland. It is unclear at this point in time what the intent for this money was to be.

A copy of this report and the photos will be emailed to my lawyer. I have decided that I will hold onto this information until I can meet with the general. As usual, it will be my goal to guide Monroe onto the straight and narrow.

Marna shuffled to the next report. She cleared her voice and started reading again.

December 10, 2003

One week ago, I had the chance to meet with Brigadier General Monroe Turner regarding the sale of arms in Baghdad earlier this year. I presented him with the evidence and assured him that my lawyer had a copy with instructions to publish if some harm came to me or my family.

Monroe told me that the sale of arms was actually at the direction of the CIA. They were trying to trace the flow of arms through the Middle East, and they were using Abdigar as a cut-out man in the operation.

He said they were hoping that the chaos of the impending war would loosen the security around the arms network. They wanted to flush out the players on both ends.

When I asked him the results of the operation, he said the subject was classified, because the operation was still in progress.

Unfortunately, because of the nature of the clandestine operation, he was unable to provide any details or documentation. There was nothing that he could show to a member of the press or even a close friend.

I told him that his version of the story was plausible. But I also said that I would continue my agreement with my lawyer. If any harm came to me, the lawyer had instructions to publish my findings.

I have since learned that he has been trying to find the identity of my lawyer.

April 12, 2012

This report will not be published. I am only documenting what I have found for my own personal records.

I have confirmed the real reason General Monroe Turner was selling surplus US arms to the dealer in Baghdad in 2003. It was not under orders from the CIA or any other authority but rather for personal and political gain.

The operation that General Turner was running was outside the bounds of the law. The attached documentation proves that the munitions were stolen from a base in Turkey, then delivered to Abdigar for money.

The attached documentation uncovered by this journalist, indicates that similar thefts have been taking place for at least twelve years. General Turner has established an entire network for the arms sales.

Given his position, he and his team would modify Army inventory reports, then just steal entire warehouses full of arms. In other cases, after they had sent out obsolete weapons scheduled for destruction, they simply diverted the shipment.

It is my belief that General Turner is motivated by the US strategic failure in Vietnam. He believes that a stronger military is the key for saving the lives of soldiers in the future. His goals in his promotions have always been to strengthen the military. He has used every tool at his disposal to obtain greater military strength for the United States.

Now, the general is running for the Senate. He is using the funds from his illegal corporation to finance the political race. I have no doubt that his goal is to continue his quest in strengthening the military, but he hopes to do it from his Senate seat.

I am facing an ethical dilemma. I have proof that my friend and former lover is involved in illegal activity. I know he's doing it for reasons that he believes are correct. But I believe it is wrong. In 2003, I confronted him, but he did not change his ways. In fact, shortly after my meeting with him, I found myself on the FBI's watchlist—I know this was no coincidence.

On the one hand, I want him to be brought to justice. But on the other hand, I cannot betray my friend. Therefore, I am torn.

I have decided that I am just going to let it ride and pretend that I don't know what he's doing. Future generations may judge me for my inaction.

This report will also be filed with my lawyer to be released upon my death.

CHAPTER THIRTY-NINE

Jackie was fighting for her sanity, knowing she would be sucked under at any moment. "Just a few more minutes," she said out loud, gritting her teeth.

Across the table, she saw the senator's nose twitch. Red was running up his neck, and his eyes were wide with anger. There was an errant strand of hair that had become detached from his normally perfect hairdo, as if to indicate that even his follicles were raging. His nostrils were flared, as if trying to suck large quantities of oxygen into his brain for the impending battle.

Jackie tapped the key on the top of the table to cover the noise of the safety being released in her lap. Under the table, she wrapped her right hand around the 1911, testing its weight. She made sure it was pointing in the correct direction—away from her, Marna, and Warren.

"How's your presidential bid coming, Senator?" Director Williams snarled. "I heard that your campaign was well funded." His voice was thick with the envy that he'd carried since twelfth grade. For a moment, Jackie thought he was going to try strangling Turner right there.

"Are you enjoying your position as Director?" Turner shot back.

Their eyes blazed into each other's. Reginald had actually bared his teeth. Monroe feigned a placid smile, but it came off more like a snarl.

"Enough! You had that fist fight in high school," Jackie snapped. "Guess what gentlemen," she said, bringing the subject back to bear. "The FBI doesn't have a leak. Nobody inside your organization is selling secrets. The man who sent Grizzly after my family is right here in this room."

It was so quiet that you would have been able to hear a mosquito fart. Both men stared at her, unblinking. They were each practically drooling with rage.

The room swayed again. She wanted nothing more than to just curl up in a corner with her little warm dog and just let Dr. Alois Alzheimer's disease drag her under—or whatever flavor of dementia she had. *Not yet*, she told herself. Jackie dug the teeth of the key into the palm of her left hand, trying to maintain control of her mind.

She looked at the key. It was the key to Aaeesha's treasure. The most powerful key in her life. This key represented the sum of her life's work... She stopped herself. She was drifting.

She looked across the table into the livid eyes of the men whom she had considered her friends of many years. She knew that this was the moment of truth. One of these men had tried to kill her and her family. One of these men was about to try again—and this time he might be successful.

"Marna," Jackie said, getting the woman's name right for a change. "Would you please go get me a cup of coffee?"

"Huh?" Marna asked. "Coffee? Now?"

"Yes, please."

Marna stood. Jackie saw both men shift their eyes. She realized that no matter which direction Marna used to get around the table, she was going to be within reach of one of the men. Somebody was going to grab her for a hostage. Not good.

"Wait," Jackie said, stopping Marna in her tracks. "Go curl up in a ball on the floor in the corner of the room, and make yourself as small as possible."

"What? Jackie, what's happening?" She heard fear shaking in Marna's voice.

Jackie didn't say anything, so Marna sighed and sat on the floor in the corner of the room. Her arms were wrapped around her knees. She looked at Warren, but he just shook his head—his eyes telling her to do as told.

Jackie reassessed the situation. On her far left, standing in the corner was Warren Banks. He had his Glock on his hip. His hand was on the butt. He was a big man—young and capable of extreme violence should the need arise. He was a soldier, a Marine. He was smart--probably the smartest man in the room. If he had stayed in the Marines, he would have gone all the way to the top. He was 250 pounds of brawn and brains.

Next to him, sitting at the table, was Director Williams. The man who had always played second fiddle to his best friend, Monroe. He wasn't currently military, but he was sharp, cold, and cunning. He was a dangerous man. His greatest weapon was between his ears, and Jackie was a little short in that category at the moment.

Directly across from her was Senator Monroe Turner. He was a killing machine. He'd risen through the Army far enough to collect his star. He was strong and tough. He'd survived the combat of Vietnam, Iraq, and several conflicts in between. He wasn't worried about Warren. He knew the young genius would have to get through Williams first, and in that time, he would have done whatever he had come to do.

At the far right, was the door to exit the room. Left-to-right, it was one, two, three, four—Warren, Williams, Turner, and the door. Three soldiers, one senile old lady with a .45, and one exit door. Who was going to try to escape? Who was going to live, and who was going to die?

Marna was out of play and safely in the corner—or as safe as one could be when bullets were about to fly.

The tension in the room was thick as a dust storm. Everybody knew they were at the precipice.

Casually, Director Williams reached his hand out on the table. Jackie noticed his fingers were close to the envelope with his name on it.

She glanced at Warren. She couldn't remember his name. But Jackie had spent enough time with soldiers that she could read his expression. His eyes said, "I've got your back. I've got this guy." He glanced at Williams, pointing with his eyes.

Jackie felt the weight of the Smith and Wesson in her hand. Even though it had been in the security lock box for years, she could still smell the gun oil, even from the distance of two feet. She remembered that it was Aaeesha's husband's gun. She knew that Aaeesha's fingers had touched this very same handle... No! I'm drifting again!

"So, which one of you sent Grizzly?" she asked, staring into their eyes. "Was it Monroe, the star quarterback, who never had a failure? Or was it Reginald, who always played second string—the man whose jealousy was his greatest asset and his Achilles heel?"

She leaned over the table. "Who was it?"

She glanced again at Williams and she instantly knew who had hired Grizzly. Williams was telegraphing his moves—his hand crept closer to the folder. He was going to grab the envelope and run. She knew in that instant that Williams hadn't been the one to give the kill order—he was only thinking about himself.

His problem was that he'd have to get past Turner on his way to the door. He also had to worry about Warren. But his eyes said that he was going to take his chances. The cost of failure was too high. He had no choice—that packet had to be destroyed. His eyes said that he was willing to risk his life to be the sole owner of that information.

She looked into Turner's eyes. They were wild with anger. In them, she could now see the icy sheen of murder. She could smell the adrenaline coursing through his pores.

She remembered that day in his office when he had sent her to Columbia with Grizzly. The man had been hoping that she'd catch a bullet. Her friend. Her lover. He had wanted her dead back then. He was determined to bring that to fruition today.

The senator was on the edge of his seat, muscles tensed. His face said that he thought he could control the situation. There was an edge of confidence about him. His body language said, "I've got this licked. I've got a secret weapon that can beat a senile old lady, a washed-up FBI director, and a rising FBI agent star." His eyes said, "I'm a soldier, and I'm the best, and I'm about to win. I can salvage this situation." He was coiled as tight as one of those huge springs that's hooked to a garage door. Jackie could read that his spring was about to snap.

His eyes also confirmed what Reginald's creeping hand had betrayed. Reginald wasn't the murderer—it was Monroe. He always thought he was above the law. He always felt that the end justified the means—even if it meant putting a hit on his former lover. Strengthening the Army was his life's purpose, and nothing was going to stand in his way. Nothing had changed since that day they had sat in the Corvette.

"Why?" Jackie asked, looking into his eyes—pleading him to stop the foolish game. His silence spoke louder than any words.

Jackie moved the muzzle of the pistol—honing in on the man that she'd loved. He didn't know that she held a .45 pistol under the table, pointed at his gut. Jackie's face was gentle, telegraphing nothing of the death she held in her hands. She allowed the senility to creep to her countenance. Her face said, "I'm clueless. I'm just an old lady. Nothing to look at here, folks. I'm just a pretty face." It was a look that she had practiced for years. She smiled sweetly, and for a moment, she felt the tension ebbing. For just a second, she thought that perhaps her sweet smile could avoid the coming bloodshed.

Suddenly, time went into slow motion as the room exploded. It was almost as if a green light had lit, and everybody knew it was time to hit the gas pedal. It was like the beginning of the Kentucky Derby—Jackie had been there once. She'd seen the explosive burst of flesh and muscle when the gates had opened. The sudden stillness had become unfettered action. Although, in the case of the Derby, the only thing on the line was money and glory. However, in this situation, Jackie knew somebody was about to die.

She saw Williams' hand reaching for the envelope. In his mind, if he could destroy the evidence, then life would be good. Sure, somebody might gossip, but without solid proof, he could continue life as he knew it. And he liked the way things were. He wanted to keep the status quo.

Jackie didn't have time to worry about Williams. She had other things to occupy her time and attention. She had to rely entirely on Warren to solve the little problem of the head Fed. Although she couldn't remember his name, she knew Warren was a competent and honest man—albeit flawed. But who wasn't? She certainly had no room to throw stones. And at the moment, she was a little too busy to toss rocks, even if some had been available. So, she ignored Williams and trusted Warren to do his job.

In the same instant that Williams' hand shot forward, Turner stood, roaring like a lion. His hand went under his jacket, and Jackie saw the glint of silver in his hand. She waited until the big, Dirty-Harry-looking revolver cleared his jacket. She realized that the man wasn't roaring, but instead was screaming, "I'll kill you!"

Out of her peripheral view, she saw Williams grab his envelope. He turned and tried to run, but Warren's huge fist pounded into the man's temple. She saw Reginald's eyes roll into the back of his head and begin his descent toward the carpet.

By now, Turner's big gun was tracking toward her head. She knew she only had another second to live. Jackie realized that she had no other choice. She didn't even bring her gun from under the table. Instead, she just began pulling the trigger.

Bang! Bang! Bang! Bang! **Bang!**

Some people will tell you that there's not much difference between a .45 ACP and a 9mm round. But those people have never seen the effects of those bullets up close. From her lap, Jackie fired point-blank using the "zipper". Meaning that she put one into his groin, into his stomach, into his chest, and tried to put one into his head, but missed on the forth shot. She zippered him all the way up his body. Shooting at him through the table, caused jagged splinters to fly into the air. The wooden table in front of her split down the middle from the force of the bullets flying upward from her hand cannon in her lap into the body Monroe Turner, senator and presidential hopeful.

In the time it took Jackie to fire four, Turner had fired one at her from his .357. Jackie had the advantage; all she had to do was pull the trigger. Monroe had to stick his hand into his jacket, pull out his gun, aim it, then fire. It was no contest. It wasn't even a fair fight. But Jackie wasn't interested in a fair battle; she had stacked the deck.

Flames belched from the man's chrome revolver. Turner's bullet grazed her neck and buried itself into the wall behind her.

Jackie's former lover and childhood sweetheart stood before her, dead on his feet. His eyes were glassy and unfocused. Behind him, Jackie could see that the wall was painted red with his blood and intestines.

She thought of the good times—the moments in high school when she had watched him trot out onto the football field. She remembered how she had cheered him on—how she had kissed him after the team had won state.

Those eyes. Though glassy now, they had been the first thing to draw her heart. Other girls had chased him for his ass; but for her, it had always been the eyes. She remembered the warmth and kindness that drew them together as teens. Everybody else saw the tough guy, but she had seen his heart. But he changed. They had all changed.

She remembered the feel of his hands on her breasts, during that illicit love affair. She could still feel his hot, passionate breath on her neck as he entered her body.

She swallowed, realizing the gravity of her actions. The dead man stood before her as her accuser—the man she had loved. The man she had killed.

Time resumed its normal pace. Almost everything in the room fell to the floor. Senator and Presidential hopeful Monroe Turner fell like a sack of dead fish. Director Williams dropped unconscious from the blow delivered by Warren's bowling-ball-sized fist. The splinters of the table fell to the floor, and the now split table collapsed on top of the fallen men. The neat packets of intelligence reports had been scattered, and papers were fluttered about like hoarfrost.

Jackie was still sitting in her chair—a smoking gun in her hand. Warren was still standing in the corner, nursing his bruised knuckles. Marna was cowering in the corner, screaming at the top of her lungs. Not that it mattered much—Jackie's ears were ringing so loudly from the gunshots in the small, enclosed room, that she could barely hear Marna's voice.

Jackie let the gun fall from her fingers. She looked at the body of the man she had loved and began to cry. At first it was a sob, then a choke, then she was wailing at the top of her lungs.

Years of grief, anger, and evil ripped through her body, causing spasms to cascade through her torso. She had spent her life living in the gutters of the world—first in the slime of politics, then in the abject horrors of war. She knew that the evil environments had seeped through and tainted her soul. Her mother had told her to make the world a better place, but in the end, she had been the one changed. The hammer had become the sickle—she had been beaten on the anvil of life. She had failed.

She was shattered by the grief for her dead daughter, her husband, and her best friend. In her mind, her family's deaths were all her fault. Every one of them had lost their lives because she had tried to make a difference. The cost was too high. And on top of all that, she herself had been corrupted.

She remembered the children of war. She had wanted to save every one of them. But in the end, she had been powerless and ineffective.

Now she had killed her first love. He lay dead at her feet, perforated by the hollow points fired from Aaeesha's husband's gun.

Jackie's keening was inconsolable. Her howling was beyond hysterical. She knew she was going into shock. The dementia that had been held at bay by the vault key, rolled over her like a freight train.

She was vaguely aware of Marna's gentle hands leading her from the room. In the corner, she saw the tear-blurred outline of Warren on the phone—apparently calling for backup. But Jackie was too far gone.

She hiccupped and allowed herself to be led away. Once the security guard recovered from his own shock, he found Jackie a chair and handed her a glass of water with a trembling hand. Marna found her coat and wrapped Jackie to keep her warm.

Within minutes, the vault was flooded with cops. But Warren wouldn't let anyone into the conference room until the FBI arrived.

After they arrived, one of the federal agents, a kindly looking woman, tried to ask Jackie questions. But Jackie couldn't remember a thing. "My brain has turned to Fruit Loops." Then she began a fresh round of tears and wept for her own lost soul and mind.

CHAPTER FORTY

The air felt fresh and cool against her cheek. Jackie sat on the porch of her own house and looked out at the red and gold leaves that had begun to fall to the grass. Beside her, six-year-old Milly played with a doll, pretending that the toys were a booth at the shopping mall.

Out in the yard, Katrice was performing the insurmountable task of raking those falling leaves into bags. But it seemed to Jackie that no matter how fast Katrice raked, the leaves fell faster. Chucky was supposed to be helping, but he seemed more interested in jumping in the piles and laughing wildly. Jackie looked at the pair blankly for a moment. She realized that, although she knew *who* they were, she couldn't remember their names.

Cassie snuggled warmly in her lap, occasionally sneaking in a lick of love against her fingers. The dog sniffed, then nuzzled her nose, hoping that Jackie would pet her some more. It was apparently Cassie's lucky day, because Jackie gave her what she wanted.

Jackie realized that there was a blanket in her lap; it had bows and snaps and zippers. She couldn't remember what her daughter-in-law had called it. Her hands seemed to have a mind of their own and were going through the motions of snapping and zipping.

A young lady stepped out onto the porch—Jackie couldn't remember her name. She was pretty sure it was her daughter. "Bye Jackie. I'll be out late. Katrice will come over to feed you and put you to bed."

"Who's Katrice?" Jackie asked.

"That's Mommy's name," Milly said from the porch floor. She pointed at the woman raking the leaves. "I'm Milly, and this is Marna."

Jackie had the urge to hold the little girl. The girl-child had become the most important thing in her life as of late.

"Hi Marna." A huge, handsome man walked up the steps. He planted a fat kiss on the young woman's lips.

The man turned to Jackie. "Hi Jackie." He patted the little girl's head. "Hi Milly." He then fluffed Cassie's ears. The dog gratefully licked his hand.

"Who are you?" she asked. She seemed to be asking that question a lot lately.

"I'm Warren. I'm here to take Marna on a date." She saw the two exchange a knowing look.

"I have something for you," he said, laying a manila envelope in her hands.

"What's this?" she laughed. "A present?"

"Yeah. It's the file that Reginald Williams had on you."

"Who's Reginald Williams?" she asked.

"He's the former FBI director. He was indicted because of what you…" His voice trailed off. "You know what? I'm going to take care of this for you." He took it back from her hands. "I'll make sure it gets burned." He stuffed it into the inside lining of his jacket.

"You're going to burn my present?" she asked, disappointed.

He nodded. "You'll thank me later."

"I'll pick up a present for you when we go to the mall," Marna promised.

Jackie smiled. "You always were my favorite," she said.

Warren came up onto the porch and sat beside Milly. He looked up at Jackie. "I'm so proud of you. You saw that your memory was fading, and you set things right. In spite of all your challenges, you finished well."

Jackie watched a brilliant red leaf as it helicoptered its way from its lofty home in the tree toward the ground. Somehow, she knew it was a representation of her life—flaming in glory but destined to die. She knew the man sitting at her feet had said something important, but she couldn't remember what it was.

Warren sighed and stood. He patted her knee. "I only hope I can say the same thing when my time comes." He held his hand toward Marna. She ducked under his arm and grabbed his waist.

The two turned to go, but Jackie stopped them. "You know, I once ended a war," she said proudly.

The two looked at each other surprised. "You remembered something," Marna said.

"Make sure you use a condom," Jackie said loudly.

"What's a condom?" Milly asked.

Ignoring the inappropriate comment, Marna came back up on the porch and gave Jackie another kiss on the cheek. There was a tear in her eye. "I love you so much, Mom," she whispered.

THE END

Don't worry, Marna will be back in *The Dementia Encryption Enigma*.

THANKS AGAIN

This is Ed Eby. Thanks so much for purchasing *Before the Memories Fail*. As a thank you gift, I would like to give you a free PDF copy of the sequel, *Marna*. As of this writing, the rough draft has been completed and the novella is in editing. Send me an email at AuthorEdEby@gmail.com to sign up.

I've also completed the rough draft of the third book of the series, *The Dementia Encryption Enigma*. I don't yet have a release date, but I'll keep you informed if you join the mailing list. I promise I won't spam your inbox.

ABOUT THE AUTHOR

In his professional life, Ed Eby served as the Network Engineer for the USPS Engineering Center for nearly twenty years. He did a short stint as the Lead Engineer for the IRS Network Operations Center. He currently works at WorldVenture, a Baptist Missions organization. This latest job allows him to leverage his technical talents to help people all over the world.

From 1985-2000, Ed volunteered as an Assistant Pastor in the Ghettos of Washington DC. He did a lot of street ministry, prison ministry, and outreach to drug addicts, homeless, and the downtrodden.

Ed has many hobbies. As a musician, He released a CD in 2000 entitled Ed Eby and Friends. The CD is comprised of songs that he has written and features former #1 selling artists from several genres of music. He currently plays bass at a local church.

Ed is a long-distance shooter. He has hit a pop can at a half-mile, and a gallon jug at over a mile. His favorite rifle is his 6.5x284. He regularly shoots eight-ounce pop cans at 550 yards or golf balls at 300 yards.

Other hobbies include woodworking, photography, and of course, writing. He loves hiking, hunting and camping.

Ed lives in the mountains west of Denver. He enjoys the rugged Rockies and loves seeing deer and elk in his front yard.

He is married to his beautiful wife, Sue. They have two adult sons. The oldest is a sculptor and the youngest is a professional musician.

Ed has been plagued with long-term chronic autoimmune illness. In 2018 it was diagnosed as Lyme's disease. In addition to a GoFundMe campaign, the proceeds from this novel will go toward the treatment of this debilitating disease.

CPSIA information can be obtained
at www.ICGtesting.com
Printed in the USA
LVHW082356060119
602965LV00010B/148/P